"I have so... Gavin said, withdrawing an envelope.

"Don't you want to see what your mother left you?"

What was he up to? I didn't trust him. "This better not be a joke."

"The monks gave it to me when they thought I was your father."

I vaguely remembered the conversation. It had happened on my last day at the monastery, the day Gavin kidnapped me. "Why did you wait so long to give me this?"

Gavin looked at me blankly. "You weren't ready."

KAREN DUVALL

KNIGHT'S CURSE

www.LUNA-Books.com

LUNA™

Recycling programs
for this product may
not exist in your area.

KNIGHT'S CURSE

ISBN-13: 978-0-373-80340-8

www.LUNA-Books.com

Printed in U.S.A.

Dear Reader,

Chalice is a modern-day knight descended from an order of female knights that existed in the Middle Ages and actually used hatchets to defend their homes when the men went off to fight. In Chalice's twenty-first century world, that order still exists, but the female knights are the progeny of angels. The abilities they inherit are their most powerful weapons. And with angels come magic… and beings who wield the forces of darkness and light.

Be sure to watch for more stories about the Hatchet Knights and the supernatural threats that confront Chalice and her sisters.

Karen Duvall

This book is dedicated to my children: Malia, Rick and Renee.

I have so many people to thank for supporting me along this wondrous journey.

First, my critique group, who read my early drafts and offered many insightful comments: Shannon Baker, Lawdon, Janet Lane, Vicki Kaufman, Jameson Cole, Bonnie Smith, Heidi Kuhn, Margaret Bailey, Michael Philips and Alan Larson. Second, Rocky Mountain Fiction Writers—an amazing organization that sponsors one of the best writers' conferences. Their professionalism is unequalled by any other writers' group.

And of course, my wonderful husband, Jim Duvall. This poor man has put up with my spacey days, my constant tapping on the keyboard, my blabbing about people he doesn't even know because they live entirely inside my head, and all the clutter in my office. He always believed in me even when I wasn't so sure I believed in myself.

one

STICKS AND STONES MAY BREAK MY BONES,
but I'd see them coming long before they hurt me. I would
hear them, too. Maybe even smell them. My abilities came
in handy at times.

But today they were more like a curse.

Through a cracked and filthy window, I watched two
jeeps filled with soldiers carrying machine guns park on
a hill above the monastery. They wore military camou-
flage that hardly camouflaged them at all. From the way
they slouched off into the olive trees, I knew they believed
themselves unseen, except that I had seen them quite well.
I noted each stitch on their clothing, every whisker on their
unshaven faces, even the color of their bootlaces.

I blinked behind thick sunglasses that shielded my sensitive eyes from the harsh midsummer sun. It was nearing

dusk so my eyes didn't hurt as much. I had just turned thirteen and was now able to see better in the dark than in daylight. I preferred the night anyway. It was quieter after the sun went down.

My family of Maronite monks kept me away from the Lebanese villagers who stared and gossiped about the way I looked. The local kids who should have been my friends threw rocks at me, and even when they whispered behind my back, I could still hear them. I could hear a bee leave its hive from a mile away.

I should have told Brother Thomas about the soldiers, but I had trouble pulling myself away from the window. I felt like a hooked fish, the bait of my own insatiable curiosity. Just a few more minutes. What harm could there be in that?

Two civilian-looking men stayed behind with the jeeps. My keen eyes zeroed in on the taller one, blond and blue-eyed, who stood beside a ruined pillar of an ancient structure that had once been part of a heathen temple. I saw the man's anger as he swatted at biting flies that buzzed too close to his face, his mouth moving with words I couldn't hear while wearing my earplugs. So I took them out.

"Damn vile country," he spat, his English carrying the cadence of a Brit like the monk who had taught me this language. Addressing the pudgy man beside him, he added, "The bitch will pay, I promise you that."

I winced at the words, but not because of their meaning, which made no sense to me. It was his loud voice that bit through my skull and vibrated painfully between my ears. I struggled to separate his voice from other noises nearby, like the buzzing flies, the rustling olive trees, the bleating goats in the courtyard. Head aching, I concentrated, focusing only on the words that took shape inside my mind.

"Faisal, radio the men. Make sure they're in position."

The man he had called Faisal wore a striped hijab and, when he nodded, the turban of fabric wobbled on his head like one of Cook's *moghlie* puddings.

Something wasn't right. A warning bell chimed inside my head, but I ignored it. I was too mesmerized by the Englishman walking down the rocky path toward our chapel. He held himself with confidence, not crouched in wariness like the men dressed as soldiers. This one didn't try to hide. Brother Thomas must be expecting him.

I replaced my earplugs and inhaled deeply through pinched nostrils, hoping to catch a muted whiff of the foreigner, but he was too far away. If I removed the swimmer's noseclips I always wore, I'd be assaulted by the myriad smells outside. I'd wait for him to come closer so I could identify the scents on his clothes and body. That would tell me what I needed to know.

He stepped through groping fingers of long shadows and skirted the scaffolds that leaned against decaying chapel walls. He scowled up at a tent of heavy canvas that replaced large portions of the missing roof. A small goat trotted in front of him, and he kicked at it, brushing at his crisply ironed slacks as if they'd become soiled.

I scrambled down off the crate I'd used to reach the window, and crept barefoot along the uneven floor of a hallway leading to the chapel. A thick wooden door stood slightly ajar, and I knelt beside it, peering through a two-inch gap to watch.

On the opposite side of the room, the Englishman stuck his head inside and called, "Anyone here?"

Brother Thomas, a short middle-aged man in a tan robe that fluttered around his ankles, hobbled toward the voice. He stooped as he walked, as if to avoid hitting his head on a low ceiling, though he cleared it by a good six feet or more. "May I help you?"

The stranger stepped inside and folded his arms across his chest. "I believe you have something that belongs to me."

The monk frowned, then his leathery face broke into a smile. "Ah! Gavin Heinrich! You have arrived sooner than I expected. So pleased to finally meet you." He bowed, his expression anxious while saying in heavily accented English, "You have come for our Chalice?"

I swallowed the lump of ice that suddenly formed in my throat.

The man called Heinrich cocked a brow and leaned back on his heels. "I've come for the girl—"

"Yes, yes," Brother Thomas said, bobbing his head and stepping closer. "The girl, Chalice. That is her name."

No. This wasn't possible. My home was here, at the monastery. No way would I go anywhere with this man.

"And the other item?" Heinrich asked.

Thomas looked confused. "Other item?"

Heinrich made a huffing sound as if annoyed, then relaxed his jaw as if it would hide how tense he was. But I could see it in his eyes. His lips curved in a half smile when he said, "The letter. My wife gave you a letter before she died."

"Of course, of course. Forgive me. I am old and my memory is not so good anymore." Thomas chuckled, but quickly sobered while clearing his throat. "Your wife said we should give it to the girl when she comes of age."

When Heinrich stared down at his feet, the monk's bright eyes softened. "Forgive me, sir, for my late condolences on your loss."

I noted how the man's expression of anguish appeared forced. I'd seen that look before, on the faces of actors in the village during performances of summertime plays. His soft words of thanks sounded unnatural coming from his hard, thin-lipped mouth. I realized then that he wasn't a good man.

"How awful to learn of your wife's tragic death from an old Lebanese newspaper. If we had known how to contact you when it happened..."

Head still down, the Englishman held up his hand in a halting gesture. "I understand."

"I assure you we did all we could to save her, but she had lost so much blood. Did you ever find the man who shot her?"

Heinrich neither spoke nor looked up.

Thomas cleared his throat. "Well, I suppose she was lucky her little plane crashed so close to the monastery. If it hadn't, we might not have been in time to save the baby."

Baby? They couldn't possibly be talking about me. I knew my mother had bled to death after giving birth to me, but not from a gunshot wound. I'd always assumed I'd been the cause.

Heinrich's audible swallow sounded authentic. Maybe he was nervous about his lies. "I'm in your debt, Brother Thomas. Your kindness won't go unrewarded."

"Would you like to see your daughter now?"

"Chalice, is it?" Heinrich asked. "Yes, very much."

Thomas turned away.

"Excuse me, Brother Thomas, but is Chalice aware of what her mother left her?"

The monk halted midstep and swung back around to face him. "Her mother asked us to keep it a secret until she was old enough to take responsibility for herself. We have done so. Chalice knows nothing about it."

Heinrich smiled, as if relieved. "I'm happy to abide by my late wife's wishes. Just bring me the letter, and I'll keep it safe."

The monk's eyes squinted with uncertainty, but he nodded and motioned toward another monk standing in the shadows. He spoke to him in Arabic, then said to Heinrich, "Brother Francis will get it for you while I fetch the girl."

When I saw the smug look on Heinrich's face, I felt sick to my stomach.

Brother Thomas headed my way. I stood, rage at his betrayal making my body shake. My first impulse was to run away, flee to the village and hide. But then what? I'd read about the outside world in the newspaper and understood how dangerous it could be for a thirteen-year-old girl alone. Those in the village who knew me would just bring me back here. I had no friends but the monks who had raised me.

As ideas for escape eluded me, Brother Thomas pushed open the chapel door. A thin smile twitched on his lips. "Chalice, my child. I was just coming to get you." His eyebrows tangled together in a concerned frown. "Is something wrong?"

He spoke to me in Arabic, and I replied in his language. "How could you?" I asked, my voice breaking.

Understanding shone in his eyes. "You heard us talking."

"I'm not going away with that man."

"That man is your father." He huffed a blast of breath out his nose. "I'm only thinking of what's best for you. We're monks, Chalice. We love you, but we've done all we can. You've grown into a young woman and deserve more than this." He gestured at the crumbling walls, the hay-strewn hallway with the tilted floor, the cracked windows. "Mr. Heinrich is a rich man who can give you everything you need and want...."

I glared at him, unable to stop the stinging tears that slipped free. I swiped them furiously from my cheeks and whispered harshly, "Now I understand. You sold me to him."

"It's not like that," Thomas said, though guilt etched the seams of his weathered face. I knew that look because it was the same one I'd seen after catching him in a drunken stupor. "He is your father."

"My mother would never marry a man like that," I said,

jabbing my finger toward the chapel. "He's pompous and cold."

The monk wiped a hand down his face and sighed. "You don't know that."

"If he's my father, why would he bring bodyguards here with him?"

Thomas frowned. "Bodyguards?"

"Didn't you see them? Ten men are outside hiding behind rocks and trees. What makes the Englishman so special that he needs protection?"

The monk shook his head and shrugged. "Your father has great wealth and can afford to do whatever he likes." He straightened and tucked both hands in his robe pockets. "I've had enough of your foolishness, girl. Come along now."

The pulse in my neck beat so hard I could almost taste it in my throat, and the instinct to run grew stronger. Slipping a hand under my muslin shift, I fingered the knife sheathed in goatskin strapped to my thigh and was reassured by its presence.

He saw me do it. "None of that, not today. I need you to behave. Your father has traveled thousands of miles from America—"

"America?" I set my anger aside for the moment. I'd always dreamed of visiting the United States. It was the land of hot dogs, Disneyland, Barbie dolls and hip-hop. I knew of American music from listening to songs that filtered through headphones worn by an occasional tourist in the village. The sound had been wonderful, and I wanted to hear more. "But that man has a British accent, not American."

Though I still had no intention of leaving with the man called Heinrich, curiosity brewed hot inside me. America. And he had known my mother. I had to get closer to him, smell him...

"English or American, he's still your father. Let's go," Thomas said with impatience.

I allowed him to steer me into the chapel, his work-roughened fingers warm at the back of my neck. Standing in obedient silence, I watched Heinrich roam the modest room while scrutinizing pieces of religious art scattered across rotting walls and splintered tabletops. He seemed to appraise their value, but nothing here was worth much. Not even the child he'd come to collect. What could he possibly want with me?

Brother Francis entered the chapel carrying an envelope. Far younger than Brother Thomas, the monk kept his gaze cast to the floor as he handed over the precious letter Heinrich had seemed so eager to get his hands on. He accepted it reverently, then carefully tucked it into his shirt pocket.

I vaguely recalled what he and Brother Thomas had said about the letter. Something about my mother bleeding to death from a gunshot wound, though I knew that couldn't be true. My mother had died in childbirth. I had killed her just by being born.

Heinrich finally noticed me. He appeared tense at first, then slouched with his back against the wall, hands in his pockets, his legs crossed at the ankles.

Thomas glanced between Heinrich and me. "She's an unusual girl, Mr. Heinrich. Please be patient with her."

Heinrich frowned. "Do you mean she's...simple-minded?"

The monk shook his head and spoke as if I weren't in the room. "No, sir. She's extremely bright. We have schooled her ourselves, but we reached our academic limits two years ago. We purchased many used textbooks in Beirut for her to study, but I'm afraid it's not enough. The child is bored, which often makes her..."

Looking irritated, Heinrich barked, "Makes her what?"

Thomas winced. "She's a spirited child with great imagination. Too inquisitive sometimes, and this causes mischief."

Heinrich pushed away from the wall and stepped forward. Kneeling before me, he spoke to me as if I were five. "Chalice? I'm your father. Say goodbye to your friends now because it's time for us to go home to America."

I stared at him while shaking my mane of inky-black hair that I'd been told looked just like my mother's. The sun had disappeared beyond the horizon and votive candles perched on an altar cast flickered light across the man's face. He looked amused by my large sunglasses and the swimmer's noseclips that pinched my nostrils shut.

Standing up, he smiled. "Isn't it too early for Halloween?"

Thomas came up behind him and said, "Chalice is extremely sensitive to light, smell and sound. You can't see the earplugs, but I'm sure she is wearing them."

Heinrich gazed down at the monk, a pleased expression on his face. How odd that he'd appreciate my freakishness. "And the cause of this sensitivity?"

Thomas shrugged. "We don't know, but we think it's a result of her traumatic birth, that it might have affected her brain. The village doctor says she is perfectly healthy. Just a bit, how do you say, *high-strung*."

The man grinned at me and said, "Won't you say hello to your father?"

My spine went rigid and I fisted my hands at my sides, lifting my chin in defiance. Using the Queen's English in a deep voice that even I knew sounded too mature for a child, I said, "You're not my father."

"Chalice!" Thomas came toward me as if to deliver a reprimand, but Heinrich grabbed him by the shoulder to keep him back.

"It's all right, Thomas," he said coolly. "She's a teenager. She can't help being belligerent." He couldn't see me glare at him from behind my sunglasses. "Chalice, you look a lot like your mother. Did you know that?"

I gasped and leaned toward him, my confidence shrinking as I bowed my shoulders and tilted my head, my inquisitive nature getting the best of me. "How well did you know my mother?"

"Very well," he said smoothly, just like a father speaking calmly to an agitated child. "After all, she was my wife. Let me have a better look at you? Let me see if you have her pretty eyes."

Wary as a mouse before a cat, I removed my sunglasses, then immediately covered my eyes with both hands. "It's too bright!"

Heinrich reached out to pull me deeper into the

shadowed corner of the chapel. I yanked away from his touch.

"You prefer dark places?" he asked.

I squinted and nodded, the needle-sharp pricks of light making my head pound. Blinking a few times, I finally opened my eyes all the way. I knew they were a strange color, gold and turquoise, and I was ashamed of how different they made me look. Mildly surprised by my reaction to such dim light, Heinrich seemed satisfied with what he saw. Brother Thomas had told me many times that I had my mother's eyes.

I tried to back away, but he grabbed my arms to hold me still. "What's wrong, Chalice? You don't have to be afraid of me. I'm your father."

I kicked at his shins with my small bare feet and my noseclip popped free. I grimaced at the unwelcome odors. "No! Not my father. I *know* you're not!"

"How do you know?"

Thomas scurried over to try separating us, but Heinrich shoved him away. "Don't interfere."

"You mustn't be rough with her," Thomas said, his voice rising to an anguished whine. He tottered from side to side, as if unsure what to do. "She's a precocious child, but still only a child!"

Heinrich ignored him. "What makes you so sure I'm not your father, Chalice?"

I stopped struggling, but he continued to hold me by the forearms. "Your blood doesn't smell like mine."

"You can smell my blood?"

"As well as the pesto you had for lunch today. The dirt on the soles of your shoes is not from this country. Your expensive soap doesn't hide the stink of your sweat." But it was more than sweat that offended me. His stench made my eyes water. I turned my face away and sucked in a breath. "I smell on you the deaths of others."

He released me only so that he could get a better grip around my waist, but I ducked from his grasp. I whirled out of reach and lifted my dress to seize my blade. A long, slim butterfly knife glinted in the faint glow of the votive candles. Crouched with the blade poised to strike, I backed my way to the chapel door.

Heinrich chuckled, looking relaxed with his hands in his pockets. "What a delight you are, Chalice. Such fire in your soul! You and I have a wonderful future ahead of us."

"I won't go with you!" I was ashamed of how my voice cracked. My tears flowed freely now, and the hand holding the blade shook with rage. "Burn in hell."

His arching brows made him look clownish, but no less evil. "I probably will. But for the time being, I need you and your special…skills. You're so much like your mother."

I swallowed, still wary of him, but more attentive now to his words. He'd known my mother, had spoken to her, maybe even touched her….

His elongated shadow cast by the altar's candles flickered on the wall behind him. "Felicia was just as special as you are, you know. Too bad I couldn't convince her to work for me. You, however, are young and can be molded into the thief I need."

"I won't steal for you or anyone else!" I shouted, my defiance and fear at war with each other.

"Not now, but you will. And I think you'll be very good at it." I saw amusement in his cold eyes; he enjoyed my fear, even seemed energized by it.

"I must ask you to leave, Mr. Heinrich," Thomas said in a quavering voice. "You have misrepresented yourself and I'm calling the authorities."

Heinrich flicked his wrist, fingers splayed, and a zigzag of green lightning flew from the tips to strike Thomas in the throat. The monk grabbed his neck, eyes bulging, as he struggled to breathe.

"What did you do?" I was paralyzed with awe at seeing what I could only describe as magic. "You're hurting him! Stop!" I wanted to run to Thomas, shake him to make him breathe again, but my fear of Heinrich doing magic on me froze me in place.

Bending as if to tie his shoe, Heinrich yanked a small pistol from an ankle holster and fired. Brother Thomas froze when the bullet pierced his forehead. The monk hadn't yet fallen and I could do nothing but stare in shock as he slid bonelessly to the floor and Heinrich rushed over to grab me.

Machine-gun fire sprayed above our heads just as Heinrich drew back his fist. Though stunned, my mind worked well enough to guess the shot from Heinrich's pistol had been a signal to his men outside. I stared at the fist aimed at my face, the knuckles white, the backs of his curled fingers sprouting fine hairs as pale as those on his head. He wore a ring on his middle finger, its ruby center surrounded by Sanskrit letters that I could read with crystal clarity. They spelled the word *Vyantara*.

Then I saw only darkness.

two

IT'S BEEN TWELVE YEARS SINCE MY ABDUCTION from the only family I'd ever known. I traveled nearly six thousand miles across the Atlantic Ocean to arrive in the U.S. with a man pretending to be my father.

I was a thief now, trained by the Vyantara, an international organization of nefarious magic users who profited from the sale of charmed and cursed objects I stole for them. I hated those people, but they adored their spooky old relics that did some very nasty things. It amazed me how much people would pay for an enchanted Native American medicine bag with the power to cause cancer instead of cure it, or a picture frame that told the future by revealing how the subject in the photo would change over the years. Today I drove down the long driveway toward a Georgian mansion, destined for another heist. Brother Thomas never would have approved.

Before every job I pulled, I thought about the old monk and his monastery. I'd give anything to return to that simpler life, but the monks were dead, murdered by a madman and his soldiers.

I could put myself in a better mood simply by calling on childhood memories, like the birthday I'd received a box of beloved *Archie* comics that were five years out of date. On my thirteenth birthday, Brother Thomas had given me my first *Tiger Beat* magazine. It was so old that half the teen celebrities featured were, by that time, married with children of their own. I didn't mind. I'd been obsessed with America as a child, but if I'd known then what it would take to get me here, I'm pretty sure I'd have picked a different hobby.

The tattoo at the base of my skull throbbed to remind me of who and what I was. I belonged to someone now, my freedom stripped from me like hide from a rabbit in the talons of a predator. I could almost feel those talons now, the same razor-edged nails that had tried ripping out my heart three years ago.

I allowed myself a final shudder at *that* unpleasant memory, then parked the rental car in front of an enormous house propped on pillars like a Greek palace. It was showtime.

I paced across the columned porch of the Grandville's Georgian mansion, my designer heels clicking a staccato beat as I waited for someone to answer the door. I checked my watch, then stood on tiptoe to peer through the

stained-glass window mounted at the center of the elabo-
rately carved door. I rang the bell a second time.

"Rich assholes," I mumbled and returned to my pacing,
giving my watch another cursory glance. My time was precious. My seventy-two-hour limit would be up soon, and
if I tried to extend it, my life as a human would be over.

The click of a door latch caught my attention and I
positioned myself, smoothing the front of my charcoal-
gray slacks and straightening the collar of my suit jacket.
Pinching my nose, I ensured both nose filters were well
concealed, then blinked over the tinted contact lenses that
hid my gold and turquoise eyes. The armor protecting my
senses was irritating but necessary to my sanity and my
disguise. I took a second to run my hands through impos-
sibly straight hair, fluffing the short shag cut to try giving
it some volume. On a good hair day, my do looked like a
halo of raven feathers. On a bad one, more like a well-used
bottlebrush. Today was somewhere in between. My plastic
smile was barely in place when the door swung open.

"May I help you?" drawled the short, stocky gentleman
whose bow tie looked gathered far too tight at his neck.
His jowls poured over his collar in fleshy folds and it made
me wince in sympathy for him.

"Margaret Malone of Samuel Crichton and Company," I
said, thickening the British accent I hadn't completely lost.
I had to conceal my real name. Chalice would be way too
conspicuous, let alone identifying. I was a thief, after all. "I
have an appointment with Mr. Grandville."

"Are you the antiques appraiser?" Short and Stocky asked,

his drawl Southern and his tone chillier than a frozen dai-
quiri. Must be the butler. He glanced over my head as if
expecting someone else.

"I'm alone," I assured him, handing him my card and
nodding toward the foyer behind him. "And yes, I'm the
antiques appraiser. May I come in?"

The man dipped his head and opened the door wider,
stepping aside to allow enough room for me to pass.

He peered down at the card, eyes narrowed with suspicion as he glanced from me to the card and back again. "I'll
fetch Mr. Grandville."

"Thank you." I stood at the center of the round foyer
and surveyed my garish surroundings.

Noticing my interest, the butler said, "I apologize for the
decor." He sniffed, his gaze wandering to the walls. "The
decorator is a relative of Mr. Grandville. A bored, delusional
old aunt who thought she could decorate a house filled with
rare antiques. The woman has no taste."

I nodded in agreement.

"Wait here, please," the pudgy man said, then turned on
his heel to go in search of his employer.

I continued my survey of the foyer. Nineteenth-century
European oil paintings hung beside bad imitations of Hi-
eronymus Bosch. Hideous. African masks were mounted
on walls of flocked wallpaper, the pink-rose designs a hor-
rifying contrast to the fanged mouths of baboonlike effigies.
The room looked like an exaggeration of a Victorian tag
sale.

I shuddered. This wasn't my thing. My taste was far less

eclectic. I was an art historian who appreciated the cultural richness of period art in all mediums and forms from all over the world. But I knew enough about antiques to pose as an appraiser, my ruse for getting inside this house.

The object I was to swipe wasn't nearly as offensive as what I was used to. Gruesome as it was, the mummified hand of the martyred Saint Geraldine from the Crusades of the eleventh century had the power to reclaim memories from the womb. An odd power, and not particularly appealing, yet the Vyantara were desperate to add this freakish item to their collection.

"Ms. Malone!" A cheerful, gray-haired man in his late sixties, tastefully dressed in a casual blue sweater over herringbone trousers, bounded into the foyer and held out his hand. "Thank you for coming on such short notice. Douglas Grandville, at your service."

I extended my hand, which he shook vigorously, covering it in a two-handed grasp. I tried not to wince from his rough touch. The way he was pumping my arm you'd think I was some long-lost relative he hadn't seen in years. What was he so happy about? Probably to know he'd finally be getting this crap out of his house.

"My uncle Malcolm, may he rest in peace, was a pack rat. He liked to overindulge in his little, uh, treasures." Douglas waved a hand at the obscenities around us before gesturing toward a closed set of double doors. "There's more."

I felt my smile wobble. "More?"

He grimaced and nodded. "I'm afraid so. But the day is

young so you have plenty of time to go through my uncle's collection. Could be a diamond or two in the rough, eh?"

The grumpy butler joined us, his eyes brightening when Douglas mentioned the word *diamond*. Well, well. Suspicious *and* greedy. I might use that to my advantage.

Douglas steered me through the doors into a den complete with wingback leather chairs, dark cherrywood furniture and large animal heads that leered from the wall above the fireplace. I felt sure I'd seen this exact same setting in at least a half dozen films from the forties. "Can I get you anything? Soft drink? Iced tea?"

I turned around slowly, taking in Malcolm's treasures as nausea crept around the pit of my stomach. Lots of stuffed things everywhere—Malcolm had obviously been fond of taxidermy—but there were also some paintings, a few sculptures and ceramics, all of which were covered in several years' worth of dust. Maybe Saint Geraldine's hand had crawled underneath something to hide of embarrassment.

"Nothing for me, thank you, Mr. Grandville," I said, forcing a smile into my voice. My lips peeled back involuntarily. "An interesting room."

"Quite." Douglas cleared his throat. "I have appointments the rest of the day so you won't be able to reach me. But if you need anything, my butler, Andrew, is happy to oblige. Just yell. He's always within earshot." The jaunty gentleman turned on his heel and marched from the room. Andrew hesitated, giving me an appraising and untrusting look, before following his employer out the door.

"Lord, help me." I rolled my eyes and pulled a clipboard

from my briefcase. I turned around, making a slow survey of the room, then got to work.

It took a couple hours of sifting through crap before I finally finished. Andrew the butler made a constant nuisance of himself, always checking in on me to ask when I'd be done. If he didn't leave me alone, I'd never get away with what I'd come here for. I had to figure out how to distract him.

"Andrew?" I called from the doorway of the den. "Would you come in here, please?"

The stout little man appeared within seconds, an apron tied around his waist and his sparse hair disheveled as if he'd been exerting himself. He probably served as maid as well as butler, which didn't surprise me. The home's interior was shabby.

"I'm finished," I told him. "There are a couple of items here that you'll need to show Mr. Grandville when he gets home."

"Of course, miss," the butler said with a curt nod.

I led the way inside the den, where I'd made quite a mess. I heard Andrew's quick inhalation of breath as he took in the condition of the room. We both knew who would have to clean it up.

I sidestepped a bookcase I had pulled from the wall and wove a path around several stacks of leather-bound volumes in a variety of shapes and sizes. "Sorry," I said over my shoulder. "I'm very thorough when I appraise. No stone unturned. But I believe Mr. Grandville will find the disarray was worth the trouble."

Andrew tucked in his double chin and gave me a dubious look.

"Yes, well..." I stepped over a pile of stuffed animals—not the plush kind—the tip of one very expensive shoe getting caught in the open mouth of a snarling badger. I kicked at it to free my foot and the animal's head broke off. "Sorry."

I approached a wooden pedestal supporting a floral ceramic jar that could hold a gallon of cookies, something I was craving at the moment since I'd skipped lunch. A small section of white with red-and-orange blossoms was visible through the dense accumulation of dust and vintage cigar smoke. "I'd say this piece is worth between forty and fifty thousand dollars, depending on how it does at auction."

Andrew's eyes widened. "I beg your pardon?"

Gotcha. I lifted the corner of my mouth in a half grin. "It's an early eighteenth-century piece of Kakiemon porcelain. Very rare. And in extremely good condition once it's cleaned up." I leaned forward and blew on the jar, causing a cloud of dust to rise in my face. I coughed and fanned the air with my clipboard. "As I recall, it has a twin, though I couldn't find it here. Does the late Mr. Grandville's collection extend to other rooms in the house?"

Andrew's eyes sparkled. "I, uh, I'm not sure."

I smiled. "It may be a good idea to check. If both pieces were sold together, they would bring a considerable fortune at auction."

I could practically hear the gears turn inside his head.

"This painting here," I said, lifting a realistic rendering of a lake scene from the stack, "is an original oil by Finnish painter Albert Edlefelt. This particular work was thought to have been lost over one hundred years ago."

Andrew looked ready to explode with excitement. He shifted nervously from one foot to the other. "Is it worth the same as the jar?"

I folded my arms and pursed my lips. "No."

He visibly deflated.

"It's worth about ten times as much."

His toothy grin completely transformed his face from a sour old crank to an enthusiastic lottery winner. I doubted the butler, or the two valuable pieces of art, would still be in the house when Mr. Grandville returned. But that wasn't my problem.

I had yet to find Saint Geraldine's hand, though it should be somewhere in the house. The Vyantara's key researcher had confirmed its delivery from the dealer in Budapest, who had sold it to Malcolm Grandville. Why the old man would want to reclaim memories from his mother's womb was beyond me. Nonetheless, the mummified thing was here and I had to find it.

"Excuse me, Andrew," I said to the butler, who was clutching the Edlefelt painting in white-knuckled fists. "May I use the restroom?"

"Of course," he said, all smiles, his eyes sparkling. A completely different person altogether. "It's down the hall, first door to your left."

I knew as soon as I left the room that he'd start going through the junk I'd scattered everywhere to look for that other jar. Either he'd be too preoccupied with his treasure hunt to concern himself with my snooping through the house, or he'd take his booty and make a run for it. My bet was on the latter.

Once inside the bathroom, I removed my nose filters, earplugs and tinted contact lenses. I'd hoped this wouldn't be necessary. Stripping away my sensory defenses was painful in a mind-bending way.

I blinked in the dark bathroom, adjusting my eyes to the brightness around me. The sink seemed to glow phosphorescent, the fixtures looked outlined in neon, and the carpet was flecked with luminous lint. I saw dried paste behind the wallpaper and counted the rings of wood grain in the oak cabinets above and below the sink.

My ears stung from every sound that vibrated inside the old mansion. I sucked in a breath, trying to ignore the stench. If I didn't get out of the bathroom this minute, I'd soon be kneeling before the commode of a hundred hurls.

Slipping sunglasses over my eyes to mute a visual assault, and then sliding on a pair of thin leather gloves, I stepped out into the hall.

I had studied the mansion's blueprints beforehand so I knew the layout relatively well. Tuning in my olfactory senses, I searched for moldy odors and the smell of human decay, homing in on the mummified hand. It took only a few seconds to pick up the scent coming from somewhere in the basement.

In less than a minute I found the basement stairs. I trotted down wooden steps into the comforting darkness below. Much better. I could remove my sunglasses now. Allowing my nose to guide me, I wound my way between stacked boxes and various sizes of luggage and old furniture. After zeroing in on a box no bigger than a football, I realized my search was over. I bent to retrieve my butterfly knife from the sheath at my ankle.

A Visayan knife fighter since the age of nine, I considered my butterfly knives an extension of myself. My favorite blade was the Filipino Balisong. A visiting Visayan at the Maronite monastery had taught me the art, instilling in me the spiritual merging of creation, motion and action. The Balisong symbolized these triangular forces and just holding the blade in my hand gave me a sense of power and control.

The smell of decay was strong now. I flicked the knife's latch with my thumb and the curved blade flipped out from the chamber port. Gripping the bifold handle, I used the blade to pry off the crate's lid. Nested within the excelsior was a glass box that held Saint Geraldine's hand.

The shrunken appendage looked unremarkable in its smudged container of filmy glass that had molded in the corners. I turned the box in my hand to peer at it from all angles. It resembled something from the biology lab at the private training camp I'd been forced to attend, only this wasn't floating in formaldehyde. Interesting. And way too bulky in its case to easily conceal beneath my suit jacket. I'd have to break the case and remove the hand.

I wrapped it in an old rag I found on the floor. Using the

pommel end of my Balisong, I smashed the glass, wincing at the thunderous sound it made inside my head, though I knew there was no way Andrew could have heard it.

I tenderly plucked the wrinkled hand from its bed of satin, surprised at how supple the flesh felt, how firm the bones were despite its age. This wasn't nearly as disgusting as the dried-up lion's testicles I'd had to steal last month. An African shaman had blessed them and—boy oh, boy—what a ruckus that little heist made.

Something strange was happening. The fingers of the hand grew warm as I held them close to my chest. I felt a tingle trickle up my arms, my neck and across my scalp. My pulse raced, the sound like beating drums between my ears.

I heard a woman crying. Deep, racking sobs that shook me to the core. The weeping echoed around me as though coming through water and I heard a muffled voice. "Remember, little one," the woman said. "Our people need you. Find them. And whatever happens to me, know I love you always."

I had people? I tried to focus on the woman's watery words and realized this had to be my mother's voice. What had she meant? I concentrated, trying to hear more, but she had stopped talking. I sensed I was in an alien place far from any mansion in Georgia. All I heard now was the roar of an engine, its idle drowned out by the amniotic fluid of my mother's womb. Where had my mother been when she spoke those words? If I had to locate the people—my people—who needed me, I had to find out where to go.

A low, animal growl forced my attention back to the present. Blinking my way to full consciousness, I glanced down into the chocolate-brown eyes of a Rottweiler.

"Nice doggy," I muttered to the animal who was baring its fangs. Damn, but I hated the thought of hurting an animal—only this was no ordinary dog. Its aura was bright red and spikes of black lightning flared from the edges like an electrified crown. The animal was possessed by a hellhound; the perfect guard dog for an eccentric collector of bizarre artifacts. What had old Mr. Grandville used to bargain for this monster? His own soul? I drew in a breath to calm myself. I could outrun the beast. Or at least I could try.

I closed my knife, slid it back into its sheath, and backed my way to the stack of crates, kicking off my four-hundred-dollar shoes along the way. The dog gave them a disinterested sniff, then barked and advanced a step. It lunged forward and I leapt onto the tallest crate.

Being only five foot two had its advantages. I easily fit into tight spaces, and at only ninety-five pounds, I didn't have the burden of extra weight to carry around. Speed was my advantage in most cases, but I'd never had to outrun a hellhound before.

"You look out of shape," I told the animal, though its broad chest was probably more muscle than fat. It growled at me again. I hopped onto another stack of boxes, then flung myself toward a web of pipes that ran across the ceiling. The dog followed, jumping up and snapping at my heels as I hung there contemplating my next move.

The pipes snaked toward an exit that I remembered from the blueprints. The door opened out to a garden, and a hundred yards from there was a ten-foot fence. Beyond that were acres of forested land, where I had stashed my Ducati motorcycle the night before in case my mission was compromised. It appeared I wouldn't need the rental car anymore, which was fine with me. It had been as much a ruse as my Margaret Malone business cards.

Using my best Tarzan imitation, I swung from pipe to pipe, the hellhound barking and leaping at my every move. I half expected to see Andrew at any moment, unless he'd already skipped off with his loot.

"Ms. Malone?"

Shit! Andrew heard the dog. Now what? I couldn't answer him because then he'd know I was down here.

"Where are you, Ms. Malone?"

I bit my lip and waited, the dog settling down enough to sit, panting, and stared up at me with its eyes glowing red. All I knew is that I had to get the hell out of there before I became Devil Fido's chew toy. Douglas Grandville would be scraping what was left of me off the concrete for weeks.

I was now dangling above the door that led to freedom. Once I started moving again, I was sure the hellhound would start foaming at the mouth and launch into a canine frenzy. I had to find a way outside without getting my throat torn out. Saint Geraldine's hand shifted against my chest, and as I angled my arm to reach inside my shirt to grab it, the hand's fingers slipped through mine and fell to the floor.

I started to go down after it, but the beast beat me to it. Its jaws clamped on to the hand like it was a rawhide bone.

I kicked at the dog. "Shoo! Get away from that." It dropped the hand, but continued to guard it, making it clear he'd take my hand, too, if I were stupid enough to come any closer.

My stomach tightened. My mission had failed. I had a choice to make: be ripped apart by a hellhound, or suffer my master's punishment. It wasn't a tough decision.

While the dog occupied itself as the hand's protector, I dropped to the ground and curled my fingers around the doorknob, giving it a twist. It opened instantly. I dived out the door and slammed it shut behind me.

Night had fallen and stars dotted the sky with sequined brilliance that made my eyes sting. Squinting, I sprinted barefoot toward the ten-foot fence. Thankfully it wasn't electric. I scurried up the chain link and dropped to the other side.

I dashed for the shrubs that hid my motorcycle. Once my nose and earplugs were back in place, I fired up the Ducati. My fury was acute and focused as I said to the night, "You want that damn hand, Heinrich? Then you can come back and get it yourself."

three

IT TOOK ME TWO DAYS AND ONE CRUDDY
motel to finally reach Gavin Heinrich's sprawling estate
outside metro Chicago. Riding a motorcycle through back
roads and side streets to avoid detection takes its toll on a
girl's patience, but I was motivated. I'd failed to do what I
was assigned and I wanted my punishment over with. But
even more important than that, my seventy-two-hour time
limit was just about up.

The itching between my shoulders had increased, an unpleasant reminder of what would happen if the restrictions
of my bond were stretched too far. The skin hadn't broken
yet, the tips of unformed wings waiting for an exit through
bone and flesh. I wouldn't metamorphose for another hour
or so, but the shift had already started. My tattoo pulsed in
rhythm with my heartbeat. As much as I hated to admit it,

I needed Shui. Since I was bonded to him, he was the only one who could stop my transformation.

I stood outside the enormous mansion, once again waiting for someone to let me in. Déjà vu. But instead of politely ringing the bell, I gave the door a couple of swift kicks with my booted foot.

The man who flung open the door with the same impatience I felt wasn't Gavin's butler from last week. This new one was thirty pounds lighter and at least ten years older, with thick gray eyebrows as long as whiskers on a cat. Without a word, he looked pointedly down at the shallow dent my boot had made in the varnished wood.

"I'm here to see my father," I said curtly and without inflection. The word *father* always left a sour taste in my mouth as Heinrich and I both knew it was a facade.

The new guy scowled. "I was unaware Mr. Heinrich had any children."

Feeling edgier than ever, I huffed and pushed the man aside, forcing my way into the house. "Hey, Gavin!"

Mr. New Guy went ashen, his mouth falling open as he glanced frantically up the spiral staircase. "Ms., you can't barge in here—"

"The hell I can't," I said softly, my silken tone having a dangerous edge. Minutes ticked by like a time bomb and I needed my fix. I needed Shui. "Where's John, the other butler?"

New Guy blinked. "Who?"

I snorted and wiped sweat off my upper lip. "Probably dead. Gavin goes through at least two of you guys a year."

That was a warning, and I only hoped he picked up the hint. Hey, I was trying to save the guy's life.

If New Guy was pale before, he was chalk-white now.

"Chalice, my dear." Gavin Heinrich descended the stairs, his smile charming and his eyes cold as a snake's. He wore a black silk smoking jacket over black trousers, his thick silver hair combed into a style better suited for a younger man. But Gavin didn't look anywhere near his seventy-plus years. He had his own methods for staying young, none of which involved plastic surgery. "I'm so glad to see you made it home safely."

"This isn't my home," I said stiffly. But no matter where I lived, I would always be his prisoner. "I have my own home, thank you very much."

"My mistake." He reached the landing and sauntered toward me, Mr. New Guy gazing at him with new respect and something akin to horror. Gavin ignored him. "I keep forgetting you prefer that little cement-blocked apartment of yours to this architectural marvel with every comfort you could want."

I shuddered. Yeah, I knew the kind of "comforts" he was into. It made my skin crawl. Folding my arms, I glared into his ice-blue eyes. "That was one hell of a job you sent me on. You owe me."

He arched his brows. "No, dear. You owe me." He held out his open palm. "Give me Saint Geraldine's hand."

An icy flush covered me from head to toe. I backed up and spun around, a prickle of fear nipping at the base of my spine. I couldn't deal with his anger right now, not with the change so close. Remembering past punishments, I could almost feel the sting of his leather whip on the backs of my legs.

Taking a deep breath, I pretended to study the decor of the foyer that was so different from the Grandville mansion. Gavin's was tastefully creepy, like the set for *The Addams Family* but without the dust and cobwebs.

"I'm waiting, Chalice," Gavin said, his tone frosty. "Where is it?"

"I don't have it." I turned to face him again, but from a safer distance. "It got eaten. I think."

Gavin's eyes widened and his jaw muscle twitched. He furrowed his brows. "Eaten?"

"There was a hellhound you didn't warn me about, and the hand…" Damn, I should have figured out how to get it away from that stupid beast. I couldn't let Gavin see my concern—signs of weakness were like catnip to him—so I shrugged my shoulders and leaned against the wall, feigning boredom. "I accidentally dropped it, and when I tried picking it up, the beast attacked me. Not my fault."

Gavin gave me a long, searching stare, but he didn't look angry. Just…pensive. "Yesterday I checked the voice mail I'd set up for our phony appraisal business. There was a long message from Douglas Grandville."

"Yeah?" I tried to smile in spite of my worries. Pretense. Oh, yes, I was very good at pretense. I couldn't survive without it. "What did he say?"

Gavin began to pace. "He said nothing about the hand

of Saint Geraldine, but he was none too pleased with the condition of his uncle's den."

He stopped pacing to glower at me. "Grandville told me the pedestal where a cookie jar once sat is now empty. And there were six spots on the wall where paintings used to hang, but he counted only five stacked on the floor. Oh, and his butler is missing. Would you happen to know where any of these things might be?"

"The butler did it."

He stared down his nose at me, his mouth pulled severely down at the corners.

"I'm serious. I told the butler about the Kakiemon porcelain piece and the Edlefelt oil I'd appraised at several thousands of dollars. He was very excited when I told him there was a twin to the vase, and if he could find it, the pair would be worth a fortune. I figured his greed would distract him while I stole the hand, and it worked."

Gavin nodded. "Yet you failed to bring me the saint's hand."

Well, shit. I thought I could talk my way out of whatever trouble I'd put myself in. It had worked before, but this time I'd be punished, and I had a pretty good idea how. Sweat trickled down the sides of my face and I could tell by the way Gavin narrowed his eyes that he knew how close I was to shifting. I wouldn't beg and he knew that, too. He waited to see how long I could last.

Looking down at my feet, I drew out an already long pause before asking, "Did Mr. Grandville call the police?"

"Of course." Cool as ever, Gavin resumed his pacing. As

always, he had the upper hand. "Not that it matters to us. The fake address on your business cards led to an empty lot, and the phone number was for a voice-mail service where neither of us can be traced."

All his loose ends were tied in neat little bows, but this time I had no package to deliver.

"Samuel?" Gavin glanced at his butler. "My daughter and I will be in the basement study. Prepare us some refreshments. Cappuccino and biscotti."

"I hate biscotti," I said, hiding my anxiety with petulance.

"Forgive me. Make that chocolate-chip cookies." He waved a dismissive hand at the new guy—Samuel—and gestured for me to precede him downstairs to the basement. "Chalice, you and I need to talk."

I started down the stairs, my mounting apprehension like a silent beast crouched low in my belly.

Cold as a dungeon, the stone basement always reminded me of something from an old movie set. I compared a lot of what I experienced to movies because what I learned from film and TV were about all I really knew of the world. I usually worked alone, had no friends and even my training had been solitary, except for the instructors who came and went on a daily basis. My college education came from CDs and DVDs; there had been no ceremony when I received my Masters in art history.

Gavin had purposely kept me secluded, claiming that my sensory disability made it necessary to limit my exposure to the outside world. His excuse was his concern for my health and safety. Yeah, right. The man was a sadist. And he owned me.

When I rounded the corner into the enormous study, my blood went still in my veins. Gavin's gargoyle, Shui, sat hunched on a perch in the center of the room and he gazed at me with hungry eyes. He was about the height and width of a bar-size refrigerator, his gray, scaly skin appearing dull in the dim light, his bat wings folded back but quivering with tension. Cocking his head, the blue baboon face sneered while issuing a low hiss. The thing looked a lot like a flying monkey from the *Wizard of Oz,* only bigger and ten times uglier.

I hesitated, repulsed by the monster that would save me from becoming exactly like him.

Jutting my chin at the gargoyle, I said to Gavin, "He looks bigger than he did three days ago."

Gavin glanced at me, then at the abomination on its perch. He lifted both eyebrows and gave me a curious look. "Perhaps that's because he's eaten recently. Haven't you, Shui?"

The gargoyle hissed again, only louder this time.

Well, there was my answer to what had happened to the other butler. Lucky for me, I wasn't on the menu.

I'd only tested my bond with Shui once, about three years ago. I had no way of knowing for sure that going beyond seventy-two hours without any contact with Shui would turn me into a beast as ugly and mean as him. Where was the proof? The tattoo on my neck had been made with a mixture of ink and Shui's blood. The shaman who put it there had warned me what would happen if I broke the rules. I was thirteen at the time and his threats scared me, but as I got older, I embraced my inner *b*s: bold, bitchy and bad. I'd felt compelled to test the bond. And it almost killed me.

I was riding my Ducati, speeding through the Illinois countryside, when the itching began. Then the burning. My entire body felt on fire. I pulled to the side of the road and ripped off my helmet. My ears rang with rushing blood that coursed through inflamed vessels, the cells inside me consumed by the curse of transformation. I looked at my hands and watched the nails curve into claws just as the stabbing pain in my back hunched me over, forcing me into a crouch. The pulsing between my shoulders was the worst part. My skin ripped as the tips of two leather wings began pushing their way through flesh and bone. The thunder of beating wings sounded overhead and Shui soared down from the night sky. Not to rescue me, as I had hoped, but with something far more lethal in mind.

He'd tackled me to the ground and grabbed my chest in his talons, ripping through my rib cage to get at my heart. If it hadn't been for Gavin's interference with a spell to paralyze him, my heart would have become Shui's evening snack. But Gavin wouldn't let him kill me yet. I hadn't outlived my usefulness as the Vyantara's thief.

Now I could grudgingly admit to having new respect for the gargoyle, though the old hate for him remained. Walking through Gavin's basement, I locked eyes with Shui while running my fingers across my chest and over the scar created by eighty-five stitches. He scared me, but I couldn't keep my mouth shut. "Why don't you fly your wrinkled gray butt back to Oz where you belong, freak."

Shui growled, the rumble so deep I felt it through the soles of my boots.

"That's the last thing you want him to do," Gavin said without turning his attention from the wall of a dozen silent but animated television screens. He liked to stay current on world events. "You need him too much."

Damn him for being right. More anxious than ever now, I tried without success to shrug off my mounting panic. I faked indifference by collapsing onto the leather couch in the center of the room, and then tugging my Balisong from its ankle sheath. Flicking open the blade, I pretended to clean my nails. The instinctive need to protect myself made the muscles in my neck bunch into knots.

I heaved what I hoped sounded like a bored sigh, though I was anything but bored. Wound up so tight it felt like my muscles would spring from my skin, I stretched my arms above my head and yawned. "Do you want to talk, or did you bring me down here just to watch television?"

He turned his back on the TVs and stared at me. "You screwed up."

I shrugged, but my nerves vibrated with warning. The itching between my shoulders was getting worse. "I already explained that it was an accident. Not my fault."

"I need the saint's hand."

Swallowing hard, I sat up straight and glanced over my shoulder at Shui. Gavin knew what *I* needed, the bastard.

"I'm no longer that scared little girl you kidnapped and brought to America. I'm twenty-five years old, well educated and with money of my own—"

"Money *I* gave you."

"Money I earned from the jobs I pulled for the Vyantara."

He squinted as if thinking that over, then lowered himself to sit on the arm of the leather chair opposite me. "Yet you still live like a pauper."

As if that mattered to him. "It's my choice. I can live any way I want."

"Aside from your obsession with designer clothes and the work of unknown, mediocre artists, you leave yourself almost nothing to live on. What money you have you foolishly give away to charity."

He probably knew what brand of toothpaste I used if not the name of my favorite breakfast cereal. "So what if I do? It's my money. And it's not like I have any kind of lifestyle to support." Giving money away never totally assuaged my guilt for thieving, but it helped. A little.

An annoying smirk tightened Gavin's lips.

This conversation was going nowhere. I was sweating so much now that my designer T-shirt had stuck to my back. I tried to sound calm when I said, "It's time, Gavin."

He frowned and the deep creases in his forehead added character to the typically bland expression on his face. "I think you can last awhile longer, eh? I'm curious to see how this whole transformation thing works. I've only seen it once."

I clenched my fists. "Damn it, Gavin!"

He smiled, showing his teeth. "Fifty years ago Shui was a striking young man. A real lady-killer, and I mean that literally." He chuckled. "Unfortunately, Shui killed the chancellor's daughter, and that's one faux pas the Vyantara won't tolerate. We take care of our own."

I bet they did, not that I gave a crap. Shui was the only gargoyle the society had that I knew of, though I assumed there must be others. Gargoyles made excellent assassins, never leaving behind any trace of their victims.

"He'd been an ordinary human before, though more coldhearted than most. He was a psychopath, and that aspect of his character didn't change with his shape. Just as well. He's a heartless killer, and the best we have." Gavin cast an adoring gaze at the monster sitting quietly in the shadows. Shui's eyes glowed bright as twin moonbeams.

Gavin was torturing me for his own entertainment. The heat of anger rose to my cheeks, adding to the burning pain already there. Panic made my nerves jump. I concentrated on taking deep breaths to maintain a calm facade because my slow-to-boil temper was about to explode. Jaw rigid, I barely ground out, "You know what I need."

He reached out to pat my hand. "Yes, dear, I know. Perhaps if you had retrieved the item I sent you for, I wouldn't need to go to these extremes."

Unbidden tears burned my eyes and I blinked them back. I recalled hearing my mother's voice tell me I had people waiting for me… The very idea of remaining as this man's slave was unthinkable. Unimaginable. Undoable.

"You've always done a good job for us, Chalice. But if

you can no longer perform as you were trained, perhaps it's time you worked for us in a different form."

My calm demeanor shattered. The consequences of killing this bastard where he stood would be death, but at this point, I no longer cared. My sense of self would be gone once I changed into the creature I despised. What was the point of living if I couldn't be free? Why continue on only to live in constant fear for the rest of my life? Not to mention the overwhelming loneliness. I couldn't do it anymore. It wasn't worth it.

Gavin had to die.

He must have noticed the change in me because his expression became puzzled, then suspicious as he jumped to his feet. I was on top of him like a fly on dung, toppling him backward onto the chair. My Balisong sang through the air as I swiped the blade down, aiming for the throbbing artery in his neck.

The thunder of flapping wings came just before Shui's claws gouged my wrist, letting my blade only graze Gavin's skin. Shui's grip tightened, his nails piercing deep into my flesh and forcing me to cry out. If he clamped down hard enough, he'd surely sever the hand right off my arm. I dropped the knife.

"That's enough, Shui," Gavin said.

The gargoyle didn't move. His hot breath crawled over the top of my head, rustling my hair, his stench sifting through the barrier of my nose filters. I fought the reflex to gag and turned my head. Yet at the same time, I craved what he could give me. Shui could stop the transformation that would force me into becoming the monster he was.

Gavin glared at the gargoyle. "Shui, let her go! Now!"

The creature growled and reluctantly released his grip. But he remained close, gripping the back of the chair with his feet as he leaned against me, possessive and threatening.

"Let him do what he has to do," I said through clenched teeth. The pain in my wrist was excruciating and warm blood from the puncture wounds dribbled onto my jeans. I shifted forward and the gargoyle followed. "If you won't let him touch my tat and stop the change, I'll kill him. I'll do it with my bare hands."

"You're being ridiculous," Gavin said, rising from the chair and stomping to a ceiling-tall bookcase. He yanked a red towel from a shelf and tossed it to me. "You know better than anyone that it's impossible to kill an immortal creature, especially a gargoyle." He tugged a white handkerchief from his robe's breast pocket and dabbed at his neck. Waving a hand at my wound, he said, "Put pressure on that before you get blood all over my rug."

What difference would adding my blood make to the countless bloodstains already there? I'd picked up on the old blood years ago.

I wrapped the towel around my wrist and heard Shui inhale deeply before a low moan rumbled inside his broad chest. The smell of blood was exciting him. And more blood was about to spill as the skin between my shoulder blades stretched.

I clenched my jaw and held my breath. "Shui's stench is

making me sick." Head down, I rolled my eyes up at Gavin and imbued my scowl with malice. "Make up your mind. Either be rid of my human self, or stop me from changing. Choose now because in one more minute, there'll be no choice to make."

Acting as if he hadn't just come within an inch of losing his life, Gavin barked an order at Shui, who bent his head toward my neck. I closed my eyes and tried to ignore the stink. The gargoyle's tongue swiped across my skin, its moist heat lingering where the tattoo scorched my flesh. As disgusting as it was to have this monster's saliva seep into my body, relief was immediate. My skin started to cool, the itching stopped. Normalcy returned. At least for the next three days.

Shui flew back to his perch and Gavin cocked his head, offering me a sardonic grin. "That wasn't so bad, was it? I admire your fortitude, Chalice. Your humanity is far too precious to have it disappear behind a pair of leathery wings, though I don't doubt you'd make a lovely gargoyle. I'm just not ready to give you up. Yet."

I was still seething, my mind conjuring ways I could make his life as miserable as he'd made mine, but I didn't discount what he just said. The word *yet* left its imprint on my mind. I wasn't free of Gavin's threat and wondered if I ever would be. "Consider me punished. Can I go now?"

"You haven't had your cookies and cappuccino yet."

I closed my eyes to shut him out. The man was off his nut. His spells, potions, charms, curses and the rest of his abracadabra bullshit had fried more than a few of his brain cells. When I opened my eyes, I found him kneeling in front of me, his lips curved in a smile that looked almost sincere.

"I have something for you." He reached into the hip pocket of his robe and withdrew an envelope. He tried to touch my good hand, but I jerked it away. Just the thought of his fingers on me made me ill.

Lifting both eyebrows in a quizzical arch, he asked, "Don't you want to see what your mother left you?"

My breathing stopped midbreath. What was he up to? I didn't trust him. "This better not be a joke."

"No joke."

I let him place the envelope in my upturned hand.

"The monks gave it to me. They said your mother wanted you to have it when you grew up."

"Why did you wait so long to give me this?"

Gavin looked at me blankly. "You weren't ready."

"But I am now because...?"

He gestured for me to open the letter. I glanced at the envelope, its edges brittle, a single word scrawled on the outside. *Chalice.* I swallowed, feeling the sting of tears, and blinking hard to make them go away. I wouldn't cry. Not in front of Gavin. I turned the letter over and noticed the flap was loose. It was too much to hope that my privacy might be respected for once. I glared up at him to let him know it wasn't okay.

He shrugged. "Just read what's inside."

I pulled the page free and smoothed out the fold before holding it up to the light. A blank piece of paper.

I gritted my teeth against the hope I'd been tricked into feeling. I'd actually believed this was a message from my mother. Her words written just for me and no one else. Longing swelled my heart as I remembered her voice warbling through the liquid cocoon of her womb. The saint's hand had let me hear her and this note could have gifted me with more of her words.

I made as if to crumple the letter in my fist, but Gavin lunged at me and grabbed my wrist. His fingers clamped down nearly as hard as Shui's talons.

He said one word. "Don't."

"You're messing with me again." I tried to yank my arm free, but he held on. "First you torture my body, now my heart. You're a sick man."

His thin smile grated on my nerves. "That may be, but I'm not messing with you now." He narrowed his eyes. "You need to read that letter."

"I can't. It's blank."

"Is it?" He let go of my wrist and I stared hard at the clean white paper. "Take out your contact lenses."

Before touching my eyes, I held the letter to my nose and sniffed. A chemical smell. I withdrew one nose filter. The overpowering stench of rotted meat and sulfur coming from Shui almost erased all other scents in the room, and I had to focus extra hard on the paper in my hand. The odor was unmistakable. Bleach.

"Now look at it."

I didn't want to take my contacts out in Gavin's basement. Nightmares lived here. I always saw too much and I feared it would drive me insane someday.

"Block out the ghosts, Chalice. Just focus on the letter." He sighed and returned to his chair, sitting slowly while studying me. As if he didn't trust me. Smart man. "Use your discipline."

Oh, yes. My self-discipline was stellar. But when emotions were involved, my concentration pretty much sucked.

I removed my contacts and made the mistake of letting my gaze wander to the shadows where Shui crouched, his wings folded close and taloned feet gripping his perch. But he didn't sit alone. I squinted in the bright glare of Gavin's forty-watt lamps and watched the fluorescent particles of energy swirl around the gargoyle, who was oblivious to them. The energy appeared like smoke in the form of people, fading and then coalescing again into the incorporeal twins of their dead selves.

"Ignore them." Gavin followed my stare to where the shades of Shui's victims hovered. He couldn't see them with his eyes, but he knew they were there. He possessed an extra sense that I didn't, a sixth one that perceived the rarified energies on the planes beyond this one. Hocus-pocus crap, but real enough for anyone with the faith to believe. What I saw was real, too, but on a totally different level.

I looked at the letter in my hands. How could I not have seen this? My lips stretched into a smile that hurt my face and I had to touch my mouth to prove to myself it was real. I'd had very few reasons to smile, but now I had a good one.

"It's from her!" I said, ignoring the fact that my audience

were my two worst enemies. "She says—" I stopped and frowned, watching the pale gray letters on the page form words I should keep to myself. I lifted my head to find Gavin leaning so far forward that one flap of Shui's wings would toss him off the chair. I refolded the letter and tucked it back inside its envelope.

Color rose in Gavin's cheeks to make him look less like a corpse and more like the furious sorcerer I'd grown to hate over the years. Much better. Angry Gavin I could deal with. Insane Gavin was too unpredictable, and therefore more dangerous. I felt most comfortable around those who acted as I expected them to.

His voice contained, but stressed to the point of breaking, he said quietly, "You little bitch."

I smiled again. I liked when our interactions were balanced. Actually, I preferred the scale tipped more to my side, and right now it was closer to me than it had ever been. "What's the matter, Gavin?" I asked sweetly. "Couldn't your badass Vyantara buddies decipher my mother's message?"

He didn't answer, but I felt the heat of his glare. In fact, without my contacts in, I could see extreme emotions leak into people's auras. His was bright red. Shui sensed it, too, because he growled from his perch to let me know he was paying attention.

"They couldn't, could they?" I asked. "Because she used bleach mixed with some unknown ingredient to make the ink to write something only I could read. You need me to tell you what it says."

Gavin crossed his arms and relaxed his face, his demeanor growing calm. "You and I can help each other."

"The only help I want from you is to get your fucking monkey off my back." I leaned in to him, picking up the pungent odor of charmed ointments he used to ward off aging. He smelled of camphor and pepper. "Just tell me how to do that, and I'll tell you what's in this letter." A letter I hadn't yet read but for the first word: *Find.*

He looked thoughtful for a few seconds before saying, "Kill him."

Surprise raised my voice an octave. "Kill Shui?"

The gargoyle growled, topping it off with a hiss.

"When he's dead, he'll turn to stone, and you'll be free of your bond. Simple." Gavin tilted his head slightly back to gaze down his nose at me. "A deal's a deal. Now, what does your mother's letter say?"

His answer was too easy. There had to be a catch. "How do I kill Shui? Gargoyles are immortal. You reminded me about that a few minutes ago."

"They are immortal, but there's a loophole. You just have to know what it is." He gave me a sly look before his face brightened, his attention focused behind me.

"Samuel! Just bring it here." He motioned for the butler to lay his tray on the heavy, oak coffee table beside the couch. "Fresh baked cookies, yes? Very nice. You can go."

Samuel spotted Shui and blanched. "Sir, is that a monkey?"

"Yes, it is," Gavin said. "Now run along. I'm having an

important conversation with my daughter and I want no more interruptions."

Samuel's hand shook as he pointed. "But it has wings—"

"Leave!" Gavin shouted, using his sorcerer's voice. The deep cadence resonated against the stone walls and shook the contents of the tray. Samuel backed up, nearly falling over his own feet before turning to disappear up the stairs. Knowing how Gavin's pneuma spells worked, I expected the butler would forget all about Shui by the time he reached the top step.

Gavin looked at me, puzzled. "Where was I?"

"Loopholes."

His eyes narrowed, but he grinned. "That's right. Loopholes."

Silence. He wasn't telling me what I needed to know. "So how do I kill Shui?"

Gavin's confused expression returned, though it was more theatrical now. "You said all you wanted to know was how to break free of your bond to Shui, and I told you. How you accomplish that goal is another question. Quid pro quo, my dear. Quid pro quo."

Bastard. He'd screwed me over. Well, not entirely, because I was now one step closer to freedom than I'd been an hour ago. Heart heavy with losing my bargaining edge, I glanced at the letter in my lap and slipped it slowly from its envelope.

four

"I'LL KNOW IF YOU'RE LYING," GAVIN TOLD ME,
his snake eyes trained on my face. He scrutinized my lip
movements, eye blinks, even the way I worked the muscles
in my jaw. I did a mental eye-roll. This was so typical,
and so totally my fault. I'd never managed to perfect my
poker face, and now I had no choice but to read aloud my
mother's letter, word for word.

My mother hadn't written it in cursive. In fact, the characters were printed in Sanskrit that I'd have to translate.
There was no salutation, so her note could have been to
anyone. My throat swelled with a sadness I couldn't express
in front of Gavin. I wouldn't give him the satisfaction. I
held back a sigh while noting how few words there were
on the page. Was this all she had to say to her daughter?

"Get on with it, Chalice." Gavin's lips thinned into that

angry line I knew so well. His stiff posture revealed a tension he usually kept hidden. It was rare that I ever had something he wanted this badly.

I let out a breath and scanned the short message that made no sense. "Find the Fallen and you'll find your father." I glanced up to see Gavin's eyes widen, his lips curling into a bare smile. He was obviously pleased to hear whatever this cryptic note implied.

"I don't get it," I said, disappointed.

"I'd always suspected, but never knew for sure." He stood and began to pace. He couldn't think without moving. "Your father was an angel. That's why you are the way you are, as well as your mother, and her mother, and all the Hatchet Knights before her. Now we can trace it back to how it first started."

My breathing hitched. Though Gavin once told me I was a descendant of the Hatchet Knights, an order of female knights who'd fought in the Crusades nearly a thousand years ago, my heritage was only a point of personal pride. I used to think the knights were extinct and until my experience holding the saint's hand, having ancestors meant nothing to me. Now I hear I'd been fathered by an angel? I hadn't given much thought to who my father *really* was. It could have been the gardener or the milkman for all I cared, but what mattered to me is that he had hurt my mother. Abandoned her. Let her die alone. But a fallen angel? My religious studies at the monastery came flooding back to me. The only Fallen I knew of were… "That's impossible," I said, my heart beating in my throat. "The Fallen are demons."

There was a bounce to Gavin's step as he quickened his pace. "Not all of them. Besides, they didn't start out that way. Committing sin is what makes an angel fall from grace. And it only takes one sin for that to happen. 'Fornication is a sin against God. Sin is transgression of the law of God.' Book of John, chapter three, verse four."

Brave words from someone who sinned on a daily basis, but to Gavin the Bible was just a reference book, not a religious icon. I shook my head, refusing to believe an angel could mate with a human. Fallen or not, there was no way an angel had anything to do with procreating me; I was about as far from angelic as anyone could get. Despite my denial, my heart raced and my mouth went dry.

I wouldn't let my emotions get the best of me in front of Gavin. So I switched my train of thought to something more academic. I knew about angels and demons, demonology having been an important part of my training as a thief. I'd met a few demons, even had one as a teacher, but I hadn't had the pleasure of an angel's company. Pixies, faeries, trolls, elves, among other fey folk, were common within the circle of influence I'd been forced into. Other than what I'd read in the Book of Enoch, I questioned the existence of angels because I'd never seen one. And the Fallen? Nothing but a myth. My mother's message had to be code for something else.

"There must be more in Felicia's letter," Gavin said, stopping midpace to stare at me. "Finish reading."

I slumped back on the couch and shook my head. "I swear that's all it says."

He scrutinized me for a second and jerked a nod.

I checked the letter again, noticing something scribbled at the bottom, but it wasn't a word. It was a drawing. Gavin noticed the change in my expression because his eyes grew hard. "So there *is* more."

I considered lying, but that would be futile. He'd catch it without even trying. My mother's drawing looked like a doodle, some thoughtless strokes of ink as if she tested its potency on the paper. But the drawing was symmetrical and looked suspiciously like a divination of runes.

"I think she drew rune stones," I told Gavin, tracing the design with my finger. I knew the symbolism of runes from my studies in European art history. Some scholars believed they originated from the Turkish alphabet, others thought Greek or Roman. Regardless of how the system got started, its purpose was to foretell the future. "It's a spread of the four elements."

"Earth, fire, water and air." Gavin resumed his pacing, still with his eyes trained on me. "She must have been divining something for you. What symbols did she use?"

I sucked in my lower lip and bit down, thinking. I realized that I could tell him the truth *and* lie at the same time. Would he know which was which? "Harvest, Wisdom, Dice Cup and Thorn," I said, listing the signs out of order. I bit my lip harder and tasted blood.

Gavin rushed to his desk and snatched up a notepad and pencil, thrusting both in my face. "Draw it for me."

I sketched the four runes my mother had drawn, only I reversed their order. This would affect the divination's meaning and I had no idea how. I wasn't a fortune teller.

I'd have to find out the real meaning behind my mother's message some other way.

I held my breath when I handed Gavin the notepad.

He grabbed it from me and, grinning, he said to the drawing, "You thought you were so clever, didn't you, Felicia?"

Damn. What had I done? "What does it mean?"

"I thought you knew how to interpret the runes." He raised his brows and gave me one of his superior looks. But he was wrong. I knew the correct order of my mother's runes, I just didn't know what it meant. "It's a warning. This tableau tells me the silver veil is closed to the Fallen's spawn."

Which would be me, *if* my father was a fallen angel. But there was no such thing. My mother's message was symbolic, not literal. Any skeptic would recognize that, but because Gavin was a sorcerer, he couldn't. He was all about spells and rituals; science be damned. My mind, on the other hand, was open to anything I could see, touch or smell, whether it be magic or science. I'd learned long ago how to adapt to the world I'd been thrown into.

He'd said *the silver veil,* which was rumored to be the entrance to the first and lowest level of the seventh heaven. Except there was no documented proof the plane existed. Kind of like the Fallen. My, what a coincidence.

"The Fallen don't exist," I said. "The concept is religious dogma." If all I had to go on were predictions and visions, what other conclusion could there be? Still, the very idea gave me a chill. My father, a fallen angel? "Look, you know as well as I do that angels are supposed to be pure spirit. So if they're not flesh and blood, there's no way an angel could fornicate—"

"Oh, they're flesh and blood, all right," Gavin said with a knowing smirk. "Out of the twelve orders of angelic beings, the lower orders can manifest as human if they want to. I'm guessing your father was a guardian of the twelfth order, the Arelim."

I had to laugh. That was ridiculous. "You mean like a *guardian* angel?"

"Exactly." He folded his arms and the black silk of his robe slid back to reveal flesh so pale I could see a thread of purple vein through the surface. "Even I used to have one."

"No way."

"Well, not now, no. I had it killed a number of years ago. I used it to bargain with a demon."

That didn't surprise me, but it didn't convince me, either.

He cleared his throat. "But that's neither here nor there. Point is, your father was more than likely a guardian angel, and I wager he had belonged to your mother."

Gavin returned to his chair and sank into it with a flourish. Heaving a sigh like the weight of the world had just risen off his shoulders, he said, "I know what we need to do."

And by "we" he meant to include me. Which was okay because I had vital information now. I had a rune divination I needed interpreted, which might help me gain my freedom somehow. A thrill coursed through me that I had to hide. This felt right to me, as if I could really make it happen. Except like almost everything in my life, it would come at a price.

Why had Gavin waited until now to give me my mother's note? What was so special about today as opposed to last month, or last year? He said I hadn't been ready until now. I think it had something to do with me reaching my breaking point today. I'd become more of a handful. Change was in the air.

"There's someone I need you to see," Gavin said, hands steepled, the tips of his index fingers touching his lips. "Someone very special who never talks to anyone, but I know she'll talk to you."

I couldn't help being wary. "Who is she?"

"You know her." He tapped his mouth again. "In fact, you two just met. She's the original owner of that hand you were supposed to bring me."

That should have stunned me, but instead it made sense in an odd, behind-the-looking-glass kind of way. The connection I'd made with the saint's hand is what resonated for me. The woman still existed, just not in the usual way. "I thought she was dead."

He tilted his head left to right. "Not completely. All that's left of her now is her head. Her other body parts were parceled off centuries ago. We'll find them eventually."

"So where is she?"

"Denver."

"Colorado?"

"Saint Geraldine, or what's left of her, is entombed at the Cathedral Basilica there. We had her moved when it became too dangerous to keep her at the Sultan Ahmed Mosque in Istanbul. The political unrest in the Middle East is such an inconvenience." He grimaced as if tasting something sour.

"The cathedral is a beautiful church built by one of our own members over a century ago. You'll be impressed."

Dizzy with anticipation, I tried to be the compliant thief Gavin expected. "So Denver is where you're sending me next."

His grin tilted one corner of his mouth. "Saint Geraldine may be the only one who can help us find your father."

Autumn was damn cold in Denver. I was thinking this while standing on the sidewalk outside the Vyantara's Fatherhouse in Denver's warehouse district. I arched my back to stare up at the redbrick building that used to be a factory. It looked abandoned now, though I knew a modest number of sorcerers, witches and other magic users resided within. Three angry-looking effigies of gargoyles glared down at me from stone shelves just below the roofline. I wondered if they'd ever been alive. Probably, considering the rare death of a gargoyle rendered it in stone.

A gust of wind blew a flurry of fallen leaves around my ankles and I stiffened. Was it wind, or something else? I'd never visited the American Fatherhouse before, but I'd been to a few in other countries. My trips abroad, which were always to steal a magical object coveted by the Vyantara, never lasted but a day or two since I couldn't be away from Shui any longer than that. It took only one day at a Fatherhouse to feed an eon's worth of nightmares. If it was supernatural, it likely lived in or around a Vyantara Fatherhouse.

I removed one nose filter and sniffed the air. An animal stench permeated the night, mostly fecal, and the stale odor hinted at its age. Must have been a stockyard nearby years ago, but not anymore.

Peering up at the stone gargoyles, I saw shadowy silhouettes that skulked around them and pulsed with whatever darkness still smoldered inside the dead creatures' corpses.

Slipping out one of my contacts, I could see that energies of the night, particularly this close to the magic wielders inside, coalesced in clusters of shapeless shadows. A few flickered with light, meaning life still seethed within them. I fingered the bottle of salt water I habitually carried to nullify curses and hexes. The water didn't always work, but I had my Balisong as backup. If it breathed, it could bleed.

"Welcome, Chalice."

I spun around, grabbing my knife from the sheath I'd strapped between my shoulder blades. Crouching low, I put my weight on my back leg, ready to leap at my assailant head-on. I flicked the blade open and held it in my left hand, my right palm flat against the pommel.

Having only one contact lens in place skewed my vision. It was a lot like looking through a kaleidoscope, the images fragmented, and my depth perception wobbled. The effect left me queasy.

The large person standing before me—at least I think it was a person, though it could have been a troll—took a quick step back and held both arms up as if to ward me off.

"Hey," its surprised voice said. "I'm only the welcoming committee, the Vyantara's housemother. Truce?"

I closed my unprotected eye and studied this committee of one. It was definitely female and she wore a colorful but shapeless caftan, the huge dress bulging in all the right *and* wrong places. Her pale face held wide, innocent eyes, and she had a Kewpie-doll mouth that she pursed as if to whistle or blow me a kiss. I lowered my knife and she released a breath that made her sizable bosom deflate to more normal proportions. Her hand fluttered against her chest and she blinked while fanning herself with a handkerchief that seemed to have materialized out of thin air. "Dear me, child. You gave me a scare."

"Sorry." I closed the knife and slipped it back in its sheath, my heart still pounding with the surge of adrenaline. "You startled me."

"Your father mentioned you were skittish," she said, eyeing me up and down. "But he didn't tell me you weren't much bigger than a pixie."

I ignored the comment, but not the reference. "Gavin isn't my father," I said curtly, needing to get that straight right away. "He kidnapped me and I've been his slave ever since." I waited for her reaction.

She nodded, her forehead creased with concern. "How awful." Her gaze wandered to the bag at the curb. "Your luggage?" She turned her back on me and waddled over to snatch up the bag like it weighed no more than a loaf of bread. As if I hadn't just confessed the most horrendous events of my life, she said casually, "Let's get you settled in your room, shall we? And you can tell me all about the kidnapping and any other nastiness you've been forced to endure, hmm?"

Like I'd willingly share anything personal with the Vyantara. What I just told her was a memorized response I had perfected in my teens. I'd taught myself to bleed the emotion out of it so that it couldn't be used against me. Getting it all out in the open was my best defense against inquisitors looking for my weak spots.

Halfway to the stairs that led to the front door, she spun around with her right hand extended. "For goodness's sake, where are my manners? I'm Zeppelin, but please call me Zee."

I curled my smallish hand around her massive paw, and quickly let go. I didn't like touching people if I could help it. Since I couldn't wear a body glove 24/7, my daily analgesic lotion usually sufficed, but not always. Direct contact with people sometimes gave me a rash. It was a psychosomatic response. I had trust issues.

"Has Shui arrived yet?" I asked, before following her up the stairs.

"Trains can't travel as fast as jets, dear," she said over her shoulder. "I expect he'll be here tomorrow. And so will your fa... Sorry. I mean so will Gavin Heinrich."

I'd much rather Shui fly here under his own steam because he'd get here faster. But despite the wings, gargoyles were not strong flyers. They could travel short distances of up to five miles without any trouble, but anything longer was too exhausting for them. They were bottom heavy, or at least Shui was.

Once up the steps, I crossed the threshold into the massive building and, heaving in a shallow breath, I felt a surge of panic when an invisible weight squeezed my lungs. I coughed and tossed Zee a puzzled look.

She nodded. "Stay calm and give yourself a minute to acclimate. I realize how overwhelming it is to be in the presence of so much magic all at once, but it's temporary. I promise."

I wasn't so sure, but my breaths soon became less labored, and I exhaled in relief. "What just happened?"

"Think of the Fatherhouse as a pressure chamber of supernatural energy." She waved a hand at the high ceilings, then at all the filled cases and shelves artfully arranged throughout the enormous room we'd just entered. It looked like a museum. "We're surrounded by curses and charms, not to mention a few entities encased in some of these objects. That's a lot of power all in one place."

"I hope you keep it well contained." I imagined the pent-up energy as a bomb ready to explode. The other Fatherhouses I'd visited hadn't been nearly as ominous as this one, but at least six months had passed since I had stayed at the house in Switzerland. Could be that all Fatherhouses were like this one now. That was a disturbing thought.

Zee shrugged like it was no big deal. "Wards. They keep the energy in and everything else out. There's one at every door and at each window upstairs." Her smile made her pudgy cheeks bulge. "You have nothing to worry about, dear. Come, let me show you your room. Your, uh, Gavin says you're an art historian."

I scowled. "Yeah. So?"

"You're going to love this."

She ushered me into a freight elevator the size of a small bedroom and pushed the up button. The open walls allowed me a view of the entire downstairs as we slowly climbed toward the second floor. Steel beams braced the first level's ceiling of what looked like the original wood used to build this place. The planks were dark, pitted, splintered and scorched. We arrived at our destination with a clang and shudder of cables and pulleys. I followed Zee out of the elevator, noting how this floor's ceiling wasn't as high as the one downstairs. This level was sectioned off by a hallway lined with closed doors. It felt claustrophobic compared to the wide-open space below.

Zee preceded me to a door near the end of the hall, where she used a key to open it. A skeleton key, which meant that it probably opened *all* the doors here. I made a mental note to remember that. It would save me the trouble of using my lock picks should I decide to go exploring. For now, I focused my curiosity on the room I was in.

Zee moved her three-hundred-pound-plus body aside and I stared at the enormous apartment, a king-size canopy bed taking up its center. She wasn't kidding about the art. Original oil paintings took up nearly every inch of wall space, beginning at about four feet from the floor. It was remarkable and, like everything else here, overwhelming.

"So what do you think?" she asked, her eyes squeezed to slits within the fleshy folds of her smiling face. "Really something, huh?"

Yep, it was something, all right. And I was no dummy. I might not have the talents of a skilled magic user, but I'd been around magic long enough to know what was what. These paintings had been planted here for a reason, possibly spying, or as portals for astral traveling from one point to another. As much as I appreciated art, I wasn't too keen on sleeping with it. I doubted I'd be able to shut my eyes for more than a minute in this room. I'd constantly feel like I was being watched.

"It's nice," I told her, faking a smile. I didn't feel comfortable here, but so far I didn't feel threatened, either. As long as the Vyantara needed me, I could count on staying relatively safe. I pointed at my bag. "That must be heavy for you."

She glanced at the soft suitcase hanging from her left hand and her Kewpie-doll lips formed an O of surprise. She giggled. "I forgot I was holding it." She set it down on the floor and stepped to the window to gaze out at the night. It was then that I realized there hadn't been any windows downstairs, just up here. Addressing me without making eye contact, she said, "I heard your mother was a knight from the Order of the Hatchet."

This brought me up short. Gavin never talked to *me* about my mother, yet he'd talk about her to someone else? Whenever I tried to bring her up, he would change the subject.

"I suppose you plan on taking up your mother's shield." Zee gave me a piercing look, followed by a raise of her eyebrows. "That is, if you even have her shield?"

I ignored her and leaned against the bed, realizing it was so tall that I'd need a stool to climb up onto it. I had no shield, yet, but Zee didn't have to know that. I'd find it eventually.

"To become a knight, you must serve as page and squire first. You did know that, didn't you?"

I didn't know that, but I crossed my arms and glared at her as if I did.

Her smile broadened, reminding me of Gavin. "Have you met any of the others yet?"

Others? My heart tripped over itself while struggling to keep a steady beat. I tried not to show shock, but failed.

"Oh, my. I'm sorry," she said, making a theatrical attempt at sincerity. "I just assumed you knew."

I cleared my throat and swallowed, remembering my mother's words: *Our people wait for you. Find them.* In Zee's own befuddled way, she'd just confirmed what I had longed to hear. And she acted delighted that I didn't know who or where the other knights were. If they existed, I'd find them.

She stepped away from the window and held out her arms as if to give me a hug. I backed away. "My goodness, Gavin wasn't kidding about you being skittish."

"I'm not skittish. Just cautious."

Zee looked me up and down. "And skinny. Are you hungry?"

"A little," I said, feeling a gurgle in my stomach that was as much hunger as it was nerves. "I thought I'd walk down the street a few blocks to one of the pubs for a quick bite." But it was the Cathedral Basilica I wanted to see. I had to talk to Saint Geraldine, and I'd rather not wait until Gavin got here. I had an agenda of my own.

She shook her head. "That's not a good idea."

What the hell? "Why not?"

"You don't know the city and you could get lost."

I laughed. "I don't think so. I have a map and Larimer Square is only a few blocks from here."

"You're not going anywhere." The pretty smile vanished

and her dark eyes grew darker, the pupils taking over her irises. I couldn't remember what color her eyes had been, but they were coal-black now. Even the whites were gone. What was she? Not just a housemother, obviously. But whatever she was, she was pissing me off.

I lunged for the door and it slammed shut in my face.

"Relax. You'll like it here, Chalice. I promise. And you can wander the streets to your heart's content, just not tonight."

The back of my neck prickled, and it wasn't my tattoo. "Because?"

Even her smirk was like Gavin's. I wondered if the two were related. "Because I said so."

Could this discussion get any more juvenile? I glared at her, then grabbed the doorknob, which turned easily in my hand. I yanked the door open and stormed out into the hall. Because I was dressed for the elements with my heavy suede jacket and Somé Gutierrez boots, I knew I could brave the night without shelter if I had to.

I raced down the hall toward the elevator, expecting someone or something to leap out from behind one of the closed doors. But nothing did. Practically falling into the room-size elevator car, I tossed a look down the hall. Zee wasn't following me. This might be easier than I thought.

When the elevator door opened at the bottom, I jumped out before the car stopped moving. Silence. From all directions. The quiet totally freaked me out. The front door looked to be half a block away, so I took off toward it. Every step forward seemed to set me back two more. The distance increased with my pace, the door shrinking with my every move. So I ran. And the faster I ran, the farther away the door.

Only one thing left to do. I stopped and stood dead still. Where was Zee? I gazed up at the loft on the top floor. Vacant.

Spur-of-the-moment game plan. I removed the bottle of salt water from the inside pocket of my jacket and slid the Balisong from its sheath. Though my eyes stung in spite of the dim light, I could still make out the dark image crouched in the shadows, standing in my path. A green halo surrounded it, pulsing with a life force better suited for its home beyond the black veil. I was about to encounter my first Fatherhouse demon.

No way would I let this thing mess with me. I was on assignment and too important for the Vyantara to lose. But by the way it was looking at me, my soul might be just the tasty morsel it sought.

The demon's body shuddered, a zigzag of energy shooting through it like a television screen that struggled to hold its signal.

I advanced slowly and the creature's eyes began to glow red. It was shaped like a man and about as tall as one, but its skin was a deep blackish-purple, its bald head covered in scales instead of hair. Its body was draped in some kind of furless hide. I stepped up close to it, our faces inches from each other. My nose twitched with a quick sniff. Cinnamon and whiskey, and neither came from my friend here. The creature had no scent because it wasn't actually in the room with me. I held my breath and advanced another step, passing right through it.

Relieved, I strode forward with purpose, the door a normal distance from me now and no longer shrinking. From above me I heard, "Excellent, Chalice! You did very well for your first encounter with one of our wards."

"Thanks," I yelled back, but didn't look behind me. I was too focused on getting myself outside.

"I don't think you realize how lucky you are."

Lucky? Like hell.

"Seriously, Chalice. If you'd tried running from it instead of confronting it head on, the Maågan would have popped through to this side and killed you on the spot."

My stomach lurched, but only a little. She was bluffing.

I yanked open the door and stepped outside into the chill Denver night to head for the mummified saint who might just have all the answers.

five

ONCE I WAS A COUPLE BLOCKS AWAY FROM the Fatherhouse, I unfolded the Denver map I'd brought with me. It looked like walking to the cathedral would be something of a hike. Fine. I had plenty of time. It was only half-past midnight so the evening was still relatively young. I rarely made it to bed before dawn anyway. And at this point, I had no idea where I was going to sleep because it damn sure wouldn't be in that room full of ghastly paintings.

I traveled three more blocks with my contacts out, letting my gaze wander to the shadows beside buildings and around thickly shrubbed landscapes. I didn't perceive any auras or odd gatherings of energy particles like those that surrounded the Fatherhouse. I took one last sniff of the chilly air before sliding all my filters back into place.

Zee had been testing me, which I supposed was fair since I'd tested her first. No two Vyantara members ever trusted each other and being on guard every waking minute got old. Someday I hoped to let my guard down, to really count on someone and get close to people who cared about me, who I knew would be there when I needed them. People who would protect me, like the monks had tried to do. They were gone from my life, but I'd find others to call family someday. If I did have people, like my mother had said, I would root them out from wherever they were hiding.

I turned down an alley for a shortcut when I felt a mild prickling sensation at the back of my neck. Someone was watching me. At the same moment, a man suddenly appeared in my path. And I do mean suddenly because he materialized out of nothing. He was stark naked, too. Considering how close I was to the Fatherhouse, I shouldn't have been surprised.

He crouched as if ready to fend me off, so I didn't disappoint him. When threatened with attack, even a defensive one, I always fight back.

I sprang at him feetfirst while reaching over my shoulder for my blade. His hands cupped my heels and he flipped me backward, forcing me to somersault in the air and land on my feet. When I stood upright, he was gone. Then he flashed into existence a few feet to my left. He disappeared once more, reappearing in the same spot he had stood the first time.

"Stop winking in and out," I shouted and prepared to

make another go at him. He hadn't hurt me, just defended himself, so I didn't consider him a threat. Not yet, anyway. But anyone who could vanish and reappear like that had to be dangerous. "You're making me dizzy."

He vanished again.

I ran a hand through my hair and spun around. "What do you want?"

There was a rustle in the leafless bushes behind me. He showed himself again, but out of the shadows instead of thin air, and this time he wore clothes.

He let me study him, an amused smile curling one corner of his full lips. He looked just a few years older than I and wasn't terribly tall, maybe five-ten at most, black hair, medium complexion. His eyes were crescent-shaped, very Asian, but the color was too pale. I'd have to see him in better light than a street lamp, but what I saw of him so far was enough to make me want to see more.

He held out both hands, palms up. "I'm not a mugger."

"No, you're a flasher." My muscles tightened in anticipation. I'd had too many supernatural surprises for one night and it was wearing on me. I wondered at the extent of this man's powers and if he could make other things besides himself disappear. Taking a deep swallow, I composed myself and tried not to give him attitude, though I wanted him aware I had plenty of nerve. "You didn't answer my question. Aside from exposing yourself, what do you want?"

"To get your attention." He approached me slowly and I backed up a step. "Did it work?"

"What do you think?"

"That you'll listen to what I have to tell you. It's important."

I scrutinized his sincerity, unsure if I wanted to trust a man with the balls to go naked in public, pun intended. "Just because *you* think it's important doesn't mean *I* think so. What the hell are you?"

He clasped his hands behind his back. "Why don't you take out your contacts, Chalice, to get a better look."

He knew my name, and he obviously knew who I was. Though the notion unnerved me, it was a relief not having to pretend I was someone else for a change. I stared at him, half expecting him to vanish again, but apparently this ability had something to do with his clothes, or lack of them.

He motioned at my face. "I mean it. Take a look."

So I did. His aura didn't glow green like other Vyantara members. In fact, he didn't glow at all. Alarmed, I backed away even farther. "You're not alive."

"I'm very much alive." He smiled and when he did, a silvery luminescence surrounded his body. It was a color I'd never seen on a human aura before. "See?"

I squinted at him. "You can control your aura?"

He nodded and thrust out his hand. "The name's Aydin Berkant."

I ignored his offer of a handshake. "Tell me how you do that." This aura thing was too strange. Forget strange, it was impossible. Not to mention the disappearing part.

"Pleased to meet you, too," he said, dropping his hand but not his smile.

I popped the contacts back in to get a normal view of

him. He looked like just a regular guy in a denim jacket and faded blue jeans. The jacket hung open to reveal a white T-shirt that had some kind of saying on it, but all I could make out was the word *world*. I felt tempted to look closer and read the whole thing when the image of his naked body flashed through my mind. Oh, hell. My face turned hot enough to singe my hair.

I narrowed my eyes and crossed my arms. "Okay, talk."

"We have a few things in common, you and I. Special abilities. The Vyantara." He jerked his head toward the street. "I'm on your side, you know. Want to get a coffee? I know a great place that caters to people like us. You'll like it."

People like us? That was cryptic, not to mention unsettling. "I don't know you."

"Not yet." He winked. "But you will. Come on. I don't bite."

I frowned and thought that over. Vampires didn't have auras, either.

"I know what you're thinking." He grinned, showing straight white teeth. "I'm not a vampire."

"So you read minds, too?"

"No, but I'm pretty good at reading faces. And you're terrible at hiding your thoughts." He offered me his arm. "Coming?"

So I didn't trust him. What else was new? If he was Vyantara, then going with him would prove me a good little slave, which might earn me points after the stunt I just pulled with Zee. And if he *wasn't* Vyantara, that was even better. He claimed to be on my side and I could sure use an ally. Too bad tonight's agenda didn't include a coffee date with a stranger who could vanish at the drop of a hat and take with him every stitch of clothing.

"Sorry, no can do. I have an errand to run," I told him.

His smile disappeared and a look of concern crossed his face. "Need some help?"

I shook my head. This guy was a kook. A handsome kook, but still a kook.

"The city is dangerous for a woman alone. Especially at night."

I flicked open my knife. "I can take care of myself."

He cleared his throat. "I'm sure you can." He studied me hard, squinting as if trying to see through my skin to the real me underneath.

"Take a picture. It'll last longer," I said, rolling my eyes as I closed my knife to slip it back into its sheath. "Look, Mr...."

"Aydin. Aydin Berkant."

"I'm in a hurry, Aydin, so if you don't mind—"

"You're looking for information," he said, his expression shrewd.

I blinked. "How the hell would you know what I'm looking for?"

"Because I know who you are, remember? I know a lot of things, and I'm happy to share them with you. Like I said, I'm on your side." He headed off down the alley. "I'm in the mood for coffee, something with caramel in it."

Watching him walk away, I began having second thoughts.

"By the way, there are lots of ghosts in the city at night," he said over his shoulder. "Spirits. Dead things. I'm not a fan, but if you are, knock yourself out. I can always tell you this important information some other time."

I was hoping to get what I needed from Saint Geraldine, but considering the hour and that I wasn't even sure I could hack my way inside the church, I knew I should settle for whatever Aydin could give me. For now. I sensed honesty behind his light-colored eyes, and he had something I wasn't used to seeing in a man. Charm. Yes, that was it. He was charming.

"Just one cup, and I take it black. None of that foo-foo latte shit," I said, the frown etched deep into my forehead. I hoped I wasn't making a mistake.

He turned around to grin at me. "Excellent choice."

My social experience was kind of embarrassing. Especially when it came to guys. I'd had crushes on a couple of my instructors during training, but it was nothing more than infatuation. They were older and I looked up to them, sort of like hero worship, and when I think back on who those people were I want to kick myself. Both were Vyantara with one-track minds and they'd left skid marks after running all over me. I had let things get too far with one in particular, but I was just a kid and he took advantage of that. If I ever run into him again, I swear I'll use my Balisong.

Meeting Aydin was the first time I'd ever made a new acquaintance without Gavin being involved. This was a new experience for me, and I liked it. A lot.

"Where are we going?" I asked Aydin, following a few paces behind while marveling at how well his jeans fit. I also liked how he smelled; sandalwood mixed with something spicy, an edgy scent that made my nose tingle. We headed away from LoDo and toward a residential area with some enormous houses that had to be at least a century old. "I thought you were taking me out for coffee."

He glanced at me over his shoulder. "I am."

"Is it far?"

"We're almost there."

I continued walking behind him, watching his easy strides and the slight swagger that radiated self-confidence. "How do you do that? Disappear, I mean."

"It's an acquired skill."

I guessed that. "Where do you go when you vanish?"

"Nowhere." He tossed me another quick look and I saw amusement in his eyes. He slapped his side. "It would be a lot easier to talk to you if you'd walk beside me."

I quickened my steps to catch up, but even though I left a good couple feet between us, I had to fight the magnetic pull that seemed to emanate from him. What was it? Did he feel it, too?

"That's better." He thrust his hands in his pockets. "I don't go anywhere. I'm still here, you just can't see me. Or I should say regular people can't see me, but *you* could without your contacts."

"How do you know that?"

"Because you can see ghosts. And in essence, that's pretty much what I become." He smoothed a hand over his jacket and looked down at his jeans. "Which is why I can't wear clothes when I make myself invisible. There'd be no solid mass for them to hang on."

I stopped walking. "You become a ghost?"

He turned and walked backward so that he could face me as he talked. "It's complicated. I lose my solid mass and become transparent. All those energy particles you see that form a ghost are essentially what I become when I, uh, vanish." Looking sheepish, he added, "I'm sorry if I shocked you by showing up naked. I had to show you I was different to get your attention."

Oh, he'd gotten my attention all right. The hot blood rushing to my face was evidence of that. He faced forward again and I hurried to stay even with him. "How do you know these things about me, about what I can see? Who told you about my eyes?" I wondered if he knew about my other senses, too.

He shrugged. "Lots of flapping gums in the Fatherhouse."

"And you live with those people?" That was disconcerting.

"They don't know I'm listening."

Considering his ability to vanish at will, that made sense. "So you're a thief, like me."

"Bingo."

I felt a little thrill at hearing that. He was like me. Not exactly like me, but the closest I'd ever come to finding another person remotely similar to myself. The so-called friends Gavin arranged for me to pull jobs with were nothing special. It was always me who took the most risks because I could see, hear and smell better than anyone else.

"Here we are," Aydin said, leading me down a driveway to a dark two-story house with a columned porch. But he didn't walk up the path to the front door. He went on around to the side and headed for a staircase leading down to what I assumed was a basement.

I stopped on the top step, a sense of caution preventing me from following him. "There's no coffee shop down there."

He stared up at me. "Yeah, there is."

"Where's the sign? The lights? The parking lot filled with cars? I don't hear any people talking or coffee mugs clinking." I'd begun to think this might be a trap. Even if it were, I imagined it couldn't be much worse than something Gavin might come up with. Or Zee, with her ridiculous portal paintings. I felt eager to get inside and find out.

I followed him down the steps and through the door.

Still no sign, no lights, no noise. "Aydin, come on. What's going on?"

"I'm taking you for coffee at my favorite coffee shop. What do you think?"

It was obviously an *underground* coffee shop because the basement walls funneled into a tunnel of dirt and rock. Bare bulbs hung from the ceiling, and the farther we ventured in, the lighter it became. Finally I saw a rusty, old tin sign that said Elmo's.

So maybe Aydin really was on the level, and this was a

real coffee shop, but it would definitely go out of business if Elmo didn't work on getting some exposure. Did he even advertise? And who wanted to have coffee inside a dirt tunnel? The door to the entrance was made of wood, the hardware on it rusted and very old-fashioned. Maybe it was some new restaurant trend. I'd heard of a place in Southern California where meals were served in pitch darkness. The appeal had something to do with it being a journey of the senses. Sounded scary to me. I liked to see what I was eating.

"After you," Aydin said.

I palmed the copper door handle and pushed. The heavy plank heaved on its hinges and a rush of voices and heat spilled out into the tunnel. The light was so bright that I had to shade my eyes. There were a lot of people here, if I could call them that. They were of varying sizes and colors, some with hair, some without, and a couple with so much hair that clothes would have been redundant. The hairy ones were chimeras. Not the literal kind from Greek mythology that had a lion's head, goat's body and serpent's tail. The faces of these people were human. The bodies? Not so much.

"Hey, Elmo!" Aydin called over the din of happy coffee drinkers. And they were indeed happy—lots of laughter to go with the music playing through speakers mounted high on the dirt walls. "Elmo, I've brought someone I'd like you to meet."

The festive atmosphere was more of what I'd expect inside a pub, but my senses detected no alcohol. I slipped one nose filter free and inhaled the aroma of coffee and honey. And yeast. Baked treats, too? My stomach rumbled, reminding me I hadn't eaten. Looking around, I recognized a variety of magical species that I'd always associated with those who had enslaved me. I wondered if these were spies.

I edged my way to the door, snagging Aydin's jacket sleeve as I went. "We have to get out of here. These people are Vyantara. They must be spies or assassins, or both."

He laid a gentle hand on my arm, and as much as I wanted to jerk away, I couldn't. His touch soothed me and made me want to get even closer. The soft look in his eyes told me he felt it, too.

He cleared his throat and dropped his hand. "No, Chalice, they're not spies or assassins. These are my friends. And they can be your friends, too."

"They're *your* friends, Aydin, because you report to the Fatherhouse. I can't associate with these people. It's bad enough I'm forced to serve them."

Aydin sighed. "That's why I brought you here, to show you that not all beings from beyond the veil serve the dark side. There's a light side, too."

"That's hard to believe." What I really meant was that it was hard to trust.

"Because you're not supposed to know." He reached out to try touching me again, then thought better of it and stuffed his hand in his pocket. "Look, give them—us—a chance, okay?"

Change was in the air. A shift was coming. I'd been sensing it ever since I'd held the saint's hand. Maybe this was part of it. I stared into Aydin's eyes. Pale green, like frozen jade.

I nodded as if to agree, but the reservation in my expression must have been clear because he looked frustrated. It wasn't like I could easily dismiss what had been pounded into me my whole life. Light or dark, magic couldn't be trusted.

"Come on," Aydin said, his smile encouraging. "I'll buy you a drink."

six

HEAD HELD HIGH AND MUSCLES TENSE WITH discomfort, I followed Aydin as he moved deeper into the little coffee shop. I felt the stares coming at me from all directions. The music continued to play rock and roll, but the voices had died to a murmur.

I slipped a filter from my ear and listened. A few words managed to punch through the hiss of the espresso machine. I heard "gifted human" and "mother was a Hatchet Knight" and "she wears the mark of the gargoyle." Aydin knowing intimate details about me was bad enough, but I apparently had no secrets from these people, either.

My eyes stung, but I refused to cry. My chest tightened with a choked-back sob and Aydin heard it because he leaned in to me, ice-jade eyes trained on my face. Our gazes locked, and I mentally dared him to pity me. He didn't.

His grin broadened as if he hadn't just witnessed the near breakdown of a would-be knight in tarnished armor. Tarnished, hell. I had no armor, no shield, no crest but for the shameful brand on the back of my neck that marked me as a slave.

But that didn't mean I had to act like one.

I tucked my ear filter back in place and lifted my chin, straightened my back, and bellied up to the coffee bar.

A stocky little man with no neck and very long ears that had multiple piercings studied me from the other side of the counter. Bitter beer face came close to describing his expression, but the words that left his mouth didn't match. "What'll it be, sweetheart?" he asked, his deep voice at odds with his small stature.

"Elmo, this is the woman I told you about. Her name is Chalice." Aydin gave me a nod. "Chalice, meet Elmo, proprietor of this highly caffeinated establishment."

"Double espresso, please," I said. "And nice to meet you."

"Into the hard stuff, are ya?" Elmo asked. "I'd have taken you for a latte kind of girl."

"Milk doesn't agree with me," I said, secretly wishing that it did. I loved the scent of steamed milk and coffee. I imagined that's what heaven would smell like, if there were such a thing. "I prefer strong flavors."

"Because of your, you know." Aydin tapped his nose. "Your nose filters. Can't smell, can't taste, right?"

This full-disclosure crap was annoying. "That's right. But if I take out the filters when I eat or drink—"

"Other smells would overwhelm your sense of taste." He looked pleased with himself, but when he saw my expression he quickly glanced away and cleared his throat. "Elmo, I'll have—"

"A caramel macchiato. Your usual. Got it."

Elmo dropped from sight. I assumed he'd been standing on something to reach the counter because only the top of his shiny, bald head showed.

"Want to sit down?" Aydin asked me.

I looked around the shop, seeing that most of the tables were occupied. It didn't feel right. Coming here was a mistake. "I—um—I think maybe I should go."

"What? Why?"

My gaze darted around the room again, then down to my feet. "I shouldn't be here. I don't belong."

"Everyone here belongs here." Aydin gestured at the only empty table. It was round with low stools, and on closer inspection I saw it was an old cable spool. The top had been sanded down and coated with varnish, but you could still see the scars of age and heavy use etched into the wood.

"Not me," I said. "Not with them."

His frown of disappointment made me flinch.

What had I gotten myself into? Being in the same room with a supernatural species was too...awful. My skin felt like it crawled with bugs. "I must sound like a bigot to you, but that's not it."

He raised an eyebrow. "Are you sure?"

"Yes, I'm sure." I felt my indignation rise through my pores, which probably turned my face red. "I bet they're all perfectly nice people, but I'm..."

"Better than they are?"

"No!" I folded my arms across my chest and refused to

look at him. I wasn't better. Just different, and not exactly normal. I didn't like it here because these people made me nervous. They would report me to the Fatherhouse, and to Gavin. And who knew what he'd do to me then? His punishments were harsh. "I don't trust them not to tell."

"They're not Vyantara. I promise." He left the table to retrieve our coffees. He returned and placed a steaming cup of espresso in front of me. The tiny cup was old and chipped, but it looked clean. I wondered who, or what, drank from it before me, and if whatever it was had left its magic behind.

Aydin sat on the stool beside me. "Worried about getting cooties?"

I scowled at him. "I never said that."

"You didn't have to." He sipped from his mug and licked the caramel-colored foam from his upper lip. "I can read it in your eyes."

Could he also read my attraction to him there? I hoped not. I wasn't ready to get involved with anyone after what I went through the last time. It was hard to admit my feelings could be hurt, but I was all about feelings, inside and out. If only I could numb my heart.

Okay, enough of this *feelings* bullshit. "You said you had information for me. Spill."

"Not until I straighten you out on a few things." He leaned back, but the stool had no backrest and he ended up slouching forward instead. "You have a lot of misconceptions about magic and the species that use it."

I shook my head. "No misconceptions. I know who the magic users are. They're all part of the same whole. You of all people should know that." I sipped my espresso. Strong, just how I liked it.

"Do you know what would happen if the Vyantara found out about Elmo's?"

"I assumed they knew, probably condoned it. A little diversion for their members."

"Far from it." He waved his hand at the room, where chimeras, a couple of elves, a brownie, three pixies and even a pair of human-looking characters sat with each other, chatting over coffee and what looked like some kind of pastry. "If news of this coffee shop ever got out, there'd be a roundup like cattle on the prairie and Elmo's would be shut down."

"But you…"

"I'm a thief for the Vyantara, and I do their bidding because I have to. I also have a life of my own. And I spend a lot of it here, as well as a few other clandestine spots in this city, where people of our nature are free to socialize." He winked at me. "As long as we keep it to ourselves."

Free? That word wasn't even in my vocabulary. The very idea that people like us could exercise free will astounded me. Magic users on the *light side?* "Okay, I'm listening. Tell me more."

He beamed at me. "Happy to." So he did.

I was amazed to learn that chimeras like Banku, the lion man who'd been my combat instructor, were not a typically violent race.

"Depending on the human-animal combination," Aydin said, "chimeras can be gentle, wise and compassionate. They all have an innate ability for magic, but not all of them use it. Those who do don't always use it for personal gain."

I remembered a deer-girl at the Fatherhouse in Germany. She looked something like a satyr, only more delicate, her four cloven hooves petite and feminine. She painted them with pink nail polish. I had tried very hard *not* to like her, even though she was a sweet-natured creature with a habit of putting other's needs before her own. I didn't believe her sincerity. Perhaps I'd been wrong.

"Pixies, faeries and elves also have a personal choice in the direction they want their magic to take," he added. "Just like humans who have a choice between right and wrong, the supernatural races aren't so different."

On the far side of the room, I saw the dirt wall quiver as if made of liquid, and it shimmered a phosphorescent green. Elmo walked over and held up his right hand to lay it flat against the surface. *The green veil. The plane of faery.*

I gasped and Aydin shot me a look, the corners of his eyes crinkled in amusement. "It's okay. Watch."

I shook my head and took a swallow of espresso, the bitter taste flooding my mouth. "He's using his sigil to open the veil. That's the mark of a dark magician. A sorcerer."

Aydin held out his right palm and there in the center was the brand of a sigil, a symbol of his will. The ropey scar was shaped like two intertwined serpents and it had a series of dashes circling them like stitches. "Neither of us is a sorcerer. Like Elmo, my will is branded into my flesh so that I can open this veil whenever I want. Someone on the other side is asking permission to cross over, and Elmo is giving it to them."

I cringed at what might be on the other side and inhaled deeply to calm my nerves. "I've seen Gavin do the same thing when he opens the black veil, except he cuts a new symbol into his skin each time. His hands are covered with scars. I thought you needed blood to work the spell."

"Only the black veil requires blood from the spell caster."

Okay, so maybe sigils weren't associated with only the dark arts. That was comforting to know. I watched the wall soften, its liquid surface wavering like a disturbed pool, and then two people walked through. As soon as their feet touched the floor inside the shop, the wall turned solid behind them. A small, blue-furred creature crouched on one of their shoulders.

"Hey," Aydin said, a smile brightening his face. "It's Toby and Myra. And they brought Ling Ling along." He stood and waved at them to come over.

When the little animal caught sight of Aydin, it stood up on its hind legs and fluttered tiny blue arms as if excited. It wore a rainbow-colored beaded collar, and its master, the woman who I assumed was Myra, tugged on its leash to keep it still. But the creature sprouted wings and leapt into the air, pulling the leash away with it.

Aydin laughed and flapped his hands, encouraging it to fly to him. The woman rushed to catch up.

A miniature gargoyle? No. It was way too cute for that, and the wings were feathered, not webbed. It landed on Aydin's outstretched arm and began to chitter like a monkey. The wings vanished and its face suddenly looked more feline, yet the legs and tail were too long for a cat.

"Chalice, this is Ling Ling." Aydin moved his arm closer to me, the creature still attached.

I jumped to my feet and took a cautious step backward. Aydin chuckled. "She doesn't bite."

I looked for teeth but didn't see any. "What is it?"

"A Jakkaryl." He petted the creature's head and it began to purr. "Sort of a fey version of a chameleon, only it changes shape instead of color. Want to pet her?"

Heart thudding like a wild thing, I reached out to touch the animal's head. She nuzzled against my fingers. How sweet.

"Sorry," Myra said when she arrived at our table. "Ling Ling is usually so well behaved, but she's just crazy about Aydin."

I could see that.

"I'm Myra, by the way." To my relief, she nodded instead of offering me her hand. "The slow poke behind me is my husband, Toby."

Toby sidled up beside her and jerked a nod, his smile quick and twitchy. That was okay. Meeting new people wasn't my thing, either.

The pair were definitely fey. They stood a little more than three feet tall, their bodies slim and well proportioned, and so unlike the stout dwarves with oversize heads that I'd seen in some Fatherhouses. Toby and Myra made an attractive couple. Her blue hair harmonized with her pet's fur, and she wore it in two braided spirals, one above each pointed ear. Myra's pale green tunic looked crisply pressed, and her white-haired husband wore a tan canvas vest with matching slacks. This was apparently date night, and Elmo's must be the main event. I wondered what other entertainments Denver had to offer a fey couple and their furry friend.

"I'd like you to meet Chalice," Aydin said, tilting his head toward me. "She's new in town, and I'm showing her around."

Myra and Tony shared a look that made me suspect they already knew who I was. I refrained from rolling my eyes.

While we'd been introducing ourselves, the little Jakkaryl had quietly moved from Aydin's arm to mine. I hadn't even noticed. She was light as lint, and that was impossible from the looks of her. I'd expect her to weigh a couple pounds, at least. My eyes opened wide as our gazes met. We both blinked, and she pealed out a string of giggles that sounded like a laughing baby. Eerie, but it made me laugh.

What had been a feline face was now closer to that of a ferret. The body had elongated and her toenails curled into hollow pink disks. She was pure magic. And I liked her. Very much.

"We won't disturb you any longer," Myra said, grabbing Ling Ling gently by the scruff of her neck. She looked like a kitten now. "Come, Lingy. I'll get you a sweet."

The animal continued to giggle softly as her owners carried her away.

I heaved a sigh. "Wow. I want one of those."

"She's adorable, all right." Aydin's gaze followed the little family to a table they'd chosen close to the veil. "She's proof positive that magic isn't all bad."

I lifted one shoulder in a half shrug, not ready to be too agreeable. A lifetime of caution couldn't be tossed away in a single night. My past had shown me that magic was cruel and dark, existing only to fulfill selfish desires and to harm others. I was happy to know this wasn't so, but I still needed time to adjust.

Now that the excitement was over, Aydin appeared suddenly weary, dark rings of fatigue settling around his glazed eyes. He didn't look well. "I think we should adjourn class for tonight. You have a lot to absorb."

"Are you okay?"

He wiped a sleeve across his sweaty forehead. His eyes appeared feverish, and the look in them was surprisingly hungry. "I will be. What time is it?"

I shrugged. I didn't wear a watch. A quick glance around the room found a furred wrist bearing a timepiece similar to a watch but twice the size. Probably so that he could see the numbers through all that fur. All that *unwashed* fur. He smelled like a wet dog. "Uh, excuse me?" I approached his table. "Do you have the time?"

"For which side of the veil?" he asked, his feral eyes roaming over me from head to toe. "Never mind. This side, of course." His human face lowered to read his watch, and he used a claw to flip up something like a lid. "Four-thirty."

Hearing that, Aydin stood quickly and began rubbing his arms. "Well, shit. How time flies. Hey, I gotta run."

"Are you sick?" I asked.

"No more sick than you."

His answer confused me at first, then surprise took its place. Did he mean what I thought he meant? "You're bonded."

He jerked a nod and turned his head, flipping up his hair

so that I could see the tattoo on the back of his neck. It was in the design of a flying gargoyle. Just like mine. "And my seventy-two hours are about up. Shojin is expecting me."

Oh, my God. Shojin must be his gargoyle. If he didn't get to him in time, he'd become something as horrible as Shui. As horrible as I imagined his Shojin to be. The very thought made me sick to my stomach. "I understand you have to go, but when will I see you again?"

The hunger in his eyes intensified and my body responded. It wasn't hunger, it was desire. Because I felt it, too.

"What's happening?" The words came out on a whispered breath because I was having trouble catching mine. We drifted closer to each other. The heat from his body mingled with mine, and I wanted to wrap myself around him, run my lips over the soft hollow between his neck and collarbone, feel his hands caress my sides and slide in to cup my...

Strong fingers grasped me by the shoulders and held me still. "I'm sorry," Aydin whispered, the words more like a growl. "This is what happens. I have a hard time controlling it when I'm this close to changing."

I frowned, confused. "Control what? I don't understand."

He sighed deeply. "We're both bonded, and though we have separate beasts, our connection is still there. It's strongest when we reach the end of a cycle."

Wow. "You mean people with this curse are hot for each other?"

He closed his eyes and jerked a nod. "In a word, yes."

No wonder I'd been so drawn to him. The animal

magnetism was more literal than I thought. That meant my attraction wasn't real, only a by-product of a nasty curse. "I'm so embarrassed," I mumbled.

He winced. "Don't be. You didn't know. Look, I really can't stay. So until next time…" In an instant, he was gone. His clothes, still buttoned and zipped, collapsed in a heap to the floor.

I spun around to see if he'd reappear, but he had truly vanished. I popped out one contact and squinted in the light, seeking out the energy particles I'd associated only with ghosts until now. I spied the muscular figure of a man, transparent and naked, striding quickly for the door. But he didn't open it. He walked straight through it.

Scratching the side of my head in wonder, I replaced my contact lens. I'd seen a lot of weird stuff in my life, but nothing quite like that.

My breaths came hard and fast for a minute as I reflected on what this meant. Not only was Aydin a thief like me, he was a bonded thief. He, too, had a nasty, old gargoyle attached to him. And yet he acted like a free man. How did he manage it?

"He'll be okay," said a voice at my back. I turned to peer down at Elmo's bitter beer face. "He lost track of time. I blame myself for not reminding him."

Such a kind little man, and his concern for Aydin was obvious. The two must be good friends. I smiled down at Elmo, a genuine, eye-crinkling smile that almost melted the ice around my heart. I couldn't remember the last time I'd smiled like that, but it was before I'd come to the United States.

The elf grinned. "You're a lovely girl," he told me.

"Oh." I barked a shy laugh. Only two people in my life had ever said that to me and both had been liars. They'd just wanted to get in my pants. But I could tell Elmo was sincere because he spoke from someplace deeper than his crotch. He spoke from his heart. "Thank you."

"I mean for a human." The bitter beer face returned and he tromped back to the coffee bar, toting Aydin's clothes behind him. The stonewashed jeans dragged across the dirt floor, stirring up dust.

I felt suddenly alone in spite of being inside a coffee shop filled with supernatural beings as alien as creatures from another planet. They belonged on the other side of the veil, the green veil, the plane of Faery.

Aydin trusted the people of Faery, so why shouldn't I? Except that I couldn't hang out here, at least not indefinitely. I had to return to the Fatherhouse. When Gavin arrived he'd expect me to be there and lord knew it would be a bad thing to disappoint him.

I peered over the counter and down at Elmo. "I have to go now. Will Aydin be back here tomorrow?"

Gazing up at me from beneath a white-browed frown, he said, "Yeah, but you'll probably run into him at the Fatherhouse before that. He lives there."

I needed to see him again. Our connection gave me hope.

"I have a small room in the back you can stay in for as long as you like," Elmo said. "It ain't much, but it's private. I imagine you don't get much privacy where you are now."

How intuitive. "That's right, I don't."

"Then stay here."

If I stayed, there'd be a risk the Vyantara would find out about this place. According to Aydin, there'd be a lynching if the Vyantara discovered Elmo's and I couldn't let that happen. "Thanks, Elmo. I appreciate the offer, but I have somewhere I need to go."

His eyebrows bunched together like two wads of white cotton. "Do you even know where you're going?"

"Sort of." Spooks. That's what Aydin had said I'd find in the city at night. I hated spooks. "There's someone I need to see."

"Saint Geraldine?"

My ears began to ring. How the hell...? "You know about her?"

"Sure." Elmo carried a tray full of cups to the sink. "Everyone the Vyantara brings to Denver has to talk to the saint. It's tradition."

I didn't like the sound of that. "And what does she tell them?"

"Nothing. She won't talk to just anybody." He grunted while stepping up on a stool to reach the faucet. "The ones who tried were sent away."

"How do you know this?"

"Aydin told me."

Aydin had suspected the destination of my "errands" and steered me away from the cathedral. There was a history there, he knew what it was, and he was protecting me. Or was he protecting Geraldine *from* me?

If Geraldine was some sort of oracle, could she possibly give me the answers I longed for?

The cot creaked when I sat down and the dirt floor at my feet radiated a chill right through my boots. I told myself I'd only stay at Elmo's until the sun came up. Ghosts were less active during the day.

"I'll start a fire," Elmo said before I could complain of the cold. "Let me close up shop first."

Within a couple of minutes I heard him talking to his customers. Nosy person that I am, I got up to see what was going on.

"Okay, folks," Elmo said. "Daylight's just an hour away. Time to close up."

Someone said, "Aww, come on. I haven't finished my latte." Then came the laughter, followed by more good-natured complaining. Stools scudded across the dirt floor as people got up to leave. I heard footsteps, some made by stomping shoes and others by clip-clopping hooves.

I peeked around the corner and watched as one by one, Elmo's patrons passed through the curtain, stirring up lines of energy that zapped the air like tiny lightning bolts. I caught a glimpse of deep emerald foliage dotted with bright colors that might have been flowers. It happened so fast I couldn't tell for sure.

The two in the group who were human—I guessed they were witches—left through the main door. I didn't doubt they were curious to follow their fey friends, but the land of Faery was off-limits to humans. At least that's what I'd been told. Considering the contradictory information

I'd received over the years, I didn't know what to believe anymore.

Elmo brushed past me to gather his barista tools and take them to the sink.

I had to know how it was possible for the fey to come and go as they pleased. Where was the sorcerer who summoned them?

"Elmo," I said. "Are you—?"

"No." He tossed some kindling into a pot-bellied stove in the corner. "I'm not a sorcerer. And neither is Aydin."

There was so much I didn't understand. I now questioned everything the Vyantara had ever taught me. Which had been lies and what was the truth?

"The fey can't cross over and then leave on their own, can they? Someone must have summoned them."

Elmo shook his head. "I invited them. Aydin must have explained that to you." He turned from the sink to face me. "The land of Faery is loaded with white magic. The fey don't need a sorcerer to open the veil for them, they just need an invitation." He held out his right hand with the sigil branded on the palm. "This is my invitation. Aydin has one just like it."

An idea came to me that made my heart jump. "So humans can cross to their side, as well?" Meaning I might have a means of escape from the Vyantara.

"I wish it were that easy." He gestured for me to follow him to the back room, where he pulled a stool close to the cot. He sat, his short legs barely touching the floor, and motioned me to sit beside him. "Where you and I are right now? This plane, the one with all the humans? It's neutral territory. Nothing stands in the way of getting to this side as long as there's an invitation. Black, silver or green veil, makes no difference. Unless you arrange for the proper wards to keep things out."

How creepy. "You mean the mortal plane can be invaded at any time? The Earth could start crawling with supernatural creatures with just an invitation?"

"Who's to say it isn't already?"

I gulped air, my throat feeling raw from too much espresso. I felt suddenly vulnerable.

Elmo patted my knee and tilted his head to one side, then the other. "I wouldn't worry too much. The Vyantara keep a low profile, at least for now. Millions of panicked mortals are the last thing they want. They prefer doing their dirty deeds in secret."

I shook my head and felt lost again. My ignorance overwhelmed me. "They taught me only what they wanted me to know, which obviously wasn't much."

"But that's about to change, yes?" He winked at me, just like Aydin had done. "You have new teachers now. It's time for you to learn the truth."

An understatement if ever there was one. I should leave Elmo's now, get out of this tunnel and back on the street. My head swam with questions and I needed to absorb everything Aydin and Elmo had told me. Knowledge was power, and I could certainly use a whole lot more than I had.

"Tell me about Saint Geraldine."

"I don't know much, and what I do know won't be helpful."

"Then tell me what you think the Vyantara has kept from me that I should know."

Elmo made a T with his hands. "Time out. Chalice, I'm happy to help you, but I'm an old elf and it's past my bed time. I'm not even sure how much I *should* tell you."

"Tell me everything," I said, puzzled by his unwillingness to answer my questions. I pointed in the direction of the door. "I'm about to head back out there, into the arms of my slave masters, and I'm completely at their mercy." The anger inside me mixed with my resentment over being helpless. I barely controlled the volume of my voice when I said, "I'm seeing the light at the end of a very long tunnel, a tunnel that's been my life for over thirteen years. I finally feel hopeful. Do you know what that means to me?"

Elmo blinked. "I, uh… No."

"It means freedom, Elmo." My eyes began to sting and I shut them to fight back stupid, shameful tears. "I thought I'd forgotten what freedom felt like, but I haven't. And I want it back. With your help, with Aydin's help, and maybe with the saint's guidance—if she speaks to me—I won't have to answer to the Vyantara anymore."

Sighing deeply, he wiped his hand over his face and yawned. "Okay, fire away."

"How do I kill an immortal gargoyle?"

"I have no idea."

Well, that was a long shot, but worth a try. "Does Saint Geraldine know how to kill a gargoyle?"

He gave me a pitying look and I said, "Okay, so you don't know that, either. But can you tell me if fallen angels exist?"

"I've never seen one myself, but I've heard rumors. You should ask Aydin."

Who was probably at the Fatherhouse right now, but I wasn't planning to go back there yet. It was time for me to go to church.

"What can you tell me about Geraldine?"

Elmo shrugged. "Like I said, I don't know much. But I do know her remains are enchanted."

Obviously. I'd held her hand and experienced its power. "Do you know how it happened?"

He appeared lost in thought before saying, "Geraldine had once been an ordinary girl living in a small Spanish village during the eleventh century, right around the time of the First Crusade. She became less ordinary when she started channeling the voices of angels."

An angel whisperer. I'd never heard of one, but there was always a first. "Was she possessed by angels?"

He shook his head. "I don't know, but her village parish accused her of being possessed. That's why they executed her."

It reminded me a lot of the Salem witch trials. "How?"

"She was hanged, then drawn and quartered. When her body parts didn't die, they were rumored to have super-natural powers. Her hands and feet were auctioned off to the magic community and profits from the sale made the greedy clergy rich. Geraldine's head stayed with the church, but the Vyantara sniffed it out. It's been in their possession ever since."

I found it curious that the saint had lived during the First Crusade. The Order of the Hatchet—the female knights my mother and I were descended from—was created because of this holy war. The order was founded by the Count of Barcelona as his way of honoring the women who took up arms to protect the town of Tortosa against a Moor attack. With all the men off to war, someone had to defend the families left behind. Who better than the wives? Made perfect sense to me.

Elmo also told me some trivia about Denver's Cathedral Basilica. I never would have guessed that Buffalo Bill Cody had been baptized there, and the legendary Molly Brown was once a parishioner. I'd have to be wary of tourists. Only I didn't think any tourists would be milling around at six-thirty in the morning.

"Thanks for your help, Elmo," I told the elf before leaving. "I'm sure I'll see you again."

Then I set out to find my way to the cathedral and the legendary Saint Geraldine.

seven

A BRISK FALL WIND BLEW AROUND ME AND I enjoyed the tangy fragrance of spent leaves in the air. I'd been told there was less oxygen in the mile-high city, but I couldn't tell. I inhaled deeply and ignored the faint scent of exhaust fumes from a distant highway that rumbled with traffic. In spite of the conflicting odors, today smelled like freedom. As fleeting as the moment was, I wanted to enjoy the experience of what my future might be like if things went my way. Then my tattoo began to throb, reminding me not to delude myself. Damn Shui. And damn Gavin for forcing me into bondage with a monster.

I rounded the corner onto Logan Street, and there it was. The cathedral, rising like a great, white dragon from the concrete and asphalt. My background in art history helped me appreciate the French Gothic architecture and

I recognized the Cathedral of Chartres as this building's source of inspiration. Two-hundred-foot spires pierced the sky, the anthus stonework an impressive accent. And there was so much stained glass! Brilliant colors, all the more vibrant when a break in the clouds passed a streak of sunlight over the windows. It looked almost choreographed, a purposeful show for my benefit. I stood transfixed on the sidewalk.

I willed my feet to move and crossed the street like a zombie. When I stubbed my toe on the curb, it startled me back to life. I had to find a way inside.

The bronze doors at the front were locked tight, so I went to the back of the church to find another entrance. Cars sputtered by in white plumes of exhaust, their drivers more intent on getting to work than checking out what I was up to. Those who commuted on foot didn't spare me a glance. It was like hiding in plain sight.

Once I found the rear door, I slid my lock picks from the little leather case I carried with me everywhere, and got to work. I was inside within seconds. And if the outside of this place wasn't mesmerizing enough, the inside took my breath away.

Out came the earplugs, the nose filters and the contact lenses. I wanted to experience this wonder with my bare senses. Eyes closed, I concentrated on a sound that was like a melodic hum that sent calmness through me like water in a stream. The scent of humanity was overwhelming, but there was also a unique sort of sweetness, a fragrance unlike anything I'd ever experienced. It lifted my spirits and brought an involuntary smile to my lips.

I'd burgled dozens of churches all over the world, and there had always been an intangible sense of purity inside each one. But this church felt different. And I guessed it had something to do with Saint Geraldine.

When I opened my eyes, the dazzling effect of stained glass reaching toward the heavens intensified. I felt drawn inside the colors, my soul wrapped in hues of cerulean and crimson. Each windowpane was haloed by its own aura of pale silver that shimmered and pulsed with whatever life force existed here, and it wasn't a human one. It was...more.

I tried focusing on the saint's remains, but her scent eluded me.

Another smell pushed its way in front of all the others, its familiarity grabbing me by the throat. It was him. It was Gavin. Shit.

"So you found me," I said to the once-peaceful air. It was turgid now, tinged with an acrid odor of Gavin's sweat and his penchant for pesto.

"It took you long enough to notice," he said, rising from a pew and turning to face me.

"I was distracted." I replaced my sensory armor, pushing the filters firmly inside my nose.

He yanked up the lapels on his black woolen coat, the tailored sleeves falling back to reveal the thick cable-knit of his sweater. "I knew you wouldn't find her."

"Find who?" Playing dumb rarely got me anywhere, but no harm in trying.

He smirked, ignoring my question. "There's a reason for that, you know. Saint Geraldine is highly valued and it's imperative we keep her safe. From everyone, and *everything*."

I frowned. "Then why don't you guard her remains inside the Fatherhouse?"

His smirk vanished and he looked far less amused. He ignored that question, too. "You know better than to go off on your own without instructions."

I shrugged as if I didn't care, but the twinge at the back of my neck came from more than just my tat. I felt enough anxiety to make my hair bristle. "Okay, I give up. Where is she?"

He held his arms up and out from his sides while looking left to right. "She's inside this beautiful church. Come with me and I'll show you."

He led me down a flight of stairs into the basement, then down a narrow hallway that was barely lit. It reminded me of the underground tunnel to Elmo's.

At the end of the hall we stopped in front of a tapestry hanging against the wall. Gavin turned to face me.

"What?" I asked.

He flashed me a grin, then went stoic. "I should prepare you before we go in."

How could anyone be prepared to confront a corpseless head? "I'm fine." Though I was disappointed. Gavin showing up here had spoiled my plan. Now I couldn't ask the saint my questions. I couldn't show her my mother's note, couldn't ask her to translate the rune divination my mother had left for me, assuming she knew how to read runes.

"She's not a bona-fide saint, you know." Gavin lifted the tapestry, using his body to shield me from seeing whatever was underneath. His hands worked at something I assumed was a combination lock of some kind. "She was never canonized by the Catholic Church because she was a pagan."

I shifted my earplug slightly so that I could hear the tumblers. Only they weren't tumblers, they were beeps. It was an electronic lock. "Pagans don't believe in angels."

He turned to scowl at me and I remembered I wasn't supposed to know anything about Saint Geraldine. Elmo was Aydin's secret so I couldn't reveal who had told me what little I knew. "Gavin, come on. You said yourself that she'd help me find my father, who you *claim* is a fallen angel, so I just assumed she must have been a Christian."

His face relaxed. "You assumed wrong. Some pagans believe in angels, we just don't call them that. They're Guardians, guides, messengers. Like angels, their purpose is to serve the divine." He turned back to his task. "What do you know about Saint Geraldine?"

I dared not lie, but I could usually get away with half truths. "I investigated how she died." He would assume I had searched the internet or studied one of the historical tomes in his library.

I heard a distinct sucking sound when the door opened and a *whoosh* of air blew past me and into the room beyond.

"Air lock," Gavin explained. "So what did your investigation reveal?"

"That she was executed, then drawn and quartered."

"You're correct. We're still looking for the rest of her remains." He motioned me ahead of him. "The hand, her left one, is probably still at the Grandville mansion. Retrieving it will be your first order of business after we finish our work here in Denver."

Great. More hellhound duty. I could hardly wait.

I blinked in the darkness. "I can't see."

"Remove your contacts."

I hesitated. Too many shadows, and therefore, too many spooks, as Aydin had called them. Harmless as they might be—and a rare few weren't harmless at all—I preferred ignorance over observation when it came to ghosts. "Why can't you just turn on a light?"

"Chalice, your contact lenses," he said in a tone that I knew meant business.

Ire burned through my pores, and I seriously considered drawing my knife. But then I'd have the entire Fatherhouse to deal with and a fight with them was the last thing I needed.

I removed my contacts and the room abruptly lightened. I was happily surprised to find it empty of any ghosts. Four blank walls painted black surrounded an ordinary wooden table. The shape of a head haloed by a thin silver aura was set at its center.

"She's still alive," I whispered.

Though I didn't understand how something mummi-fied could continue living, missing body parts or not. The leathery skin was cracked around the cheeks and temples, the nose skeletal, and her scalp a patchwork of hairy tufts. Eyes? She had no eyes, unless that's what you'd call the black raisins in her otherwise-empty sockets.

She *was* a disturbing sight. From what I'd learned about her, I had expected to see something reverent and impres-sive, not a shriveled-up dead thing that would collapse into dust at the slightest touch. But she wasn't dead, and that alone filled my heart with pity. Poor, poor woman. No one deserved to live a thousand years in that condition. No one.

"We can make her whole again," Gavin said quietly, and I was surprised to hear the hushed respect in his voice. "Two hands and two feet, that's all we need to conjure the rest of her body. Her ability to channel the voices of angels is a priceless gift the Vyantara can profit from. Do you realize how much our clients would pay to have their fortunes told by an angel?"

His question was a rhetorical one, so I didn't answer. If Gavin made her whole, he'd just use her like he was using me, maybe even bond her to a gargoyle, and I didn't wish that on anyone. She had a right to either live free, or die in peace.

"She's not speaking to you." Gavin sounded surprised. "I thought for sure she'd say something by now."

"She can't see me in the dark," I said. Though the corpse had to be blind considering the condition of its eyes. "If she could see me she might speak."

Gavin shook his head. "That shouldn't matter. I don't understand what's wrong." He maneuvered around the head so that he stood behind it, and as he did, I noticed a sudden change in the saint's expression. What there was of one, anyway. The skin around her eyes softened and I swore I saw her wink at me.

"Uh…" I swallowed and saw what looked like a scowl form on the mummy's forehead.

Gavin stepped back around to face Geraldine. "Did she say something? Take out your earplugs."

"She didn't say—"

"I said to remove your earplugs!"

Fine. So I did. Silence. Hey, I liked this room. This was cool! No sensory distractions anywhere.

"Gavin, she's not talking to me." Though I knew at some point she would. She just preferred not to have any witnesses.

Gavin ran a hand through his hair, looking slightly unhinged. Nice. The look suited him and I hoped to see it more often. "Maybe if you left me alone with her."

"That's not going to happen." He started to pace, then stopped when he saw that his footsteps caused the table to shake. "If I did, and she spoke, you wouldn't tell me what she said."

Too true. "Then I don't know what you want me to do."

"Damn it!" He didn't shout, but his whisper was forceful enough to spray spittle.

I didn't meet his eyes, not that he could see me if I did. He was in the dark, but I could see everything.

"I can't trust you, Chalice."

"I know."

"But I could threaten to withhold Shui from you if you refuse to do what I say."

I considered that. "Maybe, but I don't think you will. Would she speak to me if I were a gargoyle?"

"No."

"No," I agreed, not disguising the smile in my voice, though I should have. Complacency could get me killed, or worse. I was lucky Gavin hadn't noticed. Or if he did, he pretended not to.

"We'll come back later," he told me. "First I'll speak with

the Vyantara elders to see what they suggest. Geraldine *will* talk to you. I'm certain she will."

And so was I.

Gavin opened the metal door and stepped out into the hall, holding the door open for me to follow. I spared one last glance at Geraldine. Her emaciated lips, which could use a serious coat of lip balm, puckered and blew me a kiss. Gotta love a mummy with a sense of humor.

"I hate this room," I said, letting my gaze sweep the walls of my assigned room in the Fatherhouse. "It's creepy."

Zee let out a theatrical sigh. "I put you in here because I thought you appreciated fine art."

I stood beside the canopied bed, not wanting to touch the bedding that was probably the shroud of a long-dead sorcerer whose spirit waited for just the right vessel to possess. No way would that vessel end up being me. "Everything in this room is enchanted. I can't stay here."

Zee threw her hands in the air. "That's ridiculous, Chalice." She looked at Gavin, who stood in the room's open doorway. "Can't you talk some sense into her?"

Gavin grinned. "I've never known anyone more sensible than Chalice. Just give her a different room."

Zee's eyes widened and she did something strange with her eyebrows. She might even have winked. It was hard to tell from this angle, but her anxiety over having her plan foiled was way too obvious. I knew it! The room was rigged. The bitch was trying to pull a fast one and Gavin had caught on.

He stepped into the room and turned in a slow circle.

"Well, well. Look at this. There are the Cévennes Mountains in France. Don't we have a Fatherhouse there?" He gestured at another painting. "The Tembe National Elephant Park in South Africa was always my favorite, though I try not to visit in summer. Too hot." He straightened a frame at the far side of the room. "Is this Zurich? No, Gstaad. I haven't been to Switzerland in ages."

"All right, all right," Zee said, hands on hips. "So I wanted help keeping an eye on her. Can you blame me? She's a reckless girl, totally unreliable. I had no idea where she went last night."

I narrowed my eyes to stare her down.

"Don't look at me like that, young lady." She stomped toward me, halting within an inch of my face, though she had to bend forward to get that close. One more inch and her enormous bosom would knock me on my ass. "Respect me, or suffer the consequences." She wiggled her fingers and green sparks danced between them.

I grinned up at her round face, its shape reminding me of an overripe pumpkin. "Stop pretending to be my mother," I said. "I already have one."

"You mean you *had* one," she corrected, lip curled. "Past tense. About twenty-five years past, isn't that right?"

My throat swelled with the words I wanted to say, but I wasn't going to take the bait. Instead, I'd swallow my rage and when I finally released it, I'd let her have it. And she'd be sorry for what she said.

"Ladies, ladies." Gavin put a hand on Zee's back and her eyes closed, her expression looking as if he'd just engaged one of her erogenous zones. "Let's not bicker. There's work to be done. Shall we?" He motioned for us to exit the room, and I gladly rushed out into the hall, feeling the staring eyes from inside the paintings follow my every move. Very unsettling.

I half ran, half walked to the elevator. Zee and Gavin followed at a snail's pace.

I leaned against the cab wall as we made our descent, my head throbbing with fatigue. Though I didn't need much sleep, I needed some, and I hadn't had a wink of it in more than twenty-four hours. When the elevator doors opened, I said, "So where will you put me now?"

"Not sure yet," Zee said, sounding petulant. She still pouted over her foiled plan. "Gavin, have any ideas?"

"Not a one, but we'll figure something out."

I followed them both through the cavernous room on the main floor. There was way too much power here. Acclimate, hell. The pressure overwhelmed. I strode past a glass case filled with a number of items I recognized because it was me who had stolen them.

The Raggedy Ann doll looked innocuous in her glass cage, her big button eyes and railroad-stitched mouth an innocent facade. Except the thing packed a wallop of bad mojo. It was a soul sucker. Enchanted by a witch at the turn of the century, the tattered old doll would steal the soul of a child as it slept, and replace it with one of a demon. I'd filched it from the attic of an aristocrat in Washington, D.C., who had used it to bargain for political favors. It was no wonder I didn't trust politicians.

"Hand it over," Gavin said, holding out his hand.

I fisted my bottle of salt water, shoving it deeper in my

pocket. He knew I carried it with me everywhere. "I promise not to use it. Holding it makes me feel safe."

"Just give it to me." He flexed his fingers.

"I need protection against the curses and charms here," I said, my voice purposely close to a whine. I knew it irritated him when I sounded like a girl. "Something almost got me last night, you know. A big bad ugly from beyond the black veil."

"Throwing salt water on it would have done no good." Fast as a striking snake, he grabbed my arm and forced my hand from my pocket. He roughly peeled my fingers from their death grip on the bottle. "I'll not have you disarming the magical objects in our collection, is that clear?"

Crystal. Besides, I could always make more salt water.

The three of us entered a large room dominated by a heavy oak table surrounded by chairs in the same style. All but one chair was empty.

"Chalice," Gavin said, holding his arm out to the man who stood up when signaled. "I'd like you to meet Aydin Berkant, one of our most loyal Vyantara members."

eight

AYDIN? THE INVISIBLE MAN, AYDIN? MY HEART
banged against my rib cage so hard that Gavin must have
heard it.

Aydin stared right through me, his expression completely
blank. He'd lied to me. The bastard got me to trust him,
to follow him to a place filled with supernatural creatures
as duplicitous as he was. My fingers twitched to grab my
knife, and though I had limited talent for throwing, I'd
make an exception just for him.

"But of course you two have already met," Gavin said,
looking snide. "I trust Aydin made you feel welcome?"

I was so confused now that I couldn't even speak. I
checked Aydin's face for a change, something to let me
know our meeting hadn't been a ploy. I was usually very

good at reading people, so to say I felt betrayed was an understatement. I was mortified.

Gavin grunted to get my attention. "You had a nice night on the town? Saw the sights? Clubbed to your heart's content?"

What the hell? There had been no "night on the town" and certainly no time sightseeing. There was obviously some secret keeping going on, but I dared not breathe a relieved breath just yet.

Sounding totally reasonable and not one bit apologetic, Gavin said, "Chalice, you should understand that I had to arrange for a spy to keep an eye on you. I know how much you hate being tracked, but it couldn't be avoided. You're a very headstrong young lady and it appears Mr. Berkant kept you entertained and out of trouble for most of the evening." Head tilted back, he looked down his nose at Aydin. "But it was bad timing, eh? I hadn't taken your bondage cycle into account when I arranged for your services. I apologize."

"No need, sir," Aydin said, his vacant stare moving to Gavin's face. "I made it to Shojin in time. No harm done."

"Excellent." Gavin sat and gestured for Zee, Aydin and I to do the same. But not only was I speechless, I couldn't make my limbs move.

"Oh, dear," Gavin said, looking amused. "You were totally fooled. That's a rarity. Come now, Chalice. Get over it and sit down."

I couldn't take my eyes off Aydin. Not just because he looked more handsome in daylight than he had at night, but because he'd managed to lie so successfully to Gavin. That was hard to do. Or hard for me to do, anyway.

Aydin's eyes shifted slightly, and if he thought no one would notice, I'm sure he would have winked at me. I felt giddy with relief and my heart hammered that much harder.

"Our friend here must have demonstrated his awesome power of invisibility for you." Gavin leaned back in his chair and scowled at me because I hadn't sat down when he told me to. He yanked a chair out from the table and banged it on the floor.

I lowered myself onto its seat. "Yes." I swallowed, my mouth so dry that my tongue stuck to my teeth. "Yes, he did. Very impressive."

"Thank you," Aydin said dully.

"There's an interesting story behind his ability." Gavin tugged a cigar from a leather humidor on the table, offering one to each of us. I'd sooner kiss a Maågan demon than smoke one of those nasty things. Aydin declined, as well. Zee accepted hers with zeal.

The stuffy little room soon filled with the acrid stench of cigar smoke. "As I was saying, there's a story. Pardon me, Zee, if I bore you with what you've likely heard a dozen times."

"Oh, no. I won't be bored." Her fat cheeks sunk in when she sucked on the thick cigar that looked more like a turd. She slid it slowly in and out between her lips. So obscene. Smiling around the stogie, she said, "I could listen to you talk all day."

Gavin appeared oblivious to her flirting, but seemed

to relish her praise. "Chalice, did you know Aydin is a warrior?"

I shook my head and narrowed my eyes at the man I'd almost considered a friend. A warrior who wore faded blue jeans and a T-shirt that said I Don't Have a License to Kill, I Have a Learner's Permit.

"How old would you guess Aydin is?"

I shrugged. Aside from not giving a damn at this point, I was terrible at guessing ages. "Thirty, thirty-one, maybe?"

Gavin took a puff of his cigar. "Close." He took another puff. "He's nine hundred and sixty-seven years old, to be exact."

I shot the warrior a look, but he was too busy picking at the letters on his T-shirt to notice. "You don't say," I said, purposely sounding bored when I was actually amazed. No *human* could live that long.

"It's fascinating, don't you think? That a man can live so many centuries." Gavin waited for me to respond.

I wondered if bondage to a gargoyle had something to do with Aydin's longevity. Did it make him immortal? I was bonded to Shui twelve years ago, but I had aged normally and felt glad not to be stuck for eternity inside the body of a pubescent teen. "Is it his bondage that made him live so long?" I asked, as if Aydin wasn't in the room. He hadn't spoken a word to me, so why should I speak to him?

"No." Gavin took a pull on his cigar. "He made a deal with someone. And immortality was his reward."

I didn't like the sound of that. "Not the invisibility?"

"That, too. Actually, that was the initial deal. Aydin

fought in the First Crusade as a Seljuk Turk, helping his fellow warriors take Baghdad in 1070. He wanted to be invincible against the Christians, and a demon overheard his wish. Since it wanted the Christians to lose just as much as Aydin did, it granted him what he wanted. Invisibility hid him from his enemies, but it also took away his ability to fight. As a ghost, he wasn't solid and couldn't wield a weapon. He was invincible—and ultimately ineffective."

Bargaining with a demon demoted Aydin to a low-life, just a bare notch above Gavin in my book.

"Demons and angels love playing with humans," Aydin said in a way that sounded defensive, but I didn't think he had a case. Was a fallen angel just a demon with wings? One of the first lessons I'd learned from working for the Vyantara is to never make a deal with the supernatural. If you do, you're guaranteed to get burned.

"It cursed me." His gaze finally connected with mine. "And it forced me to endure the sin of my bargain for all eternity."

"And signing on with the Vyantara was supposed to help you?" I asked, sickened by his cowardice. Hiding from the enemy was no way to fight a war. "That's like adding fuel to the fire. What part of *damned* don't you understand?"

"He didn't volunteer," Gavin said. "He was...recruited. And bonded the same day. He and Shojin have enjoyed each other's company for over eight hundred years."

I peered at Aydin, who held his head high, his eyes focused straight ahead and not on me. But I saw the sadness there, the regret. And he did seem old to me now, as much in years as in wisdom. He had to have learned something from his mistakes. That's probably why he was so passionate about the good side of magic, the good people who wielded it, and the innocent creatures that existed beyond the green veil. I couldn't fault him for that. And maybe almost a millennium of penance made him worth forgiving. I didn't know, but I was willing to find out.

I felt suddenly feverish and the back of my neck itched. It was my tattoo. I rubbed it lightly, the flesh tender to my touch. "Where are you keeping Shui?"

Zee tore her adoring gaze from Gavin. "What was that, dear?"

For crap's sake. "Shui!" I nearly shouted the monster's name. "Where is he? I'll need him soon."

Her eyes pulled up at the corners, but her Kewpie-doll mouth was slow to catch up with the smile. "Oh, my. I completely forgot to tell you."

"Tell me what?"

She tossed a look at Gavin, who narrowed his eyes at her. She coughed into her hand. "Well, I got a call this morning that the train Shui was traveling on derailed a few miles north of the station in McCook, Nebraska. No one was hurt, thank goodness."

Every nerve in my body sizzled with alarm.

"When will he be here?" I asked, forcing calm into my voice. My gaze flicked to Aydin, whose eyes had gone hard as he stared at Zee. He didn't like her, either.

"Hmm…" She touched a lacquered fingernail to her temple. "Passengers were being bussed to Amtrak's McCook station. And so was the luggage, which would include Shui, of course. Poor creature is probably going batty by now. Who knows what effect the accident had on him?"

"Why didn't you tell me about this?" Gavin's cold, blue eyes were icier than a glacier.

Zee flushed. "I, uh, I forgot until just now."

Gavin landed a fist on the table. His sorcerer's voice shook the walls when he said, "I have work for her, Zee. I can't lose Chalice now. You know that!"

The fat lady whimpered. "I'm sorry, Gavin. Everything will be okay. She can go to McCook and meet up with Shui there. It's a little over four hours' drive from here. She can make it there in time."

Maybe. Maybe not. It was the *not* part that scared me. "Is he on a train now?" I asked, not wanting to arrive in McCook and have him not be there.

Zee shook her head. "I asked Amtrak to hold his crate."

Good thinking, Zee, you manipulative bitch.

Looking innocent, she added, "I realized there's no way the train could get him here by the time you needed him. Taking Mohammed to the mountain seemed faster."

Gavin's jaw was clenched so tight his lips turned white. "She's right. Damn it, Zee! Never keep information like that to yourself."

"You should have traveled with him," I told Gavin, the sick feeling in my stomach getting worse. I'd never make it to Shui in time. Today would be my last day as a human. "I feel sick," I said and lowered my head to my hands on the table.

A hand glided across my shoulders, the fingers gently kneading the tight muscles there. It felt really, really good. I sucked in a breath and jerked upright. "Don't touch me."

Aydin lowered himself to the chair beside me. "I want to help. I understand what's happening to you."

I wanted to say, "No, you don't understand," but he really was the only one who did. He'd been through it himself, and probably more times than I had. My eyes felt hot and they burned when I blinked up at him. My face flushed as I remembered my body's reaction to the desire emanating from him at the end of his cycle. "I'm so...I'm so..."

"You're so what?" Aydin prompted, his voice soft and low. The sound vibrated up my spine and tickled the edges of my tattoo. He comforted me and excited me all at once, yet it was exhaustion that completely took me over.

"I'm so tired." I put my head down again, feeling my energy drain through my feet and empty out into the room.

"We've got to get her out of here," Gavin said, sliding out my chair with me still in it. "Up you go."

I didn't want to move. Every muscle felt limp, and it was hard to lift my head. "What's happening to me?"

"The house is draining you," Gavin said. "It feeds on fear. Quite ingenious, really. My idea, by the way." He sniffed with self-importance and grabbed me around the waist to lift me up. "Did I fail to mention the Fatherhouse is alive?"

My words slurred as I said, "Seriously?" But I didn't care. I didn't care about anything.

"I should have given her an amulet for protection," Zee

said, and there was real regret in her voice. "She seemed so strong that I didn't think there'd be a problem."

"As with so many things lately, Zee, you thought wrong." Gavin hoisted me over his shoulder and carried me from the room. "It wouldn't have done her any good, anyway."

I couldn't keep my eyes open. I was already fatigued from lack of sleep, so having a house "feed" on me didn't help. I bounced along on Gavin's shoulder, each step knocking a shallow breath from me. Blood rushed to my head to give me one hell of a headache.

I heard a car door open, then felt myself lowered to something soft. It smelled like leather and was cool against my cheek. The rumble of an engine vibrated the cushion beneath my head and the car rolled forward, its tires crunching over rocks and dead leaves. It picked up speed, the engine humming one long, soothing note that lulled me to sleep.

"How is she?" someone asked from the front seat.

"She's waking up."

I groaned. Did I have a hangover? My body felt heavy, my head pounded and every sound was amplified. No wonder. One of my earplugs had fallen out. I tucked it back in place and pushed myself up to a sitting position. I swallowed what tasted like dust and it hurt my throat. "Water," I croaked.

A bottle appeared from over the front seat. I tried to grab it, but it slipped through my stiff fingers and fell to floor.

"I'll get it." Aydin sat in front and he bent over the seat

to reach for the bottle. "Here you go." He looked at me and blinked, his smile going stiff.

I scowled. "What?"

His smile was slipping. "Nothing. Drink your water."

I unscrewed the cap and chugged half of it. "Where are we?"

"Just outside McCook. We're almost to the station. Hang in there."

I saw the back of a silver-haired head in the driver's seat. "Gavin? I didn't know you could drive."

"You don't know a lot of things about me." He didn't turn to look at me, and he sounded annoyed.

My back hurt so bad I could hardly stand it. The skin stretched tight across my shoulder blades and I winced at a sudden, sharp pain. "Anyone have some aspirin?"

"Won't help," Gavin said. "Grit your teeth if you have to."

I was transforming. Slowly, painfully and inevitably. I tried to hold back the panic in my voice when I asked, "Can't you do something?"

The car accelerated.

I drank the rest of the water and lay back down on the seat, but had to stay on my side. My back was too tender to put pressure on. Baby bat wings were delicate things. *Shit!*

Gavin took a sharp turn to the left and tires squealed, the chemical stench of burnt rubber sifting through my filters. The car bounced over a speed bump and I cried out.

"Sorry." But Gavin didn't slow down. A minute later the

brakes screeched and the car stopped, tossing me onto the floor. "Stay down," he said.

"Why?"

Aydin turned sideways to look at me. "Because it's probably not a good idea to show your face in public."

Oh, man. It was that bad?

Gavin and Aydin left the car.

I crawled back up on the seat, keeping low, but still high enough to see out the window. The two of them were talking to a young bearded guy wearing a hat with the Amtrak logo. I lifted my earplugs so that I could hear their conversation.

"...crate with an animal inside," Gavin said.

"Oh, yeah," said Amtrak guy. "It's right over here. I guess you're the ones from the Denver Zoo?"

"Just here to pick up our monkey," Aydin told him, his face stretched with the friendliest smile. Confident *and* convincing. That man could charm the scales off a snake.

I watched all three vanish around the corner of a building, but that was okay. I could still hear them.

"Woo! What's that smell?" said Amtrak guy. "I sure hope your monkey didn't kick."

I hoped just the opposite. But considering I was about to have a major metamorphosis moment, I knew Shui wasn't dead. He just smelled bad.

"I'm sure he's fine," Gavin said, sounding all professorial and British. "Probably sleeping. He was sedated before leaving Chicago."

I heard a scuffling sound, then something metal slid

beneath wood followed by a rhythmic creaking that I imagined were turning wheels. The three men rounded the corner, the guy in the hat pushing a dolly loaded with a wooden crate twice the size of Shui.

"Cool accent," Amtrak guy said. "What part of England are you from?"

"Sussex." Gavin didn't smile. "But that was a long time ago. Do you have papers for me to sign?"

"I have a cousin who lives in London," Amtrak guy said. "I visited him a few years ago. Got to see Abbey Road."

"How nice for you." Gavin's voice had a dangerous edge, low and growly. Not a good sign. "The papers?"

Amtrak guy handed him a clipboard. "Where you from?" he asked Aydin.

"Turkey."

Amtrak guy frowned. "You sound American."

"I've lived here awhile."

The wooden crate suddenly jerked and Amtrak guy jumped back. "What the hell?" He looked down at his legs. "I'm bleeding! That fucking monkey clawed me!"

A hairy arm stuck out from the side of the crate and took another swipe at Amtrak guy, who jumped out of reach.

"If that thing's got rabies, I'll sue!" He took off his hat and swatted the paw that had incredibly long, curved nails sharp enough to slice through bone. The guy was lucky he still had his leg. "I'm callin' the cops. That thing's dangerous."

Aydin pulled Amtrak guy aside. "Look, buddy, I'm sorry. The monkey's under a lot of stress. He's a valuable animal and from what I understand of the accident, he could have been killed. And your company would have a major lawsuit on its hands."

"I don't give a damn about that," the guy said. "This is pain and suffering, man. I've got a gash on my leg and I'll probably get gangrene. I'm the one filing a lawsuit."

"That won't be necessary." Gavin slipped his wallet from his back pocket and removed a thick stack of bills. "This should take care of it."

The guy grumbled, "I don't know. It might not be enough."

Just take it, you idiot. My tattoo was on fire and I felt like tearing the guy's throat out myself. And from how I was feeling, that could happen at any minute.

Gavin threw another couple of bills onto the stack and Amtrak guy snatched the cash and shoved it in his pocket. He limped off, and from the way Gavin was staring at him, I had a pretty good idea where Shui's next meal was coming from.

Gavin and Aydin wheeled Shui's crate to the car. I think we'd arrived in a Hummer or an enormous SUV of some kind. It was hard to tell from the inside, but it had a cargo area that would easily accommodate the crate. With some grunting and shoving, the two men wrestled Shui's crate into the back, the gargoyle growling and hissing the entire time.

Gavin jumped in on the driver's side and Aydin stayed in back with me. "How do you want to do this?"

Crap. He had to watch? "I don't think Shui wants you

around." And sure enough, the gargoyle rammed the sides of his crate, roaring so loud that the people inside passing cars were starting to stare.

"She has a point," Gavin said as he steered the SUV onto the highway. "He smells Shojin on you. And he's very territorial."

"Can we leave the discussion about temperamental gargoyles for another time?" I asked, my voice rising with each syllable.

The SUV swerved around a corner and swung into the parking lot of a seedy motel. The sign said Pets Welcome. We were in the right place.

Gavin skidded to a stop. "I'll get a room. You stay with Chalice," he told Aydin. Shui growled and rammed the side of his crate again. "Shui!" Gavin yelled. "Enough." The gargoyle fell silent.

"Come on," Aydin said, and took hold of my arms to help me out. My back hurt so badly that I couldn't stand up straight. He grabbed my scarf off the floor of the SUV and draped it over my head, forming it into a hood that hid most of my face.

"That bad, huh?" I asked.

"Let's just say we don't want to upset the neighbors."

A middle-aged couple walked by and after one look at me, they shrank back, their faces leeched of color. The woman's gaze locked on to me and she took a cautious step closer. "Honey, I've got some cream that will clear that right up." She handed me a business card, snapping her hand away the second I touched it. "Give me a call."

I looked at the card. Avon.

I touched my face, fingertips running over scales the size of pennies. I wanted to scream, but my voice was locked in my throat. I'd never come this close to changing before. Agitation chewed at my nerves and I knew that if I could relax, I'd be able to slow the transformation process.

I peered over at Aydin, who was gathering plastic shopping bags from the front seat. He and Gavin must have made a stop along the way, and I'd been so out of it I hadn't even noticed. Aydin seemed so ordinary just now, a regular guy, handsome as hell, who did the same mundane things as every other human in this world. It was hard to believe he'd been a warrior more than nine centuries ago. And a coward. When he looked at me, he caught me staring and I quickly glanced away.

"I'll take care of you," Aydin said, making it sound like a promise. It made me wonder if he'd somehow sensed my thoughts.

He slid the dolly from the back of the SUV and tugged the crate toward him. Rocking it left to right, he pulled at the same time, inching it closer to the opened hatch. Shui wasn't light and the wooden crate was sturdy as hell, in spite of the fist-size hole punched through the side. Dried blood rimmed the splintered opening. I imagined Amtrak guy was already home, nursing his wound along with a beer or two—imported, of course, now that he could afford the good stuff—to help ease the pain.

"Careful," I told Aydin, my teeth chattering with chills from fever. I'd convulse soon, and I'd prefer doing it in private. "I guess we could pry off the side so that I can climb in with him." The thought of how bad it smelled in there threatened my gag reflex, but I was desperate.

Gavin came running out of the motel lobby with the key. "Let's get him on the dolly."

The three of us—four counting Shui—hurried across the parking lot to our room, which thankfully was on the first level. I stumbled and Aydin lifted me in his arms, carrying me like a baby. How embarrassing. The muscles of his biceps were firm as tree limbs, and his strong hands felt warm against my arms and legs through my clothes. He held me close, my head tucked beneath his chin, and I could only imagine his repugnance at touching the creature I was becoming. My back felt wet with blood from my split skin, my budding wings straining against the fabric of my jacket.

Gavin flung open the door and Aydin dropped me on the bed. Anyone watching would have thought us in the throws of passion, our desire for each other making our bodies sweat and our breath come hard and fast.

That wasn't far from the truth.

Passion. Lust. A carnal hunger so intense it threatened to wipe every coherent thought from my mind. Aydin froze where he lay against me, his muscles tense, and I knew we shared the same feelings.

"I *want...*" I whispered, my voice hoarse with need as I grabbed the waistband of his jeans and yanked him closer. The pain of longing forced my senses over the top.

He moaned. "I know, and I want you, too. Resist, Chalice. It's the curse taking you over. Fight it."

"I don't want to fight. I want to submit."

He hesitated before pushing himself up and off the bed.

My head throbbed so hard with the pressure of impending change I thought it might explode.

Gavin drew a knife from the inside of his jacket and watched Aydin pry the crate's boards loose with a crowbar he'd brought from the SUV. I saw that Gavin's blade wasn't made of steel. It looked more like cut stone, the edges sharp but rough. The blade appeared striated with uneven bands of purple and red, veins of black running through it from tip to pommel. The way he held it was odder still. He wielded it like a weapon, like he intended to use it against Shui. Maybe my fevered brain couldn't register what my eyes saw, but that knife… It was fabulous. I had to have it.

Two boards came free, and before Gavin could yank them completely off the crate, Shui burst out in a flurry of wings, claws and teeth. And he went straight for Aydin.

nine

AYDIN VANISHED. THERE WAS A MUFFLED PLOP
as the clothes he'd been wearing dropped in a heap to the
floor.

Shui spun one way, then the other, claws raking the
air where Aydin had stood. Gavin grabbed him around
the neck and when he shoved that odd but beautiful knife
against Shui's throat, the gargoyle froze.

"Don't make me use it." Gavin slid the knife gently over
the gray, scaly skin, but didn't cut him. From the panicked
look on Shui's face, I could tell this knife was special.

Fascinating. The knife held some kind of power over the
gargoyle. Was it enchanted? Coated in poison strong enough
to kill an immortal?

Shui's eyes closed, an expression of calm replacing his
alarm. In that instant he appeared almost human. As if

resigned to follow his master's command, he remained still, chest heaving, his leathery wings folded and tucked close to his sides.

Gavin shoved him at me. I stiffened when Shui clutched both my shoulders to flip me onto my stomach on the bed.

"Careful," Gavin said.

His claws sliced through my jacket, his hot breath bathing my neck as the room's cool air chilled my bloody back. Shui hovered close, inhaling my scent, one claw tracing an immature wing that struggled to break free. He'd rip the wing off if he could, and use it like a toothpick after dining on what was left of my human body.

But he didn't. He leaned down and ran his slimy tongue over my tattoo, letting it linger there. I didn't protest. The fever stopped almost immediately, and I felt my baby wings shrink, drawing themselves back inside my body. It hurt, but I didn't mind. I just wanted them gone.

Shui retreated and hobbled back to Gavin.

I lay on the hard, lumpy bed, silent and exhausted, and thoroughly relieved. I wondered if Aydin was still in the room somewhere. Had he witnessed what had happened, what I'd let Shui do? That was my last thought before I passed out.

I opened my eyes in the dark. An explosive memory threatened to engulf me in agony. I remembered the fear, the fever, the sense of loss when I had almost changed into—

I shot to my feet, grabbing my head with one hand while my other reached out for balance.

"Easy," said a man's voice from behind me.

"Don't touch me, Aydin." To say my nerves were on edge was an understatement. I wanted to hit something and he would make an easy target. I lowered myself back to the bed instead. "I'll be okay. Just a head rush."

"Not surprising after coming within a gnat's fart of turning all leathery and scaly." His voice sounded matter-of-fact, not teasing. I shuddered at how right he was.

I rubbed my bare arms, then hugged my chest, covering my naked breasts with my hands. Aydin had seen me half naked! "Where's my shirt?"

"Ruined." I heard the crinkly sound of a plastic bag. "I took the liberty—"

"I think you took too many liberties."

"—of picking out a new T-shirt for you. I hope you like pink."

I hated pink. I yanked the shirt from his hands and pulled it over my head. "Thanks."

He hesitated before saying, "I didn't see… You know."

He sat in the chair beside the little round table by the window. Not believing a word, I squinted at him in the dark.

He cleared his throat. "Okay, so I didn't see much. Kept my eyes closed this whole time. Promise."

"I bet you did." He was such a liar. A con man. A demon dealer. I wanted to trust him, but I wasn't sure I could.

"I would have seen lots more if I'd done what you asked."

Oh, my God. I suddenly remembered every detail. I had asked him to do me. I'd wanted to have sex and the jolt of sensation between my legs now meant I still did. "About that…"

He chuckled. "No worries. I won't hold it against you, not unless you want me to."

Every pore in my body flushed with heat. Would I ever live this down? I coughed lightly and asked, "Where's Gavin?"

"He left with Shui as soon as it got dark. Threw a blanket over him and walked him out to the Hummer. They're probably back at the Fatherhouse by now."

I rubbed my arms again and he tossed a blanket over my shoulders, careful not to lay a hand on me. Smart man. I reached back to touch the sheath between my shoulders and found it gone. I wasn't surprised. He probably thought I'd use my knife on him if given the chance, and despite being immortal, I didn't think he was impervious to pain.

Without a word, he handed me my blade still in its sheath, but I didn't strap it on. I could wait. Just holding it sent a wave of calm through me. But I'd need to replace the leather strap I used to hold it in place on my back. My body had apparently distorted enough while shifting form that it broke.

Still focused on my knife, I asked, "So where were you until they left?"

"Outside."

"Naked?"

"Yup."

"Weren't you freezing out there?"

"Nope. As long as I stay a ghost, I can't feel anything."

He hadn't materialized inside the room because Shui would have torn him a new one, literally, while tearing out his throat at the same time. Did that make Aydin a coward? Or did it make him smart? It was something to think about.

"So now what?" I asked.

"I rented a car to drive us back to Denver."

"Then why are we waiting?" I asked out of curiosity rather than urgency. I didn't care if we never went back. Not that I had a choice.

His silhouette leaned forward and light cast from the motel's neon sign outside illuminated his face. His features were tight with concern. "Are you ready for the drive?" he asked, eyebrows lifted.

I shrugged, feeling in no hurry to return to the Fatherhouse. The magic there was uncomfortably strong and it made my head hurt. Plus, now that I knew the house was alive and had an appetite for fear, I wasn't especially keen on feeding it. I had lots to be scared of. And even if I pretended not to be afraid, I had a feeling the house would know the difference.

"I'll have no place to stay when we get back."

He gave me a dubious look. "I thought you had a room in the house."

"I won't sleep there. It's rigged for the other Fatherhouses to spy on me." I watched his face to see if this surprised him. It didn't. Maybe he was used to being spied on. Hell, he *was* a spy. "How can you live in that place?"

"I don't. I live in the guest house behind it. There's plenty of room if you'd like to share it with me." His smile looked a little too sly. "It's very safe. Really."

"I'll think about it." As the old saying went, "Keep your friends close and your enemies closer." Staying with Aydin might not be such a bad idea. I was pragmatic enough to know Gavin wouldn't let me get too far out of his sight.

I was sticky with dried sweat and blood. "I need a shower." I headed for the bathroom, dragging the blanket like a cloak behind me.

The second the door snicked shut, I heard the television flick on.

Rather than switch on the light and fry my retinas, I removed my contact lenses and bathed my eyes in darkness. I wanted to see how badly my body had been ravaged by my too-close-for-comfort transformation. Letting the blanket drop from my shoulders, I peeled off the ugly pink shirt and pivoted in front of the mirror above the sink, craning my neck to check out my back. The skin was mottled with puffy red lines surrounding two puckered scars where wings had poked out from beneath my shoulder blades. I healed fast. Always had.

My face, on the other hand, had never looked so horrid. I pressed close to the mirror, staring hard at the rashy skin on my cheeks and forehead. It would be completely healed by morning, but at the moment I looked like an adolescent in serious need of extra-strength pimple cream. I scratched at a pink scab on my temple and dry flakes of skin fell into the sink. Gross.

I twisted the spigots in the outdated shower and stood

beneath the spray as hot as I could stand. I gazed down at my feet to watch swirls of bloody water circle the drain.

After drying myself off, I stuck my head out the bathroom door. "You wouldn't happen to have a clean pair of jeans and underwear in one of those bags, would you?"

He snatched a shopping bag from the floor and tossed it to me. When I reached out to grab it, I opened the door too far and flashed him. I flung the bag inside and slammed the door shut. Reopening it a crack, I said, "You didn't see that."

He smirked, revealing a dimple at the corner of his mouth. But he politely kept his stare on the TV and not on me.

The jeans were a size too big. No surprise there. The pink shirt looked silly enough, but the idiotic saying branded across the front made it worse: Talk Nerdy to Me.

I emerged from the steamy bathroom and looked at the white T-shirt Aydin was wearing. He must have bought it at the same time he'd decided Pepto-Bismol was my color. The front of his said Where There's a Will…I Want to Be in It.

But I couldn't smile. In fact, I was having a hard time feeling *anything.* I wanted to go to Elmo's and hear the fey laugh, and listen in on conversations between people having fun, even if those people were from beyond the green veil. I wanted to play with Ling Ling and watch her change from a monkey to a cat to a ferret. I'd welcome a bit of magic just to have a little joy.

Aydin's hand disappeared inside a bag of chips cradled

in his lap. He stopped chewing midcrunch to stare at me. "What's wrong?"

I was horrified to feel a tear slide down my cheek. I flicked it away. "Not a thing. Why?"

He resumed chewing and shoved another chip in his mouth. "Oh, I don't know. From the look on your face, you seem ready to bite my head off. Here." He offered me the bag of chips. "Bite one of these instead."

I grabbed the bag and dug my hand in for a fistful, then sat on the bed to eat them. Potato chips had never tasted so good.

He reached for the bag and I yanked it away. "Mine."

He shrugged and ripped open a bag of pretzels. "You're craving the salt, you know."

I licked my fingers. "No, I'm craving food. I'm starving."

"Yeah, but your body also needs salt. The salt counteracts the curse working through you and it helps get your body back to normal."

How about that. I learned something new every day in my crazy world of curses and flying monkeys. "You know this from experience?"

"Yup." He snapped the end off a pretzel. "I don't remember the exact date, but it was right after the Vyantara first got their hooks into me. I was recruited about a hundred years after my…" He waved a hand in front of his body. "This."

Meaning a hundred years after he was cursed by a demon. "So what happened that overstretched the bond with your gargoyle…what's his name?"

"Shojin." He absently rubbed the back of his neck where his tat was. "I didn't believe what the shaman had told me. I thought I could beat the curse by running away."

"How far did you get?"

He leaned back to study me. "In distance? Or in shifting."

"Both."

"About fifty miles and a full set of claws, front and back." He wiggled his fingers, which looked perfectly fine now. Better than fine. They were long and thick, and really strong. I knew that from when he'd carried me inside the room.

I heaved a breath, imagining how hard it must have been for him, especially in the twelfth century. There were no hotel rooms or showers or fresh changes of clothes. And no fast modes of transportation. Which begged the question, "If you were fifty miles from your gargoyle, then how...?"

"Shojin stalked me from the moment I escaped."

"He hunted you?"

"Not exactly. Chalice, not all gargoyles are like Shui. Shojin is different."

I choked on a chip.

"You have to meet him."

He had to be kidding. "Excuse me? I have my own vile, bloodthirsty monster, thank you very much. I think I'll pass on meeting yours."

Considering where we were and where we needed to go, I decided I was rested enough for the long drive back to Denver. Peering out at the night sky through an undraped window, I said, "I'm ready to go back now."

"Not just yet."

I looked at him and scowled. "Why not?"

He pulled an envelope from his inside jacket pocket. "I need to show you something first." Handing it over, he added, "I've been saving it for you."

I accepted the envelope with caution, unsure what to expect. Saving it for me? Since when, yesterday? We'd known each other less than forty-eight hours. I lifted the flap, which was unsealed, and peered inside before pulling out the photo that lay within. The picture was laminated, and a good thing, too, because half of it had burned away. The charred edges glistened beneath the clear plastic. I blinked and looked at it more closely. "How did you get this picture of me?"

"It's not you." He hesitated. "It's your mother."

My legs turning to rubber, I sat on the bed and clasped the photograph to my chest. I tried to ignore my thudding heart and lifted the picture to gaze into turquoise eyes flecked with gold. My eyes; the eyes I'd inherited from my mother.

"Where did you get this?" I asked, the words fading in the air between us. He cocked his head as if he hadn't heard, so I repeated the question.

"I found it in the fireplace at Gavin's home in Chicago." He shifted his weight from one foot to the other, then locked his knees as if forcing himself to stay still.

"I don't understand. When were you at Gavin's?"

"About twenty-five years ago."

Close to the time I was born. Even back then he'd known

he would meet me someday. I couldn't decide if this was good or bad, but he had a connection to my mother. "You knew her?"

He crouched on the floor in front of me. "I knew *of* her, but we never met." He swallowed, looking uncomfortable. "Soon after Gavin came back from a trip to the Middle East, he dumped the contents of a folder filled with notes and photographs into the fireplace and lit a match. What you have in your hand is all that's left. I rescued it when he wasn't looking. If he ever finds out…" Aydin made a slicing motion across the front of his throat.

But Gavin would never find out. I'd make sure of it.

On closer inspection, I could see the differences between my mother and me. Her nose was straighter, her face thinner and she had long black hair that waved around her head like ribbons of midnight. She wore a black leather jacket that flared open as she ran. She looked at the camera head-on, her expression defiant, her eyes slightly narrowed as if to challenge the photographer. This fierce woman was the mother I'd never met.

"Why did you keep it?" I asked.

"Because I knew you'd want it. Your mother was obviously a strong woman to have survived a fatal gunshot wound long enough to give birth. You deserved to know what she looked like." He eyed the picture, then focused on me. "I couldn't save her, but I hoped for a chance to save you."

Damn Gavin. It sickened me to know the man for whom I'd slaved for twelve years had killed my mother, but I could do nothing about it. I'd tried to kill him once. That didn't mean I wouldn't try again.

My mood more numb than sad, I let the photo fall to my lap. "You can't save me, Aydin."

"I realize you're living your destiny, but that doesn't mean I can't help you through it," he said, his voice deep with meaning. "I think your mother would have wanted that, don't you?"

I passed my fingers over the face in the photograph, trying to sense her through the plastic, through the years that separated us. The photo was a cold and inanimate thing. It couldn't feel my longing or my loss.

"I'm here for you," Aydin said. "I'm no substitute for your mother, but I understand what you're feeling. I lost my own family many lifetimes ago."

Yet he'd taken a big risk to give me a gift of family that I could treasure always. No one had ever done anything so selfless for me. Not even the monks.

Aydin jiggled the bed to get my attention. When I looked up, I found him smiling with mischief in his eyes. "Want to see some magic?"

I shook my head, but inside a ghost of smile touched my heart.

"It will cheer you up. I promise."

"You said you're not a sorcerer."

"I'm not, but I've learned a few tricks over the centuries. I'll show you." He stood, strode to the door and left.

"Nice vanishing act," I said to my mother's image. "But

we've already seen that trick. At least this time he's not naked."

He returned minutes later, his hands cupped around something he seemed careful not to drop. He joined me on the bed and held out his open palm. A furry, black caterpillar wiggled slowly over the sigil scarred into his skin.

"Cute." I petted the tiny creature. "But not very magical."

Aydin linked the fingers of both hands together and blew through an opening between his thumbs. Pale blue light glowed through cracks in the finger cocoon he'd made for the bug. After one breath, he stopped.

I leaned back to create more distance between us. "What did you just do?"

"Magic." He pulled away his fingers and in place of the caterpillar sat a golden-winged moth. "It's a tiger moth. Very common."

"But not at this time of year." I stared at the insect. "Your breath. It gives life?"

He shook his head. "Accelerates it. A byproduct of my immortality I discovered by accident a few hundred years ago."

I blinked, my focus still on the moth. "So if you breathed on a puppy, it would turn it into a dog?"

He quirked an eyebrow. "I've never tried it, but I think it would take more than one breath. Puppies and caterpillars aren't exactly in the same league." He stood and stepped to the door to open it, releasing the moth out into the night.

"Magic doesn't have to be bad, Chalice." He dipped his

chin toward the photo still in my lap. "If you and your mother aren't proof of good magic, I don't know what is."

I hugged my one and only family heirloom to my chest. "Thank you."

"For what?"

"For this." I patted the picture. "And for the lesson in perspective." I stood from the bed and grabbed a couple of shopping bags off the floor. "Shall we go?"

After leaving McCook, we'd barely gone thirty miles when Aydin announced he was too exhausted to drive. Considering I'd already slept more in one day than I had in a week, I didn't have a problem taking his place behind the wheel. He needed to sleep; I needed to think. I wasn't one bit lonely without conversation as he snoozed beside me.

Aydin took back the helm once we got close to Denver's city limits because I didn't know my way around well enough to find the Fatherhouse. He parked the rental in a driveway behind the old refurbished factory, close to where a small house sat sheltered beneath the enormous branches of a hundred-foot-tall cottonwood. The tree's skeletal limbs looked like claws that raked across the night.

"Home sweet home," Aydin said as he engaged the parking brake.

I opened the car door and studied the dusky little house. I'd left out my contacts because my night vision was so much better without them. I scanned the front yard where shadows crept around the base of the cottonwood and wove in and out of low-growing fitzers. "You've got ghosts," I told him.

He stiffened. "I do?"

"About half a dozen." I peered at the human shapes that faded to smoke then reformed and hid behind the pillars holding up the front porch. "They're old ones. Probably hanging around out here because they can't get in the main house."

"The wards are set to keep them out." He grimaced. "I hate ghosts."

"So do I." The chips and pretzels hadn't been filling enough so we had stopped for burgers in Sterling. I gathered empty fast-food bags from the floor of the car. "Ignore them."

"I always do." He climbed out and shut the car door behind him.

I stepped on the path leading to the front door, then froze. My nose twitched as I sought out the scent that could give me nightmares. "Your gargoyle doesn't live in there with you, does he?"

Aydin chuckled and shook his head. "Shojin lives in the Fatherhouse basement." He moved ahead of me to the front door, unlocked it and held it open. Such a gentleman.

"Thanks." I set down my armload of fast-food trash and slid my contact lenses back in. "Okay, you can turn on the lights now."

He flipped a switch and warm light poured into the living room. Modern sconces hung near the ceiling on walls painted ochre and sage, and a flat-screen TV was mounted like a painting on the longest wall.

"At last, someone with taste. Thank you," I said, while releasing a relieved breath. "I've encountered too much bad art lately."

He lifted an eyebrow. "Allow me to show you around the house. That is, if you're still sure you want to stay here."

"I'm sure." I'd made up my mind the second I walked in the door. I needed this. I *deserved* this.

He gave me a puzzled look before waving a hand at the room we were in. "The living room."

"Very retro." I took in the fifties-style room complete with a boxy sofa perched on slender wooden legs. I liked it. It felt peaceful.

The kitchen, on the other hand, was techno-modern all the way, with stainless-steel appliances and concrete countertops. "This is amazing." The house didn't look like much from the outside, but the inside more than made up for it. "Where do I sleep?"

Worry lines creased his forehead.

"You do have an extra room, right? I mean, you said…"

"I do." He leaned back on his heels. "I never have company so it's more of a storage room, but it does have a bed and a bathroom across the hall."

"Sounds perfect. Lead on."

I followed him to the back of the house and he pointed to an open door. "Make yourself at home."

I flicked on a light to illuminate a neat little room with a futon rather than a bed, but I didn't mind. Anything would be better than sleeping in the Fatherhouse. There were a lot of boxes in this room, most made of wood, and some that looked like leather trunks. They appeared to have come from different time periods, and I suspected they contained mementos he'd saved over the centuries. "Are you a collector?"

He touched his chin in thought. "You could say that, yes."

I sat on the futon and bounced a couple times. "Comfy."

"Good." He still looked ill at ease.

"Hey, if you've changed your mind about me staying here, I'll understand." *And I'll never forgive you.*

"It's not that." He gave me a tight smile. "I'm glad you're here. Really."

"What better way to spy on me, huh?" The smile *I* returned was genuine. He was growing on me and I almost felt like I could trust him. "A guy's gotta do what a guy's gotta do, right? I'd rather it be you doing the spying than some faceless sorcerer in another country watching me through a portal painting. At least I know you. Sort of." A blush burned my cheeks when I thought about the passion we'd shared. Neither of us had given in, but it was only a matter of time.

He turned serious and stepped away from the doorway to join me on the futon. "You don't know me the way you think you do."

I cocked my head and studied the stern look on his face. "Is that a good thing, or a bad thing?"

"You don't know my history, what happened to me nine hundred and thirty years ago. It's not what you think."

"Okay." I settled my back against the futon and crossed my legs. "Then fill me in. I'm all ears."

His shoulders sagged as if beneath a heavy weight, and he leaned forward, resting his forearms over his knees. "I fought for the Turks in the First Crusade between the Christians and the Muslims."

"You weren't kidding about being a warrior," I said, the gravity of his true age hitting me all at once.

He nodded and closed his eyes, frowning as if he recalled memories difficult to dredge up. "In the last battle I fought, my army was driving back enemy troops when I noticed a woman wearing a helmet and chain mail that strained against her enormous belly. She was pregnant. And she swung her sword as bravely as any warrior on the front line."

Stunned, I didn't know what to say. I knew women occasionally fought in the Crusades, like the order of knights from whom I was descended. But a *pregnant* knight?

He opened his eyes to look at me. "She was in labor, Chalice. Blood stained her tunic from below the waist. Watching her, I was barely able to concentrate on my own sword. Then I saw her go down."

I leaned forward as if watching a suspenseful scene in a movie. Only this was real, which made it all the more frightening. "What did you do?"

"I picked her up and carried her to a cavern in the side of a hill. The fighting had moved on ahead, and I could hear the shouts, the killing blows, the screams of men dying. And so could she." He stopped to swallow. "I intended to leave her there so that I could keep fighting. I didn't even know this woman. A Christian. One of the enemy. I should have killed her right then. Looking back, I sometimes wish I had."

But all this had happened centuries ago. How could it matter now? "Did she have the baby?"

He nodded. "A girl. I didn't speak her language and she didn't speak mine, but we managed to communicate somehow. Hand gestures, mostly. And we shared our names."

He stopped talking and I couldn't stand it. "So what was her name?"

"Geraldine Terranova." He sucked in a breath before adding, "You would know her now as Saint Geraldine."

ten

DID HE MEAN THE SAME SAINT GERALDINE
entombed at the Cathedral Basilica? She and Aydin had
lived during the same era, so it shouldn't surprise me they
had known each other. It made a millennium seem so much
shorter somehow. A decade or a century, time was indiffer-
ent to people who could live forever.

"Did you hear what I just said?" Aydin asked.

I nodded and cleared my throat. "I'm just taking it all
in. Can the world have really been that much smaller back
then?" I didn't expect an answer and he didn't give me one.
"It's all adding up for me now—Geraldine, the Vyantara,
the angels." I stopped. I hadn't told him anything about
what my father was supposed to be. I'd keep that bit of info
to myself for now.

Without reacting to my angel slip, he said, "Gavin doesn't

know I knew Geraldine when she was alive. None of the Vyantara know."

"That's some secret to keep for over nine hundred years." Gavin could sniff out a liar like a fox could a hare. "How'd you do it?"

"I've had time to get my story straight."

No argument there. "So what *is* your story? The real one."

He slouched back against the futon, both palms curved over the mounds of his knees. "After Geraldine gave birth, I couldn't just leave her. So I found a midwife in the village. I tried to leave it at that, but I couldn't. There was something about her, some inner light that glowed through her eyes and made me think of angels." He jerked a look at me. "You said something about angels. You know what she can do?"

I recalled my conversation with Elmo and shrugged. "Only that she'd been accused of witchcraft because she claimed to talk to angels."

He turned his gaze to a wall lined with boxes stacked high to the ceiling. I could have sworn I saw the smallest one on top shift sharply to the left, but he didn't seem to notice.

He sucked in a breath and said, "That was a strange time in our world's history, Chalice. So much evil plagued Europe and the Middle East that people didn't look like people anymore. Their bodies were contorted, faces hidden behind hoods, their hands gnarled into claws that curled like fish hooks."

Looking distracted, he tapped his chin and squinted as if that would sharpen his memory. "In the small villages around the holy city, the humans were turning into something else. They did odd things, performed miracles, cursed their enemies and talked to angels."

"What kind of angels?"

"The Fallen kind."

He meant the demonic kind. "So it was a fallen angel you'd made your deal with."

"It wasn't that simple." He scowled and a muscle in his jaw began to twitch. He stood to straighten the same stack of boxes that had drawn my attention a moment ago. Focusing on the top box, he carefully picked it up to hold it gently in his hands, treating the small wooden cube like a fragile piece of glass. "From the moment I met Geraldine, I knew there were dark powers at work in that war. The Crusaders fought an army of creatures that fed off violence, greed and hate."

I cleared my throat. "So your deal—"

"—was really a curse disguised as a gift."

"How did it happen?"

He turned the small box over in his hands. "I went to see Geraldine at the midwife's home, but the woman wouldn't let me in. I was a Seljuk Turk, the enemy, and with all the horrors happening around them, none of the villagers were taking any chances."

I was once again struck by the age and experience of this man. I studied the straight line of his nose, the crescent shape of his eyes, and those very thick, very black eyebrows that seemed to furl around his deepest thoughts. He was a living artifact the Vyantara had added to their cursed collection. A freak. Like me.

His gaze bored into me as if daring me to disbelieve what he said. He'd told me things he wouldn't reveal to just anyone, and his earnest expression begged me to hang on every word. "A hunchbacked figure approached me in the streets. A hood partially hid his face, but he pulled the fabric back when he spoke. He was pale, his hair white as clouds, and his skin smooth and hairless as a child's. He said he needed my help."

I suspected what that cloaked figure had been. "He was an angel, wasn't he?"

Aydin nodded. "I saw an enormous black feather fall to the ground between his feet. I didn't think he was carrying birds under his cloak."

I shuddered. "One of the Fallen."

"He said he knew a way for me to see Geraldine. He promised to make me invisible so I could pass through the walls of the midwife's house like mist. In return I would have to spy on his enemy and bring him secrets of the Christians' plans."

"Did you?"

He looked away. That was my answer.

"Geraldine was angry with me for making the deal. That same angel had tried bargaining with her for her baby. He knew the child was gifted because it was spawned by one of the Arelim."

My breath caught. The Arelim, guardian angels of the

twelfth order. Gavin had said my father had been a Guardian before he fell from grace.

The father of Geraldine's baby was an angel, meaning Geraldine had obviously been one of the first knights in the Order of the Hatchet. I gulped down air that had suddenly become too thin.

"What about your immortality?" I asked. "Did you know that was part of the bargain you made?"

"I didn't find out until later, when a Crusader saw me materialize outside an officer's tent and tackled me to the ground before slitting my throat. He left me for dead, and that's exactly what I thought I was. Dead. But I didn't die. The fallen angel I'd dealt with hadn't wanted to lose his investment. That's when I realized the gift granting me time with Geraldine was also a curse." He hung his head to stare at the floor. "I also realized I'd fallen in love with her."

And then his love was executed and dismembered, her withered head a trophy in the hands of his enslavers.

My gut twisted and I suddenly felt like I'd lost something, too. The one person who had given me back what I thought I'd lost forever: my mother. And now I'd lost him to a dead woman. Or rather, an undead one. I peered up into his face, but his eyes were closed. What could I say? That I understood? I really didn't. I didn't know what it was like to love someone that way. I didn't know how it felt to care so much for someone that I'd sacrifice my own soul just to be near him. I wanted to understand and to feel as deeply as he did, but it would only happen if I stayed human. I now had one more reason to break the gargoyle's curse.

"What happened to Geraldine's baby?" I asked, my head humming with questions about my ancestors.

His eyes popped open and he blinked as if waking from a dream. "She survived. Her name was Maria."

"Did she become a knight like her mother?" *And like my mother?*

He shook his head. "I don't know. Maria was still a baby when Geraldine was executed. I think the midwife ended up raising her as her own. What happened after that..." He held out his hands and shrugged.

So Maria probably grew up not knowing about her roots. She never discovered who she really was.

Geraldine couldn't have been the only Hatchet Knight to start the order. "Tell me about the other knights."

Aydin cocked his head to one side, his puzzled expression looking painted on instead of real. "What about them?"

I heaved an exasperated breath. He was stalling. There was still so much I needed to know, but he purposely held out on me. Why?

He smiled, and lifted the box he'd been holding to run his hand across the top. "What do you think is in here?"

I was dying to know, but I refused to let on how much. I didn't appreciate his mocking. "I can't say I care."

His smile widened to show a bright row of perfect teeth. "You're a terrible liar."

The small cube of wood was now balanced on his open palm. It jumped an inch and the lid popped open.

Something shiny and colorful leapt out to land squarely in my lap.

"What the hell?" I started to swat it away, then realized what it was. A frog. A tiny, jewel-encrusted frog not much bigger than my thumb. I looked up at Aydin. "Mind explaining what this is?"

"Her name is Ruby."

The tiny creature lifted its amphibian head and grinned at me. It looked like a grin, anyway. I know frogs don't have lips, but this was no ordinary frog. "What's it doing in my lap?"

"I think she likes you." He squinted at the sparkling creature and nodded as if he approved.

A living piece of jewelry. It didn't get much weirder than that. I held my hand open and Ruby hopped on. She was covered in precious stones: rubies, diamonds, amethysts, emeralds. I looked for skin showing between the jewels and found only silver. Her eyes shone like polished sapphires. I blinked at Aydin. "I've never seen anything like it."

"Because there isn't anything like Ruby. At least not in this world." He reached for the animal and she hopped up to land on my shoulder. "I think you have a new friend. She doesn't want me to put her away."

"Then don't." I turned my head to peer at the frog that was now mere inches from my face. "I don't mind having a roommate." No doubt an enchanted one, which made me wonder what else lived inside the trunks and ancient boxes in this room. Was Ruby a gift? Or a bribe to stop me from asking questions he wasn't prepared to answer?

Just as I was about ask that very thing, a vibration pulsed through the floor and a low boom sounded inside my head. Ruby leapt off my shoulder and disappeared behind the futon.

"What was that?" I asked Aydin.

"My wards have been breached."

But he wasn't a sorcerer. "You know how to set up wards?"

He stared at me and frowned. "You don't?" Not waiting for an answer, he rushed from the room and I followed.

"I knew I'd find the two of you here." Gavin stood in the middle of the living room looking pleased with himself. "Pleasant drive back?"

Aydin faced him, stone-faced and cold as a lost soldier who had fought too many battles and never won any of them. "What can I do for you, Gavin?"

Gavin grinned, but his eyes were hard. "Getting chummy, I see."

"Us?" I coughed. "Oh, yeah. Best of buds. Cowards are high on my list of favorite people, right next to serial killers and rapists." I fought to follow Aydin's example, holding the muscles in my face still and letting my eyes freeze over with indifference. I hadn't practiced the poker face much and I hoped I looked the part.

Gavin narrowed his eyes, then slid his gaze to Aydin.

"She doesn't like me much," Aydin said stiffly. "Having her stay here is the best way for me to keep an eye on her, but she doesn't see it that way."

Gavin tapped his bottom lip and studied us. "I trust you,

Aydin. You've served us well over the centuries. Chalice, on the other hand, is a loose cannon. Can you handle her?"

"You know I can." Aydin's expression didn't change. Fearful that mine would, I averted my eyes to stare hard at the floor.

"I've figured out a way to let Chalice speak with Saint Geraldine without me present." Gavin stepped to the far wall and investigated a decorative arrangement of dried reeds in a tall ceramic vase. "Aydin, I want you to go with her."

I frowned, then caught myself. Gavin didn't know anything about Aydin's relationship with Geraldine. I had to pretend that I didn't, either. It was easy to do when I thought about how much I still didn't know, and I hoped it translated to my face. Either my acting had worked or Gavin was too preoccupied with his fabulous plan to notice.

"He'll pass through the tomb walls and remain invisible while you talk to Geraldine. She won't know he's there, and he'll report back to me everything that's said between you." Gavin pulled a reed out of the vase and pointed it at Aydin. "It's the perfect plan."

I tossed a quick look at Aydin, who'd managed to maintain his apathetic facade. Even so, I swore I detected a hint of glee in his eyes.

Aydin stripped out of his jean jacket and handed it to Gavin, who folded it over his arm. The front of Aydin's T-shirt said I'm Gonna Survive. Even if It Kills Me.

I stood beside the tapestry that covered the vault of Saint

Geraldine's tomb. When Aydin unbuckled his belt, I turned away to face the woven piece of art and studied an intricately stitched rose garden made of flowering vines that climbed an arched arbor. It smelled musty.

I heard the slide of fabric along skin, then the clink of Aydin's belt buckle hitting the linoleum floor. Knowing there was a naked man behind me made my skin warm. And this wasn't just any man; it was Aydin. I felt my blush deepen.

In a few minutes, Aydin and I would be standing in front of a mummified head, having a conversation with a dead woman who wasn't really dead. Though I'd be the only one talking since Aydin couldn't speak while invisible. For all I knew, he'd be seeing Geraldine for the first time since their clandestine meetings in the midwife's home more than nine centuries ago.

"I'd like to take candles in with me," I told Gavin without turning around. I needed him to leave me alone with Aydin before he ghosted out and could no longer talk.

"You don't need light to see her, Chalice," Gavin said, sounding annoyed.

"I know, but maybe she does." I'd made that point the last time we were here. "If she can't see me, she may not talk to me."

Still facing the tapestry, I heard Gavin's theatrical sigh at my back. "I have some black ritual candles in the car. I'll be right back." His footsteps tapped down the long hallway and trailed into silence.

"Aydin?" I was afraid of turning around to find him

standing nude in front of me. Not that I didn't appreciate the male body, especially Aydin's, but I feared seeing him would light an erotic spark we might not be able to put out this time.

When he didn't answer, I *did* turn around. No one there. He'd obviously ghosted out so I removed my contacts to see him. Though it was night and the lights were dim, they were still bright enough to make me blink and squint, so I covered my naked eyes with my hands. I peeked through my fingers and sure enough, Aydin's hazy, translucent form wavered in front of me. He drifted toward the door.

"Wait!" But it was too late. He passed through the vault door and into the tomb behind it. I slipped out my earplugs and pressed the side of my head against the tapestry. Though soundproof, the door wasn't thick enough to prevent my ultrasonic ears from hearing. There were whispers. A man's voice. A few seconds later came the female response.

"Holy shit," I said to no one as I realized this wasn't the first time Aydin had paid his lady friend a visit.

The sound of approaching footsteps made me push away from the door and bank off the wall like a ball in a pinball machine.

As Gavin came nearer, his frown deepened. "What's wrong with you? You look agitated. What's going on?"

"He, uh, Aydin just…" I gestured at the door and tried to cover my surprise at knowing Geraldine had spoken to him. So I pretended to be flustered about something else. "He went in without me."

Gavin smiled thinly. "Do you have a problem with that?"

I didn't, but since I was doing a poor job of masking the emotions that animated my face, I acted like I did. "He'll screw everything up."

"She can't see him," he told me. "So don't worry about it." Moving in front of me, he lifted the tapestry and began pushing buttons on the electronic lock. A whoosh of air blew past me as the vault opened.

Gavin handed me the candles. "I'll be waiting right outside."

I nodded and slipped into the tomb. The door swung slowly closed behind me, enveloping me in incredible silence. How I loved hearing nothing for a change.

I didn't see Aydin right away. Instead I focused on the head at the center of the small table and the silver aura pulsing faintly around it. Again my heart ached for the dead woman who clung to life without a body to embrace it with.

Just like my encounter with her hand, the mummified skin on Geraldine's face appeared to soften and plump, her pale skin suffusing with a healthy glow. Her shrunken eyes filled with light before eyelids formed to blink over clear blue eyes that glimmered in the darkness. She looked about my age, maybe a couple years older. Her coral-colored lips spread in a serene smile before she said, "Hello, Chalice."

My heart fluttered like a hummingbird's. I don't know why, but I felt compelled to kneel. I also bowed my head and said softly, "Saint Geraldine."

Her laugh sounded like tinkling bells. "There's no need to be formal, child. I'm not royalty."

I stood and looked around the tomb, searching for Aydin. He stood naked in the corner. I forced myself to keep my eyes focused above his waist and when our gazes found each other, he stepped forward. "I hope you're not too surprised."

"I listened at the door and heard you two talking." Still amazed by what I was witnessing, I swallowed what felt like sawdust in my throat. "I wish you would have said something to me earlier. When Gavin saw my face just now he knew something was up."

"But you held your ground. I knew you could do it." He angled himself to face Geraldine, positioning his hands over his groin in classic fig-leaf fashion. I blew out a relieved breath. He said, "I explained to her how you and I know each other."

"I thought you might have," Geraldine said with a pleased smile. I was surprised to hear no European accent in her voice, though Aydin didn't have one, either. Assuming he'd spent time with her over the past nine centuries, I figured he must have taught her English, as well as kept her up to speed on the modern world. "We have much to discuss, and hardly any time to do it. Gavin will get suspicious if we take too long."

Panic gripped me. "I'm a terrible liar. Gavin always knows when I'm lying."

Aydin's brows arched in concern. "We'll figure something out. We have to. And your expression of detachment is improving." His lips curved in a reassuring smile.

Though pleased to have his confidence, I wasn't sure I shared it. "I have questions," I said to Geraldine. "Lots of questions."

"I'll answer as many as I can." She slid her blue-eyed gaze to Aydin. I could see she used to be a pretty girl; her beauty lived on in the enchantment that shrouded her remains. "Aydin can fill you in if we run out of time."

I reached inside my pocket for the copy I'd made of my mother's note. I hadn't wanted to take the chance of Geraldine being unable to see the invisible ink. "Do you read rune divinations?"

A tiny frown wrinkled the perfect skin of her forehead. "It's been a few centuries, but I remember. What do you have?"

I opened the copied note in front of her eyes. She blinked and her eyes glowed. "This is from Felicia?"

I gasped. "You knew of my mother?"

"Of course. I know about all the women in our order."

So it was as I suspected. Geraldine *was* a Hatchet Knight. And she'd used the present tense so that meant she knew of others who were hopefully all still alive. "Where are the other knights?"

"One thing at a time." She stared once more at the note. "Your mother wants you to find the Fallen. So does Gavin. Each for different reasons."

"Gavin made me tell him what the note said." I caught a brief flash of anger in those crystal-blue eyes. "But I transposed the rune signs. I can't interpret them myself, but I know what each symbol is. He translated what I'd given him as meaning the silver veil is closed to the Fallen's spawn."

She pinned me with a serious stare. "Then you know whose child you are?"

I shook my head. "I thought it possible my mother had used some kind of code to pass me a secret message. My father can't be a fallen angel."

If Geraldine could have nodded she would have. Instead, she gave me a slow blink. "No code. It's true that your father is one of the Fallen. As for the divination, you did the right thing. We don't want Gavin to know its true meaning."

"Which is?" I held my breath.

"Harvest is the reaping of rewards. The tree of wisdom is a shaman's rune and means transformation. Dice cup stands for fate, and thorn means change and action, or it can also mean travel."

I heard Aydin gasp.

"So what are you saying?" I asked her, my pulse sounding like running hoofbeats inside my head.

"Gavin's translation is nearly the exact opposite of what your mother saw in the rune stones she threw." She paused before saying, "She predicted you would take a journey, which has already happened. Is that right?"

"I came here from Chicago."

"Next you will learn your fate of transformation from the

tree of wisdom, who in this case is your father. A member of the Fallen."

My hands shook and it felt like tiny needles pricked the bottoms of my feet. I clenched my jaw as I tried to hide my reaction from Geraldine and Aydin.

"Are you okay?" Aydin asked.

I shouldn't have been surprised. I'd been denying this ever since Gavin first brought up the theory of who my father was, but somewhere deep inside, possibly as deep as my DNA, I'd known it was true. Still, I couldn't help feeling some shock at learning the truth and its implications. Half angel. *Me.* Who'd have thought?

"I'm fine," I said, barely opening my mouth to say it. My teeth were clamped so tight that my ears rang. "I'll be fine. Just give me a second."

"We don't have a second." Geraldine focused on Aydin. "Protecting our sisters will be harder than ever now."

"What are you talking about?" I asked. "Who's being protected, and why? What's going on?"

"I'll let Aydin explain the details. Chalice, you play a far larger part in all this than you realize."

"Hold on a minute." I was getting more confused by the second. "What part are you talking about?"

"You know about the Order of the Hatchet, but what you don't know is how the order has perpetuated itself over time." She looked to Aydin, then back at me. "We took it upon ourselves to even out the balance between the forces of dark and light. Our knighthood depends on divine strength so we bred with as close to the divine as we could. We took angels as mates."

It was just as Gavin had said. His recitation from the Book of John echoed in my mind: *Fornication is a sin against God. Sin is transgression of the law of God.* Fornicating with the Hatchet knights had denigrated the angels to the rank of Fallen.

"They were once Guardians, from the Arelim," she went on. "It became tradition for our daughters to take their Guardian as mates, and then their daughters would do the same, and so on for generation after generation. Your mother, Felicia, mated with the Arelim angel Barachiel."

I gulped a shallow breath. *Barachiel.* My fallen-angel father had a name, and that made him real. "Where is Barachiel now?"

"I don't know," she said, furrowing her brow. "I can't hear the Fallen speak, only the Arelim. And they won't tell me. Gavin wants to find the Fallen to make deals similar to the one made with Aydin. He wants to find your father because he thinks Barachiel knows where our sister knights are."

I glanced down at the note in my hand, speechless. The Fallen wouldn't be with other angels, would they? So I'd never find my father beyond the silver veil. He was somewhere else and I didn't want to think about where that might be. A place for dark things. The black veil.

"Your mother obviously had something she wanted you to do, or knew your father had something to tell you. I don't know. We don't keep track of our mates after becoming pregnant." She closed her eyes and went still for a full second before adding, "These angels of the Arelim sacrificed their place beyond the silver veil to help breed an army of special women to fight the darkness."

Whoa, whoa, whoa. This was way more than I could handle all at once. "What happens to angels who fall?"

"They lose their wings and become regular men," Aydin said. "Or they can choose to join the darkness. That choice would allow them to keep their wings *and* their powers."

Just the thought of my father cavorting with demons made a ball of fear tumble like a rock in my belly.

Geraldine peered at me with laser intensity. "A member of the Fallen can turn into something like the dark angel who tricked Aydin and cursed him for eternity."

Aydin dropped his head to stare at the floor. "I didn't know who he was."

Geraldine's voice softened with sympathy when she said, "I know you didn't."

All three of us went quiet then. The dark angel who had fathered Geraldine's daughter was the same one who tried bargaining for her baby. How horrible. I wondered what that angel had been like before choosing the dark side. Could all the Fallen be as awful?

I also wondered about my sister knights, if they were like me and possessed the same super-senses I had. I knew from years of stealing magical objects that a curse wasn't always intentional and, in my case, I had a double dose with one on purpose, the other an accident of birth. How lucky could I get?

I considered what Geraldine had said about the tradition practiced by our order. "I'm not expected to, you know, mate with an angel, am I?"

Aydin coughed into his hand, and Geraldine smiled. "No, dear. You're not."

I felt relieved and confused at the same time. "Why not?"

"As long as you're bonded to the gargoyle," Geraldine said, "your impurity prevents you from taking an Arelim mate."

"Impurity?" I asked. "If I'm supposed to be a virgin, I'm afraid I'd fail that test, too."

"Virginity is not a prerequisite for breeding," Geraldine said lightly. "As a matter of fact, our Arelim mates appreciate experience since they have none themselves. But we won't get into that now. There isn't time."

I still had so many questions, but Aydin could answer them for me later. "About my mother," I said to Geraldine. "How did you know her?"

"Gavin brought her to me when she was about your age."

My heart stopped and my knees went weak. "You spoke to her?"

"I couldn't," she said, regret in her voice. "He wouldn't leave her alone with me and I won't speak in front of him or any of the Vyantara."

"But you know that's why he's allowing me to be alone with you now, don't you? He knows you and I will talk." My flimsy lying skills would be put to the test in a big way.

She gave me a slow blink. "That's why Aydin made sure

to get involved this time. He won't let Gavin know what really transpired between us. He'll lie for you."

There was a noise outside the vault entrance and electronic beeps indicated the door was being unlocked.

"Not yet!" I whispered to the mummified head that was quickly turning back into its shriveled, lifeless self. "Geraldine!"

I looked at Aydin, who immediately ghosted out.

The door swung slowly inward, and my nerves thrummed with dread. Could I hold my countenance? Or would my face accidentally let Gavin in on secrets he wasn't meant to know?

Aydin's translucent form approached me. What was he doing? He was getting too close! His ghostly face pressed against mine, and then he passed through my skin and into my body. I heard his mind speak inside me: *I'm sorry to do this to you, Chalice, but now you must sleep.*

I became light-headed. The moment Gavin appeared from around the open door, my vision darkened. My limbs turned to liquid and as Gavin rushed at me, his frown more annoyed than concerned, he couldn't catch me before I fell face-first to the concrete floor.

eleven

I BLINKED MY EYES OPEN TO A DIMLY LIT
room. When it came into focus, I recognized the wooden
boxes and trunks lined up in stacks along three walls. This
was the storage room inside Aydin's house.

When I tried to sit up, I grew dizzy and nausea gurgled
in my stomach. I struggled to detach my tongue from its
plastered position at the roof of my mouth. My efforts made
a loud enough noise to bring Aydin into the room.

Seeing me work so hard at making my mouth move, he
left and came back with a glass of water. "This will help."

I tilted it to my lips, but stopped before taking a sip.
"Poisoning me?" I asked, though it sounded more like "ois-
honing me?"

The corners of his lips curved in an almost smile. "Sorry
for having to knock you out like that, but if Gavin suspected

you had learned something, bad things would happen. To you. By him."

I tasted the water. "You're probably right." I downed the rest and handed him the empty glass. "What the hell did you do? Possess me?"

"Not really."

Not really? My heart skipped at the thought of my will taken over by another. I'd lost control. Being a slave was one thing, but losing my will brought on a whole new kind of anxiety. I felt more vulnerable than I cared to admit.

Aydin set the glass down on a box and sat on the trunk beside it. "All I did was give you a mental suggestion. It's something old ghosts can do, too, so don't ever dismiss them as harmless."

"You hypnotized me."

He tapped his nose with a forefinger. "Close enough. I left your body as soon as you started to fall."

I touched my bruised mouth.

He grimaced. "I'm really sorry about that."

If I had known what he'd planned to do, I would have fought him. At least I think I would have. "Just don't do it again."

He made a crisscrossing motion over his chest. "Promise."

"That's a handy ability you have. I bet it works really well during a heist, especially with witnesses."

He nodded. "But let's keep it between you and me, okay? Gavin has no idea the extent of what I can do, and that's one ability I'd rather keep secret from him. He exploits me enough as it is." He stood and ambled to the doorway, where he turned to face me. "Speaking of heists, you and I have a new assignment."

I shook my head to clear it of leftover mind fog. "I thought what we just did *was* our assignment."

He quirked an eyebrow. "This new one could play well into our plans."

"Just what the hell *are* our plans? Geraldine said you're supposed to catch me up on what's going on." I held out one hand and curled my fingers toward me. "Let's have it."

He leaned his shoulder against the doorjamb, as relaxed as a thief who had just pulled a job without getting caught. He reeked of self-confidence, and I hoped some of it would rub off on me. "Since you're such a bad liar, I'm going to hold off giving you that information. Just until we've had our meeting with Gavin to get the details of our new job. Okay with you?"

I nodded, but rolled my eyes to let him know I wasn't happy about it. He was right, though. "What did you tell him?" I asked, knowing Gavin must have grilled him like crazy. "You didn't say I asked Geraldine to translate my mother's runes, did you?"

He crossed his arms and looked at me sideways. "I did, but don't worry. I lied and said she confirmed his interpretation. He still believes you can't pass through the silver veil. Then I told him the truth about Geraldine's failure to speak with the Fallen. He was really disappointed to hear that."

Good. I loved it when Gavin didn't get his way.

Aydin squinted up at the ceiling, as if peering through

the veil itself. "I hope you realize your father won't be wait-ing for you on the other side."

Good point. I chewed my bottom lip and winced. "I know. My mother's note said he chose the dark side." But Geraldine *did* say I would learn my fate of transformation from the tree of wisdom, and if her interpretation was cor-rect, that tree would be my father. I felt curious to know how demonic a fallen angel could get. Considering what Geraldine's Arelim mate had done to Aydin, it must be a lot. There was even the chance my dark-angel father hated me enough to hurt me.

"Welcome to Lying 101," Aydin said as he began my in-struction on how to improve my skill for deception. "You're already good at half truths, and you're brilliant at disguising your feelings, so lying shouldn't be much of a stretch."

"I took acting lessons to help develop my role as a thief," I said. "So I don't understand why it's so difficult for me to lie outright."

"Because the lies you need to tell Gavin are personal, and for you, a personal lie is almost impossible to tell." He whistled through his teeth and a tiny flash of rainbow colors leapt onto his shoulder. "Ruby is going to help you."

The tiny frog chirped and her bejeweled hide sparkled. "How?"

"Her jewels will twinkle when she recognizes a lie." He stroked the top of the frog's head with his finger. "So if a lie works, she can help you know what you did to pull it off."

We practiced with me telling impersonal lies about things

that didn't matter, and I did great. But if it had to do with anything close to me, even my favorite food or color or movie, Ruby would blink like a string of Christmas lights.

"You can do this," Aydin told me, looking me in the eyes with a face so still he could have been a statue. "You need to practice your facial expressions. That's where you fail every time."

Since I was so good at hiding my emotions, we worked on an exercise where I associated the lie with a feeling. When frightened, I faked it with anger, but I believed the anger. I refused to believe the fear. I even managed to fake out Ruby.

"That's the answer," he said, slapping his thighs and flashing me a grin of amazing white teeth. "Believe the lie. That's what George Costanza said."

I frowned. "You mean the guy from *Seinfeld?*" It was hard to believe Aydin watched as much television as I did.

"According to George, 'It's not a lie if you believe it.'"

It felt good to laugh, and he chuckled right along with me. This was the first time I'd seen him lighten up since he'd introduced me to Elmo's Coffee Shop.

"You're pretty when you laugh," he said, smiling while holding my gaze with his.

My own smile slipped away and my cheeks burned. I suddenly wished my spiky hairstyle wasn't too short to hide my face. "I'm a shrimp," I said, using the nickname my Vyantara instructors had given me during training.

Suddenly serious, he said, "You are not. And I'll kick the ass of whoever dares call you that."

I pictured this Turkish warrior beating up my teachers, most of whom were nearly twice his size. He'd still win, hands down.

I sucked in a breath. I could do this. I could be a good liar. "Okay, I'm ready to face Gavin. Let's get this over with."

I hesitated at the front door of the Fatherhouse, wishing I had Ruby in my pocket to give me confidence. But Aydin made me leave her behind. He said it wouldn't be safe for her, and the last thing I wanted was for an innocent creature to get hurt on my account.

He reached around me to open the door and I slapped his hand away.

"Give me a minute." I got swept up in the memory of what had happened the last time I'd been inside. I closed my eyes, willing myself to relax, and reminded myself that I wouldn't need Shui again until tomorrow. I had nothing to be afraid of, so the house couldn't feed off me this time.

"Get mad," Aydin said. "It's how you hide your emotions." He bent toward me until his mouth nearly touched my ear. His breath tickled and I shivered. "Get mad, and mean it. It will help."

I pulled back my shoulders and nodded. It wouldn't take much to make me angry. Just thinking about all the horrible curses and charms sitting on shelves, hanging on walls and filling up the glass-topped cases in the house was enough to infuriate me. Worse yet, I was the one who had stolen those things. Or a lot of them, anyway.

"You look steamed."

I answered him through gritted teeth. "I am."

"Good." Aydin grasped the door handle and pushed.

I stepped over the threshold and stomped across the oak floor toward the back of the house where the conference room was. I glanced at display cases lining the walls, and the ten-foot-tall free-standing ones that divided up the room.

I knew the house was sectioned off because most curses don't get along with each other. Also because charms, which were good magic like Ruby, made a dangerous combination when in contact with the curses. You couldn't put them together and not expect trouble. So it really was a good thing I hadn't brought along my pseudo-amphibian friend.

I passed a silver amulet hanging on the wall and it reminded me of the time I'd accidentally touched a cursed monkey's paw to a charmed medallion. With both objects stuffed in one jacket pocket, I'd ridden my motorcycle past a high school and the psychic reaction between the objects had caused a fight to break out in each classroom I passed. It had taken a half-dozen blocks of spontaneous brawls exploding on the sidewalk, street corners and in front of a convenience store to make me realize something was wrong. As soon as I put the objects in separate pockets, life around me returned to normal.

I approached the open door to the conference room. Its bloodred walls were festooned with colorful tribal masks from different countries and I guessed all of them were cursed in some way. That's the only reason they'd be inside this house in the first place.

A figure loomed in the doorway and I put on the skids before smacking into her voluminous bosom. Zee looked different from the last time I'd seen her and it appeared from her condition that Gavin hadn't been in a forgiving mood. She wasn't wearing a cheery smile of welcome today. Those cupie-doll lips were swollen, the bottom one split and scabbed. Her right arm had a fracture brace supported by a black canvas sling, and one ankle looked twice the size of the other.

My anger disappeared and amusement took its place. "Good morning, Zee," I said, sounding more happy than I should have. I was still upset with her for keeping the news of Shui's derailed train a secret from me. The woman flat-out didn't like me, and the feeling was mutual. "Been working out? Or just worked over?"

She attempted a snarl, but winced instead, using her good hand to touch her ruined mouth. I hoped this meant she couldn't talk. Her mouth would only get her into more trouble.

Gavin came around from behind her to give her a withering look. She backed away and hobbled to one of the heavy wooden chairs positioned around the table.

He turned his attention on me. "I trust you fully recovered from your fainting spell?"

I nodded, mentally groping for that thread of anger that would support my deceit. I found it easily, my rage at this man filling me to the brim. "I didn't faint."

His brows arched almost to his hairline. "Then what was it that happened last night?"

"I don't know." I moved past him to take a chair far from Zee. "Lack of oxygen inside an air-locked tomb, maybe?"

He seemed to think that over, then dismissed it. "What about the candles?"

Candles? I must have looked confused because he closed his eyes and sighed. "You insisted on having candles in the tomb. I assumed the candlelight helped?"

I'd forgotten all about that because I hadn't used them. I hadn't needed to. I swallowed in an effort to moisten my dry throat. "I didn't need them. There wasn't enough air inside the tomb to keep them lit, anyway."

He frowned and glanced at Aydin. "Sit down."

The Turk took the chair next to Zee, putting him clearly on the side of the enemy. Good move. It fed my anger, which was also good. I felt ready for anything now.

Gavin remained standing. "I'm going to summon one of the Fallen. I'm bringing Chalice's father to the mortal plane."

But I wasn't ready for that.

"The plan is to make him tell me where I can find the other Hatchet knights. But I also have a potential buyer for his services."

Aydin held his stony countenance, but there was a flicker of curiosity in his eyes. "What kind of services?"

Gavin chuckled. "You of all people should know the answer to that, Aydin. A power like yours would fetch a handsome price, and a fallen angel is just the source for such a gift."

"It won't be given freely," Aydin reminded him, raising his chin to emphasize his point. "And the Fallen have no use for your money."

"I'm aware of that. But money isn't the only currency needed to strike a bargain." From Gavin's severe tone, the subject of payment was now closed. He targeted me next. "I assume Geraldine told you your father's name?"

Molding my face with a scowl, I worked on covering up my surprise with anger. I hesitated to give him my father's name, but Gavin and I wanted the same thing this time. We both wanted to find my father, but for different reasons. I had questions, like why he chose to become a fallen angel instead of changing into a human. And he certainly wasn't off the hook for abandoning my pregnant mother, then abandoning me. "His name is Barachiel."

"Why so angry, Chalice?" Gavin asked, lowering his chin and widening his eyes to scrutinize me. "I thought you were looking forward to this meeting."

"Her foul temper is my fault," Aydin said, spearing me with a cold stare that pierced my heart. Did he mean it, or was it only for Gavin's benefit? "I've been strict with her, sir. She's eager to go out alone, but I won't allow it."

Gavin nodded. "Work on the two of you getting along, will you? I need you both to cooperate on this assignment." He paced behind Zee's chair and stared down at her with distaste. "To accomplish this summoning, I need an item that's owned by a man named Quin Dee. It's not a coincidence that he moved to Denver from London last month to accept a lucrative job offer."

An offer I was sure the Vyantara had something to do with. "And you want us to steal this item?" I asked.

He nodded. "It's an obsidian Aztec artifact used for scrying. It once belonged to Quin's ancestor, John Dee."

Aydin looked pensive. "John Dee. Ah, yes, the sixteenth-century mathematician and philosopher. I met him once." He stared at me so coldly I wanted to shrink beneath the table. Damn, he was convincing. "Dee's power to communicate with angels was legendary and he'd owned several valuable artifacts the Vyantara wanted. I stole his shrew stone for the British Fatherhouse."

Considering Aydin's age, I should have guessed he'd have had an opportunity to meet the man. I'd read about Dee during my training and found his life of angel communication interesting, if not dramatic. I wondered if Quin was anything like his great-great-great-great-whatever.

"John Dee replaced the shrew stone with the Aztec version that's rumored to be more powerful," Gavin said. "It does more than scry. It amplifies a psychic's vision to allow evocation of angels. The apparition can be witnessed audibly and visually." He resumed his pacing. "It's not just the artifact we need. We want Quin Dee, as well."

Steal a person? I wasn't comfortable with that. It was kidnapping and it struck too close to home. "Why not ask him to do it and pay him for his trouble?"

Gavin grinned. "We tried that. He hates us."

Of course he did. What sane person wouldn't?

"He's a moral and spiritual man who inherited his ancestor's skill for communicating with angels," Gavin went on. "The Vyantara are the antithesis of his beliefs."

Good for Quin. I was starting to like him already. "Even if we manage to kidnap the man, how will you force him to summon my...to summon Barachiel?"

"That's *my* problem. You just focus on bringing both the artifact and Quin Dee to me." He glared at Zee, who had clearly fallen out of favor. "Zee, I need you to prepare a room for our new house guest."

Zee stared silently down at her lap, then suddenly launched to her feet and pointed an accusing finger at me. "She's a liar!"

My heart jumped, but I concentrated on holding a neutral expression. "Excuse me?"

She held out a black stone the size of her palm. "The truth stone doesn't lie."

Aulmauracite? The meteoric rock was alleged to have the power to see truth, but I'd never seen one up close. Its surface went dull in the presence of lies, and would glitter silver in the presence of honesty. Someone was lying, and it wasn't me. At least not right now.

"Zeppelin!" Gavin grabbed the rock from her hand. "It lost its shimmer because *you're* the one who's lying. Look at it." He held it up and it sparkled. "Get out. Now! You have work to do."

Glaring daggers at me, she stood and hobbled from the room.

Gavin rubbed his forehead. "I don't have the patience for

this." He glowered up at the ceiling as if to blame someone else for his troubles. "I need a new housemother for this Fatherhouse. I can't trust Zee anymore. She's a witless witch who's lost her focus."

"She's jealous," Aydin said.

Gavin appeared genuinely puzzled. "Jealous of who?"

"Chalice."

Aydin drove us to the Cherry Creek Shopping Center, where I was to "accidentally" meet Quin Dee in a bookstore, and then coerce him into having coffee with me. The plan was for me to drug his coffee so that he'd think he was sick, drive him home and, while he was passed out, I'd search his house for the Aztec artifact. Simple.

"Now that I know there are other knights, I want to meet them," I said to Aydin's profile as he drove us down I-25 to get from one end of town to the other.

He answered me with a quick nod, but I needed more than that. "Tell me where they are."

Without taking his focus off the black ribbon of highway in front of him, he said, "Fifty knights live in the U.S. and Canada, and only a handful are still in Europe."

I thought about Gavin and his obsession with the Hatchets.

"Every knight is protected by the Arelim," Aydin said, as if sensing my concern. "Their identities are kept secret from the world and especially from the Vyantara."

"What do the Vyantara want from us?" I asked as we strode across the shopping center's frigid parking lot. Night had fallen and it was starting to snow. "Bond us all to gargoyles and turn us into thieves?" I was being facetious so his response surprised me.

"That's part of it."

I stopped to pierce him with a sharp look. "Are you serious?"

He nodded and motioned for me to keep walking. "Each knight is special in her own way, and that will make all of them valuable to the Vyantara. You have heightened senses, someone else has phenomenal strength, another reads minds, maybe uses teleportation, or telekinesis, and I've even heard of one who can do what I do."

"Invisibility. How very cool." I had assumed the knights' abilities were exactly like mine. I didn't know they would be so diverse.

He opened the double glass doors at the mall entrance and waved me in ahead of him. "Invisibility, shape-shifting, throwing lightning, causing storms—"

I chuckled. "Sounds like superhero stuff."

"It is."

We walked side by side, silent and serious, until we reached the mall directory. I wasn't a superhero. Super*thief,* maybe, and it wasn't something I was proud of. "So what do they do with these superpowers that I assume were inherited from their fathers?"

"You assume correctly." I watched him study the directory, his eyes scanning through the list of shops and restaurants. He sounded casual while answering my question, yet the words he used were grave. "Some of them work for the police, the FBI, and even a few have set up their own private-investigation businesses. Others are firefighters, search and rescue, soldiers in the military, bodyguards, any kind of job that involves protecting people. But they use their powers in secret to take down criminals from beyond the mortal realm."

Of course. The idea of ridding humanity of the diseased evil that fed on them sent an unexpected thrill through my heart. Fighting the good fight. What a glorious job.

Aydin's eyes widened and he pointed to something on the list. "There it is. Level two."

I'd already lost interest in our assignment and wanted only to continue this conversation. So the Hatchets were vigilantes. That sounded like a lonely and dangerous pursuit, but an exciting one. It was illegal, too, which made them just as criminal as me.

"According to Geraldine only a handful have teamed up together," he said. "The majority are independents, trained by their mothers." He chuckled. "Armies of one."

Trained by their mothers. I envied them. And it bugged me that Aydin didn't seem impressed by my sister knights' good works. How dare he pass judgment? "You disapprove?"

He shot me a surprised look. "And you care?"

I glared at him. "I'm not sure what you mean."

One corner of his mouth lifted in a cynical smile.

Was he being smug? I gasped and tossed him the same surprised look he'd given me. "You obviously don't respect what my sisters do."

"Oh, so now they're your sisters?" He smiled and

frowned at the same time, making him look devilish. Very sexy. "You, the lone wolf, who has no one and prefers it that way."

"I never said I preferred it that way." In reality, I hated being lonely, but I'd never had a choice.

I narrowed my eyes at him. He was starting to piss me off.

"Are you saying you'd join your sisters if they needed you?"

"Damn right I would." I folded my arms and gave him a sideways glance. Seeing his mollified grin, I finally got it. He was baiting me. "Okay, now I see what you're doing. This is a test." Being tested meant I wasn't trusted, and that hurt.

He lost the frown but the smile remained. "Guilty. I need to be convinced you're serious about getting involved. The Hatchets' lives are at risk."

I felt only slightly better knowing he wasn't the insensitive prick I'd almost believed him to be. "Explain."

He stepped over to a tiled bench surrounding a square planter filled with some kind of variegated ivy. Sitting down, he patted the space beside him, but I stayed where I was. I hadn't forgiven him yet. "Chalice, the problem reported by the Arelim to Geraldine is the knights' lack of unity. These women can't join together as a unit because if they do, they risk detection by the Vyantara, and by those from the supernatural realms. The knights are less effective alone than they could be as a team, and they're more vulnerable to attack. The Hatchets haven't fought together since their crusading ancestors did."

"So what does that have to do with me?"

He peered up at me and winced. "You're making my neck hurt. Sit down. Please."

I plopped down beside him, but left a good foot of shiny tile between us.

"You're immune to cursed and charmed objects." He pointed to himself. "And so am I. As an immortal, magical objects have no effect on me."

"What about Ruby?"

"She's an *animate,* a magical curiosity that has personality, but no power."

"She's not enchanted?"

He wobbled his open hand like the wings of airplane. "Yes and no."

"But I'd be immune if she was, right?" I squinted as I tried to puzzle this out. "Even though I'm not immortal like you."

"Your angel side combined with your bedeviled side is what protects you from the effects of magical objects."

It all sounded great except for the bedeviled part. And why hadn't Gavin ever told me any of this? "How am I *bedeviled?*"

"Because of the curse that bonds you to Shui."

"I intend to break that curse." I leaned sideways to get closer, emphasizing my point. "Does that make me a handicap to this great plan of yours?"

He sounded less confident when he said, "No. In fact,

you must be free of your bond before you can help unify the knights. Your freedom won't affect your immunity, though. It's your one and only benefit of bondage to Shui."

"Why is my immunity so important?"

"Because we need you to reclaim all the collected objects in all the Fatherhouses around the world. Or nullify them. Our goal is to reduce the Vyantara's power as much as possible."

Now that would be a task and a half, but I was willing. I'd always felt guilty for stealing those things in the first place and hoped this might bring me the closure I needed. "You've got a deal. But I get the feeling there's something else."

"There is." He blinked and looked away, his gaze returning to the directory. Staring at it blankly, he said, "You'll have to teach the knights about curses and charms, how to identify them, how to deactivate them and how to use them."

I didn't think I'd heard him right. "Did you just say how to *use* them?"

"I know how you feel about magic, Chalice, but sometimes you have to fight fire with fire. The knights aren't immune like you are. Right now they're helpless against any magic that can be used against them."

I mistrusted magic, with the exception of Ruby. And Aydin, of course. But I still held magic responsible for every awful thing that had happened in my life, and I associated it with the people who forced me to steal. Now Aydin was asking me to endorse its use? I stood up and backed away. "I can't believe you'd ask me to do this."

"There's a lot about magic you don't understand." He was clearly frustrated, his body tense and his jaw rigid. Though he had gradually introduced me to the benefits of magic use, he anticipated how I would react and was ready for it. "Why do you think I introduced you to Ruby? I knew you two would hit it off. She's a sentient creature, Chalice. I think I've already convinced you that magic isn't always a bad thing."

I thought about the bejeweled frog, the charming Jak-karyl I'd met at Elmo's, Aydin's magical breath of change and my stubbornness wavered. "Help me understand."

"There's offensive magic and defensive magic," he said slowly, as if to make sure his words sunk through my thick skull. "It's okay to use defensive magic to protect yourself, and we need your sister knights to know how it works. You're the only one who can help them."

"Why can't you do it?"

"I can. Someday." He stood to face me, his chin just about even with the top of my head. "But as a fellow knight in the order, it's *your* voice and leadership that will bring your sisters together. A new war is coming. A new kind of Crusade. And we have to be ready for it."

So that's what all this was about. But neither Aydin nor I would be any good in this war if we didn't break the curses that bound us. We couldn't help the Hatchets if we became gargoyles that served the enemy.

This is where my life had been headed all along. Even

my exposure to curses and charms could serve to protect my sisters, and myself.

Aydin tilted his head. "Are you all right? You look... different. Like someone just flicked on a light switch."

I gave him a small smile. "Maybe someone did."

Aydin's cell phone rang. "Yeah," he answered. "Already? Okay. We'll be there in five." He closed the phone and tucked it in the inside pocket of his jacket. "The Vyantara have someone tracking Quin. He just pulled into the parking lot."

twelve

I TOOK A DEEP BREATH AND JOINED AYDIN AS he made quick strides toward an escalator. Quin Dee loved bookstores and he made a weekly visit to one in his neighborhood every Monday night after work.

Aydin and I separated at the top of the escalator so that we wouldn't be seen together.

I'd only seen one picture of Quin that was a fuzzy rendition of a DMV photo. But I felt sure I'd recognize him once I saw him inside the store. Gavin had said he wasn't very tall, average build, brown hair, glasses—aka boring. I liked boring. Boring was safe.

I entered the store and, after perusing the front tables loaded with recent releases, I lifted my gaze to troll the room for Quin. Gavin had said the man liked science fiction and philosophy. I spotted him browsing the psychology section.

I wandered over to the religion section and found a book called *The Big Book of Angels*. Lovely. I carried the two-pound tome in the crook of my arm and wound through the aisles, closing in on Quin.

Peering at him from the corner of my eye, I saw he was deeply engrossed in a book called *Anger, Madness and the Daimonic*. Whoa. Heavy stuff. He didn't notice my look of surprise at seeing him up close for the first time.

The photo I'd seen had lied. This man was eye candy and not a bit boring from the female perspective. Broad in the shoulders, slim at the hip, he looked like a guy who spent a fair amount of time in the gym. He needed a haircut, but the way his nut-brown hair curled over the white collar of his shirt gave a rustic edge to his *GQ* appearance. Neat to a fault, his jeans were creased down the front and his loafers looked just out of the box. He wore a tan suede sports jacket opened to reveal a gray sweater-vest, and he smelled…yummy. It was more of a soap smell than a cologne smell. Clean, fresh, expensive.

I let my angel book slip free and fall to the floor by his feet. "I'm such a klutz," I said, bending to retrieve the book.

He quickly crouched down to reach it first. "Hey, I've read this one."

"You have?" I asked brightly, turning on a multiwatt smile that nearly burned my eyes from the inside. "Any good?"

We stood up at the same time, our gazes locked. He

cleared his throat and pushed his wire-rimmed glasses higher up the bridge of his nose. His grin was all teeth. Such a happy guy. "It's very good. Are you interested in angels?"

"Who isn't?" I asked, blinking up at him, then worrying I might be laying it on too thick. "I mean, everyone believes in angels. I saw one once." Lie, lie, lie. But this was a lie I could make myself believe if I used my imagination.

"You saw an angel?" His grin was still in place, but the beginning of a frown made his eyebrows curve into an interesting shape. "Where?"

So I made something up about an angel appearing in front of my car, forcing me to slow down at an intersection just as a bus ran a red light.

"That doesn't surprise me," he said, his eyes bright with interest. "I've heard similar stories from people whose lives were saved by a guardian angel."

If he only knew. "I think my guardian angel follows me everywhere." Though in truth I didn't think I had one. "I was on vacation when this happened."

"Really? Where?"

"London."

He grinned. "That's where I'm from."

"You have an amazing accent. So…European." I let the smile reach my eyes, which I thought were my most alluring feature in spite of my tinted contact lenses. He'd probably think me a freak if he saw their *real* color. Turquoise and gold were what you'd find on a piece of jewelry, not in someone's eyeballs.

He looked suddenly uncomfortable, as if he'd just received disturbing news. I hadn't heard anything, and an awkward silence followed.

His smile looked less playful and more polite. Wasn't this the part where he was supposed to ask me for my phone number? If so, it didn't happen.

Throughout this exchange, Aydin hung out in the science-fiction and fantasy section. He wasn't close enough to hear us talking, but I'm sure he must have caught the gist of our conversation from our facial expressions and body language. I'd giggled in all the right places, touched my hair and gazed up at Quin through my eyelashes. I slid a look in Aydin's direction to see if he still watched, and he did. Outright. It made him look like a stalker. I scowled at him and he seemed to catch himself, returning his attention to the book in his hand.

Quin spun around to see what had attracted my attention.

"Have you seen the display of new releases in the science-fiction section?" I asked, seeing that Aydin was no longer in view. I hoped it didn't mean he had *literally* disappeared. I needed his help.

"You like science fiction?" Quin asked, but he didn't sound interested. I doubted my answer would matter to him one way or the other. He took a step back and glanced toward the cash registers at the front of the store. "Me, too. Hey, I've gotta run. Nice talking to you." He flashed me an apologetic smile and walked away.

Hey, I wasn't done with him yet. How dare he ignore my feminine wiles? Starting to panic, I moved quickly to catch up with him. "I have an idea. Let's go out for coffee and we can talk more about angels."

He barely looked at me when he said, "Another time. It was very nice meeting you."

"But we haven't actually met yet. You don't even know my name." I offered him my hand, which is something I rarely did because my skin was so sensitive. "I'm Cherise," I said, using one of my aliases.

He barely touched my fingers. "Quin Dee." I'm not positive, but I think he wiped his hand on his pants as if to clean off my cooties. Talk about weird.

He practically ran ahead of me then, rushing to the cashier at the front of the store. I stopped to look for Aydin, who was still in the science-fiction section. Catching his eye, I aimed a bewildered stare at Quin, and then I shrugged and shook my head. Aydin signaled for me to come to him, then looked behind him and to either side before vanishing completely.

Surprised Aydin would disappear like that in public, I glanced around the store for witnesses. The few shoppers around me were too focused on their browsing to notice his vanishing act. Quin hadn't seen anything, either, his attention solely on paying for his book and avoiding me like a disease.

I threaded my way through the aisles until I arrived at the spot where Aydin had ghosted out. There on the floor was the pile of clothes that had dropped from his body when he lost physical form. I gathered them up, hoping I didn't look too conspicuous with a load of men's denim in my arms, not to mention the size-ten tennis shoes that clearly weren't mine. A boy of about eleven or twelve gave me an odd look before going back to the graphic novel he was reading.

I couldn't see Aydin but hopefully he'd stay with me when I walked out. The unpaid-for angel book was still in my hands so I dropped it on a stack of children's books before making my exit.

Quin stood on the escalator, heading down, so I followed him. He was about halfway to the shopping center's east entrance when he stopped to rub his temples. His knees wobbled and he held out one arm for balance while taking careful steps to a bench. He sat down and held his head in both hands.

It took me barely a second to realize Aydin had gotten inside Quin's head and must have suggested something that made the man sick. *Oh, Aydin, you bad boy.* I had a fairly good idea what my accomplice expected me to do now.

I approached the bench and watched Quin struggle to stay upright. "Are you okay?" I sat down beside him.

"Huh?" He dropped his hands from his face to stare at me. "Who are you?"

"I'm Cherise, remember?" I smiled and laid a concerned hand on his shoulder. "I happened to be walking behind you just now when I saw you collapse."

He squinted at me as if he had trouble seeing. "Oh, yeah. I'm okay, I just need to sit for a second. My head hurts like a son of a bitch."

"Can I help you to your car?" I hugged Aydin's clothes

to my chest. I still needed him to keep doing what he was doing. "Is it in the east parking lot?"

He nodded and winced. "Damn. It's like I've been drugged or something." He gave me an accusing look.

I raised my hands in a pose of surrender. "Don't look at me." And why would he even suspect me of such a thing? I was just a girl looking for a cute guy to go out with. Though drugging him had been my original plan, he had no way of knowing that. I reached for his arm. "Let me help you. Then I promise to go away. Deal?"

He nodded and stood, appearing more stable now. I led him outside and he directed me to his car. I popped out one contact lens as we walked across the asphalt lot. With my protected eye closed, I saw Aydin's ghostly form behind Quin, his right hand inside the other man's back like a puppeteer operating his dummy.

Quin's car was a late-model, silver Acura. Sweet. "Are you sure you can drive yourself?"

He nodded while auto-unlocking the driver's side door. Aydin's ghost leaned into him. Quin grabbed the open door as his knees buckled. "Oh, man. I can't do it. I can't drive. I hate to ask, but would you mind?"

"I'd be happy to," I told him, and helped him into the front seat on the passenger side.

"My house isn't far." He sounded breathless, as if Aydin were squeezing his lungs, which he probably was. "Just about five miles, in Cherry Hills. I'll call you a cab when we get there, and, of course, I'll pay the fare."

He was coherent enough to give me directions and in less

than ten minutes we pulled in the driveway of his charming, two-story Cape Cod. Very fifties. As I helped him to the front door, supporting him with his arm draped around my neck, I half expected June Cleaver to welcome us at the threshold.

The outside of the house was clean, and by clean I mean no specters hung out in the shadows. And no angels, but never having seen an angel, I can't say I'd recognize one.

Aydin trailed us into the house, his hold still on Quin. I eased the angel whisperer down on the living-room couch and Aydin merged with him completely. Seconds later, he slipped out of the unconscious Quin.

I waited while Aydin passed through a wall to go outside. Minutes later he returned through the front door as his fully clothed, flesh-and-blood self.

I gave him an apologetic look. "I tried to get him to go out with me for coffee, but he wasn't interested."

"Fool," he said to Quin's sleeping body, then grinned. "I think he was tipped off by one of his angel friends that you were bad news."

That threw me. There'd been no indication that Quin was having psychic communication with anyone or anything. "How do you know?"

"I get mental snapshots when I enter a person," he said, sounding as if his invasive tactics were embarrassing to admit. "It's hard to describe, but I could sense him communicating with someone inside his head. I didn't hear a response from whomever he linked to. Quin seemed to accept what he was told without question."

"So he's been warned about me." But if he knew anything, surely his angel friend had informed him I was a Hatchet knight, and therefore an ally. That must count for something. "He knows the Vyantara are involved?"

Aydin shrugged. "Probably. I gave him a hypnotic suggestion to sleep, so he won't be waking up for a while. Which means we have the run of the house to look for the artifact."

"But what about Quin?" I was still bothered over the whole kidnapping thing. We wouldn't steal this man and take his life away from him like ours had been taken from us. Conscience aside, it simply wasn't right. "We have to protect him."

Aydin hesitated, his expression sheepish.

"You're not thinking about letting Gavin have him, are you?"

He didn't look at me when he said, "I don't think we have a choice."

I recalled my own abduction, the memory making my heart bang against my ribs. "Of course we have a choice! There's got to be a way to keep him safe. To hide him, disguise him, something!"

"Okay, maybe." Aydin sighed and sat on the couch beside Quin. "But I hate to use the Elmo card. If Gavin ever found out about Elmo's Coffee Shop, it would be over for Elmo. I'd never forgive myself."

Elmo's? What a great idea. I'd been inside the tidy little room at the back of Elmo's shop and it would be perfect, except I doubted Quin would think so. The dirt floors might offend him, but his freedom would be worth a bit of dirt.

"There could be a problem getting Quin over there." Aydin stood from the couch and rubbed his hands together. "Oh, hell. We can figure that out *after* we find the artifact."

Since I'd already removed both contact lenses, I slipped out my nose filters next. Inhaling deeply, I caught the scent of Italian spices, probably a recent meal prepared in Quin's kitchen. There was also that yummy soap he used, the delicious smell coming from a bathroom down the hall. I identified metal, like tin or maybe solder. There was a distinct scent of other metals, as well, and I assumed he had a workshop in the house. Another odor sent a jolt of recognition through me. A memory sent me back a couple of weeks to my failed heist at the Grandville estate.

"She's here." I turned slowly in place to determine where the smell of old decay was coming from. It was Geraldine. "Part of her is in this house."

Aydin appeared from the hallway, his arms loaded with bedding. He'd apparently been searching a linen closet. "Who is?"

"Geraldine." I took a deep breath and held it. Yes, that was the same moldy odor I attributed to the hand I'd found in Atlanta. "It's definitely her."

Aydin dropped the linens. "Where?"

I closed my eyes and focused. "Basement. I think Quin has a workshop down there. He makes things from metal."

Aydin grabbed my wrist, and as much as his calloused

hand hurt my skin, I let him tug me to a staircase leading to a lower level of the house. "Show me," he said.

I knew we should be searching the house for the artifact, but I had a strong feeling we'd find it in the basement. Quin was too orderly to separate his treasures. As we neared the bottom step, I caught a whiff of old blood. It smelled human, and then again it didn't, which troubled me. I tried to sniff out the obsidian piece we were looking for, but solid stone rarely has a scent unless it's been coated with something, like blood, or dirt from being freshly dug from the ground. The closest thing to dirt I found was clay, a standard component in Colorado soil.

The blood scent bothered me. Did Mr. Angel Man use sacrifice to call his prophetic messengers from beyond the silver veil? No, that couldn't be it. Only the dark side required blood sacrifice. I recognized another blood scent, fresher than the first, as belonging to Quin himself. It was possible he had injured himself in his shop. Then again, if he used a sigil to open the veil, a fresh mark on his hand would have drawn blood. I picked up an odor of herbs and incense: sage, jasmine, lavender, absinthe and myrrh. It was definitely ritual. He might have been preparing to do some evocation of his own.

The glass case sat in plain sight on the workbench. And inside it was Geraldine's other hand.

"We have to hide it," Aydin said, sounding panicked.

His anxiety bewildered me. I thought he'd be excited to find a piece of the saint's body puzzle. I knew that bringing all of her parts together would make her whole, and as long as the Vyantara weren't involved, bringing her back would be good for all of us, especially the Hatchet knights. "Just think, Aydin. If we find her other parts, we can bring her back—"

"I don't want to bring her back." He lifted the glass box and held it up to the light. "You don't understand." He looked at me, concern replacing his panic. "If the Vyantara got a hold of this and all her other parts, they would make her whole and never let her go."

"And you're afraid they'll do to her what they've done to us."

He nodded. "She's another knight, like you, except she's one of the *first*. She knows where the other Hatchet knights are. Once alive, Gavin would find a way to make her tell."

But that wasn't going to happen. I wouldn't let it, and neither would Aydin.

I searched the workshop, focusing my eyes to see beneath layers of paint, wallpaper, cloth and carpet. I saw brick behind a thin sheet of wallpaper that had been painted over.

I ran to the wall and withdrew my Balisong from the sheath I'd restrapped to my back. Slicing the blade through the painted paper, I said, "We can loosen the bricks and see if there's space behind them to hide Geraldine's hand."

He rushed over to help me peel back the wallpaper, then used a chisel he'd found on Quin's workbench to chip at the mortar between the bricks. We loosened only three and pulled them free. I could tell right away the gap between the wall and its plywood frame was big enough for the case. Aydin tucked it inside the cubby hole we'd made and replaced the bricks.

He grabbed a wooden crate filled with coiled extension cords and slid it in front of the mess on the wall to hide our work.

"Why would Quin have her hand?" he asked, which surprised me because I considered Aydin the one with all the answers. "The man talks to angels. Geraldine was one-hundred-percent human."

She was one of the first Hatchet knights, and therefore not angel-spawned. Not like me. Yet Quin and Geraldine had something special in common. "Quin is just like her."

Aydin ran a hand through his hair, leaving behind streaks of powdery gray residue from the mortar. "I can tell he never removed the hand from its case, and that's a good sign. He respects who Geraldine was, who she still is. I'm relieved to know that."

So was I. I'd started wondering about Quin's intentions. Charlatan, or true mystic? We'd find out once we had his confidence. For now, we were his enemy, at least until he knew us for who we really were. "Based on what I know about John Dee, he left a lot behind, mostly documenta-tion of his angel communications. The hand had probably belonged to him."

Aydin studied the items on Quin's workbench. "Take a look at this."

I moved to where he was investigating a number of silver pendants. There was a scent of tin solder that told me how the pieces had been joined. "Check this out." I held up a pendant. "The Enochian alphabet. What letter is this? It looks like an *M*."

He shook his head as he took it from me. "It's an *R*. See how the middle part curves down?"

I leaned in closer. "There's a small stone setting. A crystal."

"Celestine."

"You're right," I said. "Very few crystals I know of are this shade of blue."

"Makes sense that Quin would use them in his jewelry." Aydin lifted one to the light the same way he'd studied the case holding Geraldine's hand. "Celestine is supposed to be a conduit for the celestial."

"Does it work?"

He shrugged. "Quin obviously thinks so."

"I bet he makes these to sell to people he does angel readings for."

Aydin selected another pendant. "Do you think he uses his psychic gifts for profit?"

"Good question." I began sliding out drawers in the second workbench shoved against the back wall. It seemed to serve as a storage unit. "I don't know how much he makes, but he'd have to be earning some righteous bucks to afford a house like this, plus that great car."

Aydin joined me in searching the drawers. I bent to sniff each one, honing in on the blood scent I'd picked up earlier. I was getting close.

"I found it." He lifted a black hand mirror from a bottom

drawer, peeling back sheets of tissue paper as he plucked it from its nest of excelsior.

I inhaled deeply. That's where the old blood was coming from.

"Look at this." He ran his finger along the intricate pattern carved in the stone. The design wreathed the shiny obsidian surface where the bloodstains were. The blood had been wiped clean, but I could still see it, and smell it.

"There was blood on this stone," I said. "It's old, but the scent is still there."

He lifted the mirror to his nose and gave it a quick sniff. "If you say so."

I ran my fingers over the intricate symbols carved within the circular frame. The images were both beautiful and terrifying, their symmetry perfect, their geometric unity flawless. Double-headed serpents, gods wearing necklaces of skulls, goddesses with skirts made of writhing snakes, all engraved with pictures of feathers, gems, woven fabrics and flowers. My naked eyes picked up chips and scratches in the stone, but these carvings had taken incredible skill to create. The design was amazing, and I found myself drawn in, deeper and deeper, my focus zeroing in on one detail after another....

"Chalice!" Aydin grabbed my arm just above the elbow and the pain of his rough touch brought me around. "Are you okay?"

"Fine," I said, setting the mirror down. "It got hold of me for a second, but I'm all right now." I heaved in a breath. "Angels for the Aztecs. Who'd have thought?"

"They referred to them as spirit guides or spirit messengers, which is what angels are." He ran a finger over the symbols. "The word *angel* comes from the Greek word *angelius* and means messenger."

I could never associate the bloodthirsty Aztecs with angels. Human sacrifice had been their way of appeasing their gods, and just knowing blood had been spilled on this artifact gave me the creeps. I looked around for something to put the mirror in, and found a padded envelope big enough to hold it. I held it open while Aydin rewrapped it in the tissue paper and gently slipped it inside.

"So what about Quin?" I asked.

Aydin pursed his lips. "I've been thinking about how to get him over to Elmo's without Gavin finding out."

That would be a problem. Gavin knew where Quin lived and the car he drove, so we couldn't use Quin's car to drive him to Elmo's. The Hummer was still back in the parking lot at the Cherry Creek Shopping Center. Both Aydin and I were stuck here, unless we called a taxi.

"I have a suggestion," Aydin said, looking uneasy. He clearly felt guilty about something. "We need to call in reinforcements."

"Like who?"

"Shojin."

His gargoyle? "I'm so not getting you."

He gestured for me to precede him up the stairs. "Shojin is nothing like Shui, Chalice."

"I don't believe you, but even if I did, what does that have to do with getting Quin to Elmo's?"

"Shojin and I have come to an understanding." He stopped at the basement doorway. "He'll give me a ride when I can't find other transportation."

I barked a laugh. "You've got to be kidding." How could anyone make friends with a bloodthirsty gargoyle, then turn it into a chauffeur?

Aydin went suddenly serious and I felt badly for scoffing. "I fashioned a harness for him to carry things, people included. I can call him here, load Quin in the harness and have Shojin fly him to Elmo's."

It was all I could do to hold back my smirk as I said, "And that's all there is to it?"

"That's it."

I found a huge flaw in his plan. "How were you planning to call him?"

Aydin looked puzzled. "With telepathy. Isn't that how you call Shui?"

"Hell, no!" My mouth dropped open in amazement. "Why would I want to call a homicidal maniac?"

"You need him every three days to lick your tattoo, same as I need Shojin." His eyes narrowed. "Unless Gavin keeps you two apart on purpose."

I tromped up the stairs, once again frustrated over Gavin withholding information from me. "That's the power he has over me, Aydin. I thought you knew that."

From behind me I heard, "Sorry. I didn't realize it was that bad."

No one was more sorry about it than me. I was about to tell him that, when a figure appeared at the top of the stairs.

Holy crap. We really stepped in it this time.

It was Gavin.

"Look what the cat dragged in," I said to the man standing in the upstairs doorway. I tried to ignore the sweat beading on my forehead and covered my panic with insolence. "What are you doing here, Gavin?"

I heard Aydin's quick inhalation of breath, then silence. *Oh, please don't ghost out on me now.* How would I explain the pile of discarded clothes in the basement? I hoped Gavin hadn't heard our conversation. If he did, we were screwed.

"I wondered what was taking you two so long," Gavin said, his face void of expression. "My men called to inform me the Hummer was still in the shopping center's parking lot. They said they'd seen you drive off in Quin's car. What happened?"

Since Quin was unaware of Aydin's unique skill for possession and hypnotic suggestion, I'd have to skew the facts. "Quin insisted we take his car." I wasn't lying about that part.

"He let you drive?"

I shrugged. "He was certainly in no condition to." Little did he know it wasn't drugs that had made him that way.

Gavin scowled. "Where was Aydin? He was told not to leave you alone."

"He didn't," I said. "He ghosted out and hid in the backseat. Quin never even knew he was there."

Aydin appeared beside me, his expression smug. "Once our man passed out completely, we made a quick search, and—" He slipped his hand inside his jacket and withdrew the envelope. "We got what we came for."

Gavin's thin lips tilted in a lopsided grin. "Excellent." He reached for the envelope, but Aydin hesitated. Gavin narrowed his eyes. "What's wrong?"

The Turk's eyebrows lifted and he surrendered his treasure. "Nothing."

Frowning, Gavin peered down the stairs. "Is that where you found it?"

Aydin looked unsure, and I knew why. He didn't want Gavin snooping around Quin's workshop because Geraldine's hand was still down there. But we couldn't stop him from searching. It was inevitable. I just prayed our hiding place wouldn't be found.

Gavin's stare became a shrewd, scrutinizing glare. He locked his hands behind his back. "You're both acting very strange. What's going on?"

A plan formed in my mind and I made a show of rolling my eyes. "Wow. This is embarrassing." We couldn't let Gavin's suspicions get any worse. Our secrets about Geraldine and the knights had to remain undisclosed at all cost. If we were to incriminate ourselves, let it be for something less damning.

As Gavin looked back and forth between us, I said, "Isn't it obvious?" I could easily tell this lie because I wanted to believe it. I wanted to very much. I lowered my chin and gave Aydin a coy look through my lashes.

"Oh?" Gavin looked at me blankly, then understanding arched his eyebrows practically to his hairline. "Oh!"

Aydin appeared totally lost, so I winked at him and smiled. His lascivious grin was slow but meaningful, and he had me half believing he meant it. A flush washed over me from head to toe and I knew how red I would have looked if I hadn't been standing in the shadows.

"Well, that changes things now, doesn't it?" Gavin asked, though I knew he didn't expect an answer. He was assessing. All I cared was that he stop doubting us so that Aydin and I could devise a new plan for Quin's escape. It would be much harder now. "I can't have my thieves cavorting under the same roof, or any roof, for that matter. An intimate relationship could compromise your assignment. I need you both completely focused."

"What the hell does that mean?" I asked, already dreading his answer.

Gavin looked down his nose at me. "It means, Chalice, that you and Aydin are not to see each other anymore."

thirteen

BECAUSE OF MY BRIGHT IDEA, IT HAD BEEN two days since I'd last seen Aydin. However, convincing Gavin that Aydin and I were an item actually did work to our benefit. It took the spotlight off our plan to spring Quin and our desire to break the bonds with our gargoyles. Or at least *my* desire to break free of Shui. Now that I thought about it, Aydin never said he wanted to rid himself of Shojin. He liked his monster.

My heart hurt. Having Aydin taken from me left a hole that only he could fill. It pained me to think that our attraction was nothing more than the result of having the same curse. I felt too deeply for it to mean nothing. It *did* mean something, at least to me. Was it possible our connection might be the real thing after all?

It helped that I wasn't back in that awful room filled with

portal paintings. If Gavin had put me in there, I'd have yanked every picture off the wall, stacked them like logs on the floor and set them all on fire. Instead I was given an ordinary room on the second floor. It had bars on the windows, but contained no artifacts, and was furnished with only a motel-style bed and nightstand. The television set was ancient, but at least it helped keep boredom at bay.

Zee had taken away my Balisong blade with the help of two witches and a house elf that looked like a cross between a wood nymph and a Brownie. All three had to hold me down while Zee pried the knife from my hands. I managed to cut her palm when I'd actually meant to slice off her finger, but I was out of practice. She was out of patience and conked me a good one on the noggin. I woke up an hour later with one wicked headache.

Now a prisoner of the Fatherhouse, my meals arrived on a tray and Gavin escorted me to his own room when I needed my fix from Shui. The old man hadn't said more than a handful of words to me since the night Aydin and I stole the scrying mirror. Gavin was wound up tighter than a coil of barbed wire and just as prickly. I sensed he was planning something, and whatever it was involved me.

I worried about Quin. My gut clenched when I considered the tactics Gavin might use to force Quin into summoning my dark-angel father. If he forced my sister knights into serving the Vyantara, there was a good chance he and his black-veil allies would gain enough power to tip the balance between darkness and light. A battle was on the horizon.

Aydin had yet to visit me in my "cell." You'd think he would secretly manage his way upstairs and into my room, but he hadn't. That made me mad, and then I got mad at myself for caring. It just proved what I'd known all along. No one can be trusted, not even a so-called friend who, to be perfectly honest, I wanted as my lover.

My chest tightened as I recalled everything the two of us had been through together. Though we hadn't known each other long, he'd been a constant source of support and guidance, beginning with the night we first met. And he'd given me a priceless gift to treasure always: a photo of my dead mother. Aydin wouldn't betray me. Something, or someone, was keeping him away.

I refused to stay locked up a moment longer.

I removed my contact lenses and both sets of filters from my ears and nose. Sniffing the air, I sought out Zee's scent, a sickly sweet odor of rotting roses and stale sweat. I'd also scented other people as they roamed the hallway outside my door, and though I hadn't seen them, I'd heard their voices.

Zee was close, probably perched on the chair outside my door. She couldn't stay there forever. I'd know as soon as she left her post. As for the lock on my door, I'd have to pick it open. Too bad I no longer had my Balisong *or* my case of picks.

I stood beside the door, my unprotected ears tuned in to noises in the hall. I detected six separate heartbeats; one close, the others farther away, and from the muffled echo I guessed these people were behind closed doors. Zee's heart had a *lub-lub* rhythm of lazy beats. She was a very unhealthy woman.

I slid the butter knife I'd pilfered from last night's dinner out of the back pocket of my jeans. The six heartbeats were still muffled, and Zee's were gone completely. Gavin's room was on this floor, but way on the other side of the building, so I didn't worry about him hearing me. And I'd smell him if he came close. I slid the knife point into the keyhole and jiggled it until I heard the upper pins inside the lock lift from their housing. I yanked the door open, slipped out into the hall and pushed the door firmly but quietly shut behind me. I rushed for the stairs and sped down them as fast as my short legs would carry me, jerking my head around to look back every few steps. It took me less than thirty seconds to make it down two long flights, putting me one flight below the main level of the house.

I was in the Fatherhouse basement now. A dark, colorless basement not much different from the one in Gavin's Chicago mansion. And like Gavin's place, this dank hole of rock and dirt was home to a lot of ghosts.

I pressed my back against the wall and sidestepped to the first set of doors. I heard a voice. A familiar voice. *Aydin!*

The door wasn't locked, and I was so excited that I couldn't stand staying outside a second longer. I grabbed the door latch and shouldered my way in. The room was blessedly dark enough for my naked eyes to see with crystal clarity.

"Aydin! I can't tell you how glad I am to see you. Why haven't you come to my—?"

A large gargoyle twice the size of Shui stood beside Aydin, its batwings flaring out aggressively. Its blue-black head angled forward and a beakish mouth issued a roar my sensitive ears could have done without. Red eyes blazed within an angular face so similar to Chinese folkart that its primitive beauty mesmerized me. This must be Shojin.

Aydin laid a reassuring hand on the creature's head and told it to hush. "Close the door," he told me, and I did. But I didn't venture any farther into what looked like a cell despite its comfortable furnishings and brightly colored rugs. I sniffed. Wet feathers, damp fur, but none of the rotted-meat odor I associated with Shui. Shojin smelled like a domestic pet in need of a bath.

"I thought all gargoyles looked alike," I said while slipping all my sensory armor back into place. "He's kind of pretty."

"I agree." Aydin stroked Shojin's head, but the creature continued to act hostile, glaring at me with red eyes narrowed in suspicion. "How did you get down here?"

My feet still glued to the spot, I said, "The usual way. I picked the lock and escaped when Zee left her post. I was feeling cooped up so I decided to explore the house. I didn't expect to find you here, especially not with that."

Shojin hissed.

"You hurt his feelings." Aydin was only half kidding. He focused on the gargoyle. "This is Chalice. I told you about her, remember?"

The gargoyle still looked sinister, but he lightened up on the hissing. Less aggressive now, he began to sulk. I

wondered if he sensed my affection for Aydin and was
jealous.

I wasn't about to scratch him behind the ears and coo
what a good boy he was. In spite of his sleek blue-black
feathers and regal raptor head, he was still a monster. A big
monster. I could see how he wouldn't have much trouble
flying with a human strapped in a harness to his back. I
guessed his wing span to be at least twelve feet, and his
chest was massive. Why did Shui look like a monkey and
Shojin looked like something from a fairy tale instead of a
nightmare?

"I told you not all gargoyles are like Shui," Aydin said,
watching me watch his "pet." "Their appearance is tied to
the character they had as humans. Shui is ugly and vicious
because that was his human psychotic self. Shojin, on the
other hand—"

"Does anyone know you're in here?" I glanced toward
the door, my nerves twitching. I'd been spared Gavin's
physical punishments since arriving in Denver and I wanted
to keep it that way.

"You couldn't have picked a safer place to hide." He sat
down on a burgundy corduroy couch that was two decades
out of style, but still in excellent condition. I guessed Aydin
enjoyed sharing his hand-me-downs with his gargoyle and I
wondered how much time he spent down here. There was
even a television set in the corner. Did Shojin get cable, too?

Aydin patted the space beside him. "I'm glad I was here
when you found it."

"Why, because your monster would have eaten me if you hadn't been?"

He shook his head. "Shojin's not violent."

"He's not an assassin?"

"Retired."

"Ah." I kept my eye on the beast while rushing to the other side of the room to join Aydin on the couch. "He's not an ugly monkey thing because...?"

"Because he was once a prince who got stuck in a compromising situation. He used to be one of the good guys as a human." He and his gargoyle shared a look. "At least that's what he told me."

"Telepathically?"

Aydin nodded. "According to the shaman who bonded us, Shojin was once Prince P'u Yi, older brother to Yang Jian of the Sui Dynasty in China. His brother sold him to a group of sorcerers to prevent him from becoming emperor when their father died."

That group of sorcerers had obviously been the Vyantara. "When was this?"

"610 AD."

And Shojin didn't look a day over a thousand. "If I ever tried contacting Shui with my mind, I think my brain would blow up." I glanced at the door again. "So why haven't you tried coming to my room?"

"Gavin said we couldn't see each other anymore, remember?"

I rolled my eyes. "Who cares what he says? You could have made like a ghost and snuck in."

He shook his head. "The wards on the second floor are set to detect ghosts. Kind of like a mouse trap."

So even the Vyantara thought spirits of the dead were vermin. "But you're not a real ghost."

"I am when I vanish."

Point taken. "I thought you and I were immune to curses and charms."

"Cursed and charmed *objects,* yes. But wards are different. So are most spells. In that case, we're just as susceptible as anyone else."

"So if someone threw, say, a coin at me that was cursed to turn a person blue, it wouldn't work."

"Correct." He frowned and gave me a funny look. "Not that turning someone blue would be an especially effective curse."

I rolled my eyes. "It was just an example."

"Okay, then in comparison, if someone aimed a curse at you directly to turn blue—"

"I'd turn blue."

"Exactly."

I wasn't happy to hear this. "Does that mean we can't protect ourselves from wards and spells?"

"We can, but it would mean using white magic. Are you prepared to subject yourself to white magic?"

I supposed so, but I shrugged instead of giving him an answer. "How's Quin?" I asked, hoping he might know something about the angel whisperer since Gavin wasn't talking. I knew Gavin would use me to help summon my father, and I assumed that would happen once Quin gave in.

Aydin slumped back on the couch and rubbed his chin. I glanced at his T-shirt that said I Had a Handle on Life, But It Broke.

His silence worried me. "Aydin, what's going on with Quin?"

"He's been beaten."

I was afraid of that. My breathing hitched in alarm and I twisted around to face him. "How bad is it?"

"He's still breathing." Aydin sighed and rubbed his forehead as if to soothe away a headache. "But he doesn't look good. I don't know how much more he can take."

Oh, no. I could only imagine his bruises, and it didn't take much for me to empathize with him. I'd been where he is. I had experienced Gavin's cruelty firsthand. "You saw him?"

"Only for a minute. I passed by the interrogation room when the door was open. Quin was strapped to a chair, his eyes wide open as if in a catatonic stupor. It was like he didn't see me."

"Maybe he didn't."

"What do you mean?"

I could only speculate, but my theory made perfect sense to me. "If angels come to Quin, speak through him, couldn't they just as easily control what he hears and says? His will may no longer be his own right now. I mean, consider what happened to Geraldine. She and Quin are alike in what they can do. Could she have prevented her execution by telling her interrogators what they wanted to hear? Had she had a choice? Does Quin?"

Aydin's jade-colored eyes lowered to stare at the woven rug beneath his feet. "It's not the same."

I had to agree, but that wasn't my point. "What I'm trying to say is that the host who channels information for an angel, or a demon for that matter, is *expendable*."

He glanced at me sharply. "Geraldine was a martyr."

"Was that her choice? Or the choice of the angels speaking through her? I don't know as much about angels as you do, but I don't believe 'good' angels mess with human lives. I think Geraldine was sacrificed. I think Quin is being sacrificed now."

"So you don't think he has the power to speak for himself?"

"No." Which meant he'd die at the hands of his tormentor. Gavin would kill him if we didn't act fast to intervene. "I can give Gavin what he wants. He wants my fallen-angel father."

Aydin's eyes widened. "Not without Quin's help."

I thought about the obsidian scrying mirror we'd taken from Quin's workshop. There was residue of blood on the mirror. Some of it was Quin's. The really old blood wasn't completely human, and I was certain it belonged to an angel. "There was angel blood on the mirror we stole from Quin. That must be part of the ritual for evocation. I'm half angel. My blood should work, and we don't need Quin's cooperation to take some of his."

Aydin looked unconvinced. "Chalice, you don't even know what the ritual is."

He was right about that. And as much as I didn't trust

magic, I'd have no problem using it to save a man's life—a man I felt responsible for. Quin's angels had tried to warn him about me, then I screwed everything up. Now I had to fix it.

"Aydin, you can find out from Geraldine how to perform the ritual, and then come back to tell me how it's done."

He scowled at my idea. "We can't be sure she even knows what it is."

Communicating with angels was her thing. She'd know what was needed for an evocation, even if it wasn't the exact same ritual Quin was used to. The ingredients were what mattered most, and we already had most of those. I'd been around magic users long enough to know that a conjurer's will was the real catalyst for a spell or ritual. The rest was just window dressing.

"What are you planning to tell Gavin?" he asked.

Good question. I'd have to put my refined lying skills to good use. "I'll tell him I don't need Quin's help. Then I'll lie and say Geraldine shared the ritual for angel evocation at the same time she told me about my father."

"He'll be pissed you didn't let him know this before now."

I realized that, but I'd cross that bridge as I watched it burn behind me.

Zee never made it back to her post outside my room, and I returned to my prison unseen. After locking myself back in, I slipped a note under the door with a request to see Gavin and he showed up less than an hour later.

"I understand you want to see me." Gavin stood in the doorway, his expression flat and his eyes half-lidded, looking bored. He took a quick peek at his watch as if I kept him from an important appointment.

I lay propped up on the bed by two pillows stacked against the headboard. "Where's Zee?"

"In my bed. Why?"

That was far more information than I needed to know. I shrugged, but didn't hide the disgust on my face. "Just wondering." I pointed the remote at the TV and switched it off. "How much longer are you planning to keep me locked up in here?"

His chest heaved with a silent sigh. "Not much. Do you have something better to do?"

Asshole. "Dinner and a movie?"

"Are you asking me out on a date?"

A date? My stomach turned so fast I thought I'd lose my lunch. All I'd been fed today was peanut butter and grape jelly on white bread and a glass of Kool-Aid, compliments of Zee. "If it will get me out of this museum for a few hours then yes, I'm asking you out. But only if Aydin can come with us."

His eyes flashed. "No."

Okay, no more games. I tossed the remote on the bed and swung my legs over the side. Swallowing hard, I asked, "How's Quin?"

"You're full of questions tonight." He stepped farther into the room and took a seat on a ladder-back chair by the window. "Are you that bored?"

He knew I was. The jerk. "I'd just like to make sure Quin's all right."

"He's as well as can be expected under the circumstances." Gavin slipped a cigar from his shirt pocket. "Do you mind?"

"I sure as hell do." I made a face and he put the cigar away. "You don't have to hurt him anymore, Gavin. I can do this without Quin."

Gavin squinted at me. "What could you possibly know about performing an evocation ritual?"

I bit my lip, letting my nerves show. I felt anxious and I wanted him to know it, just not the reason why. "I know the ritual because Saint Geraldine explained to me how it works."

He leaned forward in the chair. "What did you just say?"

My stomach twisted. "When Geraldine confirmed who my father was and told me his name, I told her I wanted to see him. I asked if she knew where he was, but she can't contact the Fallen. Only the Arelim. She said I could summon Barachiel myself if I had the right tools."

"Why didn't you tell me this before?"

"Because I..." Crap. What could I say? A sudden burst of realization hit me like a slap in the face. Tears filled my eyes and I tilted my head back to keep them from falling. "Because I wanted to do it by myself and without you around. Contacting my father is *my* business, Gavin, not yours. You already took my mother from me, and I won't let you take my father, too." I confounded myself with the truth behind those words. I meant every one of them.

He glared at me.

"So you can stop torturing Quin now. I'll perform the ritual for you on my own."

Leaning back in the chair, he said, "You should have told me this sooner."

I studied Gavin's stoic expression, his skin starting to redden with anger. I tossed him a pleading look. "I'm sorry, okay? Just don't hurt him any more."

He folded his arms across his chest. "Too late for that."

He couldn't mean what I thought he did. My heart did a tap dance inside my chest. "What are you saying?"

"Quin is dead."

The tap shoes went instantly still. "But you just told me..."

He stood and began his habitual pacing. "I said he was well enough under the circumstances, which for Quin happens to be dead. All he had to do was cooperate, but he'd been nonresponsive since the moment we brought him to the Fatherhouse. If you had just told me this before now—" He stopped and hit the wall with the side of his fist. "Damn it, Chalice! He could have worked for us. His psychic powers were impressive. I even had a gargoyle arranged for his bonding."

My breaths came short and shallow. I'd really blown it this time. But if the angels really had taken over his body to prevent him from working for Gavin, maybe they'd taken his soul, too. If so, he hadn't suffered. If his body had been sacrificed for the angels he channeled, he never felt a thing.

God, I hoped that's what happened. Poor Quin. May his soul rest in peace.

"Where is he?" I asked.

"His body is still in his room." Gavin returned to the chair and leaned forward, holding his head in his hands. "We'll have him cremated tonight. The plan is to make it appear that he made a sudden decision to return to England. We'll pack up his house, fake his resignation from his job, and take care of tedious details to avoid suspicion. I can fix it so that his car runs off the road and catches fire on the way to the airport." Looking pleased with himself, Gavin leaned back and slapped his thighs before launching to his feet. "Let's go."

I felt dazed and looked at him with unfocused eyes. "Go where?"

"We have a ritual to perform." He waved a hand at the open door. "Tell me what you need to get started."

I inhaled a shaky breath. "Give me a minute, okay? A man just died! Have you no heart?"

He didn't even flinch. And he didn't answer me, either.

I shook my head, though I shouldn't have been surprised. Gavin was about to wipe Quin's existence from the face of the Earth without any thought to the dead man's family or friends. And he was taking it upon himself to have Quin's house packed up—oh, shit. Saint Geraldine's other hand! Aydin would have to get it out before Gavin found it.

"Minute's up," Gavin said. "What do you need for the ritual?"

I didn't know. Aydin was supposed to find out from

Geraldine, and I assumed he was with her now. I recalled the herbs I'd smelled while in Quin's workshop. I had a hunch I'd need them, as well as something else. "Get me some of Quin's blood."

"Not a problem."

I bet it wasn't. "I also need sage, jasmine, lavender, absinthe and myrrh."

He cocked his head. "Standard ingredients for rudimentary spells. Is that all?"

No. "I'll need the scrying mirror we took from Quin's house." I couldn't believe I was going to try summoning an angel, and a Fallen one at that. Would Barachiel even come to me?

I remembered all the metal in Quin's shop, the tin and the silver. And the crystals. Whether or not he used them in a summoning spell was unknown, but it wouldn't hurt to have them just in case. "Bring me tin, silver and Celestine crystal." I felt like a total fraud. "That should be everything."

Gavin left, closing and locking the door behind him.

I clutched my head and fell sideways on the bed, my stomach tumbling with nerves. What had I done? And what would I do now?

fourteen

LESS THAN AN HOUR LATER I STOOD IN THE basement of the enormous Fatherhouse, at the center of a fifteen-foot pentagram painted on a concrete floor. They called this the summoning room. Bare brick walls rose up to meet a broad-beamed ceiling. Thanks to the light from the wall sconces, I could see rusty stains splashed over the pale floor. I could still smell the old blood.

"Use this room much?" I asked Gavin, who stood leaning casually against the wall.

He grinned like a wolf calculating its prey. "Of course. We depend on our allies beyond the veil to help us with our business dealings."

The *black* veil. I studied the pentagram, noting the Greek letters for alpha and omega imprinted on the star. The beginning and the end; the symbol of the infinite.

The pentagram was a striking rendition of an archaic mark that symbolized the human being. The five-pointed star included all five impressions of the Great Light: Gabriel, Raphael, Uriel, Michael and Samael. *Angels.* It just proved how thin the line was between darkness and light. One couldn't exist without the other.

"You ready?" Gavin asked.

Crap. Where the hell was Aydin? "As I'll ever be." An ordinary wooden chair was positioned at the star's center. Did I have to get naked for this? I was dressed for winter, from a heavy down jacket to gloves and boots. It was freaking cold down here and I wasn't about to take off my clothes.

I held my hand out to Gavin. "I need the mirror."

He lumbered toward me and slapped the beautiful piece of carved obsidian in my hand. "Did you know knives and arrow points were made from this stone as early as 2500 BC?"

Yeah, I knew. And so what? This wasn't a history lesson. I wrapped my fingers around the handle of the artifact. Obsidian was rare. Since this was an Aztec piece, I surmised that the stone had come from the Peruvian Andes. A place of intense dark magic. And I was about to taint my soul with its poison.

I gave the mirror a passing scan, reluctant to look at it too long since it had nearly entranced me the last time. *I* was in charge now and it felt damn good for a change.

"Obsidian makes the perfect cutting tool, sharp as a scalpel." Gavin slipped his hand inside his sports coat and I knew he was reaching for the beautiful stone knife he had used to threaten Shui a few nights ago at the motel. Except the stone blade of that knife wasn't obsidian. The marble-ized red-and-purple colors were unique and I wanted to know what kind of rock it was made from. I also wanted to know why the sight of it had paralyzed Shui and obsessed me.

Zee came striding into the room trailed by Shui, the gargoyle's folded wings giving him an awkward gait so that he hobbled as if crippled. He glared at me while taking his place beside his master. What the hell were Zee and Shui doing here?

"What's with the audience?" I asked.

"Witnesses." Gavin gave Shui a pointed look before add-ing, "And protection. We never know what we'll encounter when trying something new. Though I doubt an angel, dark or light, poses much threat, it doesn't hurt to be cautious."

And of course Gavin had his special knife with him to make sure the gargoyle behaved. "What about her?" I in-clined my head toward Zee, whose smoldering glare could have set my hair on fire. In fact, my scalp did burn a little and I absently rubbed the top of my head. "Is she a body-guard, too?"

He chuckled. "Hardly. She'll record the ritual for future use. I think the Fallen have the potential to be quite use-ful. A high bid for the gift of invisibility will make us a fortune."

It was all speculation. He had no idea what value the Fallen would have for the Vyantara. I didn't know what moral code they followed, or if they even had one.

However, it was reasonable to assume they were self-centered beings that acted solely on their own behalf.

"Is Aydin coming?" I craned my neck to watch for him through the door. I couldn't do this without him. I needed his strength and his courage, though I wouldn't confess this to Gavin. "I figured that since he's had experience with a fallen angel, he could help me."

Gavin gave his watch a cursory glance. "He'll be here. He said he had something for Shojin to do, and that's just as well. Two gargoyles can't be in the same room together."

Though I suspected the reason, I wanted to hear it from him. "Why not?"

"They're too territorial."

Meaning they'd fight. That interested me, especially when I wondered how they determined the winner.

Gavin checked his wrist again, then shot his cuffs. "I don't suppose you could do whatever you need to do to prepare?"

I scooted the chair back and laid the scrying mirror at the center of the pentagram. There were five bowls containing the herbs I'd requested, and one with the crystals, but something was missing that I remembered seeing in Quin's workshop. "I need silver and tin."

"The pentagram itself contains silver and tin," Zee said, enunciating each word slowly as if speaking to a child. "All metals must be present to perform a summons. You should know that."

Gavin shot her a sharp look that shut her up. He then said to me, "Proceed."

Aydin? I need you, damn it! "Quin's blood?"

He reached in the pocket of his jacket and brought out a vial filled to the brim with something black as ink. I knew it was just the lack of light that made the blood appear so dark. He handed me the vial.

"I also need a knife." I held out my left hand. "The ritual requires my blood as well as Quin's, and I have nothing to cut myself with." I hoped Gavin would offer me his stone knife, but he handed me an ordinary pocketknife instead.

I removed my contact lenses and gazed around the room. No ghosts here, which is where I'd expect to see them. There had to have been deaths at this site, sacrifices and murders necessary for a ritual that would summon something through one of the veils. With the exception of stationary green veils, a veil could open almost anywhere, but nothing could cross to the mortal plane without an invitation. I had the ability to see through a veil if it was near me, like the way I'd seen the Maågan demon on my first night in this house. Tonight would be my first time actually bringing something through on my own.

I blinked naked eyes at the doorway where a misty figure stood waiting. Aydin. He pantomimed that he'd have to get inside me. I knew what he meant, but when I considered the physical alternative, it gave me a thrill. There was no denying I wanted him, but it unsettled me to think of his ghost merging with my body. It wouldn't do for me to pass out before things even got started, yet he couldn't convey the details for the ritual any other way.

I sat in the chair and inhaled deeply while closing my

eyes. Within a few seconds, I felt another presence inside me, filling me with heat and energy. Aydin's very essence expanded each cell in my body, his thoughts and emotions like liquid fire running through my veins.

The sensation was more intimate than I imagined. Every erogenous zone in my body came fully engaged, and I squirmed in the chair while responding to his sharing. Hot didn't begin to describe what I was feeling. If I were a smoker, I'd need a cigarette after this was over.

I sensed his wisdom, his knowledge, his "otherness." Information going from his mind to mine was instantaneous. The experience was over within seconds, and I was still awake yet completely relaxed.

He also sent me a powerful sensation of calm and confidence. When he left me, the emptiness was so sudden it felt like my own soul had been siphoned away, leaving me bereft and painfully alone. The feeling vanished almost as quickly as it had presented, and I opened my eyes to see Aydin's ghost disappear through the wall.

Shaking off my disorientation, I glanced down at the tools and ingredients by my feet. All were here, everything I needed, and I instantly knew exactly what had to be done.

I combined the small bowls of herbs into one, setting the absinthe aside. I crushed the sage, jasmine and lavender flowers with my fingers, filling the room with their pungent scent. The sticky, resinous myrrh had to be crumbled over the crushed herbs before I could sprinkle absinthe over the entire mixture. I hadn't asked for matches, but I found some beside the herb bowls, an obvious ritual component I had overlooked.

I lit a match and ignited the herbs and resin. A flame abruptly flared toward the ceiling and I nearly dropped the bowl. Gavin looked ready to jump in the middle of the pentagram and rescue it if he had to, but that would have ruined everything. The painted circle around the star served as an invisible barrier between the mortal plane and the worlds beyond. Any breach at this point would nullify what we were trying to achieve.

I sat within the boundaries of a gateway, acting as its gatekeeper. I'd never before felt so in control.

I stood to position myself at the head of the pentagram. The fire had gone out of my herbs, but dense smoke swirled from the bowl and I offered it to the north, south, east and west. Crouching down to retrieve five Celestine crystals, I placed them all in the bowl to coat them in ash, then set one crystal at each point of the star.

I opened the vial of Quin's blood and poured a generous amount into the bowl. I used Gavin's pocketknife to slice through my palm, wincing at the sting of razor-sharp metal through my flesh. I held that hand over the ashes and watched my blood mix with Quin's. Using two fingers, I stirred the bloody concoction until it became a paste that I smeared on my forehead in the shape of an X. I knelt on the floor beside the mirror.

"The blood of an angel blends with that of the host who serves as conduit to connect two worlds." I touched my bloody fingers to the mirror's cold black surface and marked a spiral pattern; the symbol for creation. "I summon the dark angel, Barachiel."

Nothing happened, not that I was surprised. I'd probably missed a step. This ritual was meant to call one of the Arelim, and Barachiel was no longer a member of their club.

I shot a furtive look at Gavin, whose solemn stare made him appear more patient than I think he was. The tightness around his frigid blue eyes told me that much.

Still kneeling, I bowed in supplication to the angel I summoned. If the Fallen were as arrogant as I guessed, submissive behavior might get me noticed. A flutter of nerves ran up my spine and ice coated the pit of my stomach. Anticipation had every hair on my body standing at attention. "Barachiel, it is your blood I shed. I summon you to the mortal plane, to the human side of the veil, so that I might know the one who spawned me."

There was an immediate change in the mirror's surface. The blood and ash began to bubble, and steam rose in long streamers to twirl and spin, expand and contract. It was a lot like watching the formation of a cyclone, only far slower and at a fraction of the size.

I sensed tension from the others and only then noticed that flesh-and-blood Aydin had joined them. He stood calmly at the edge of the circle, hands clasped in front of him, his strong, handsome face angled toward me with his eyes focused intently on what rose from the mirror.

A series of colorful sparks burst within the swirling steam. The sconces on the wall sputtered before flickering out completely, but the light show at the center of the pentagram threw off enough illumination to make up for any loss of light. I set the mirror down on the ground in front of me and took a cautious step back. I blinked against the brightness and threw up my hands to shield my eyes.

A figure began to take shape. It stretched its enormous wings, black feathers gleaming with reflected light from inside the spiral.

The angel's body was human in appearance and so pale that it glowed in the darkness. He wore a short black tunic belted at the waist with what looked like a silver rope. I had to tilt my head back to gaze up into a face of frozen white marble, its eyes as black as the obsidian mirror where it stood.

The fallen angel, Barachiel. My father.

He cocked his head while gazing down at me, though it was hard to tell where his attention was focused because he had no pupils. The blackness completely filled his eyes, making him appear blind. I thought I saw stars glimmer within their depths.

"It's you." His baritone voice carried through the room with a reverberating echo. "I knew it had to be you."

I swallowed, fixated on his unnatural beauty, his skin so smooth it didn't look real. Was he real? Was he solid, or an apparition? I reached out and touched his chest, his sculpted pectorals as smooth and solid as polished stone. And just as cold.

His hand covered mine. "Daughter."

I inhaled a sharp breath that felt like needles pricking my lungs. I think I'd forgotten to breathe the moment Barachiel became visible. With the sudden burst of fresh oxygen, my blood flooded my veins with force, the rush of it causing a pounding pain behind my eyes.

I had so much to say, so much to ask, but my addled brain went suddenly blank. I was staring at an angel. A fallen angel, but still an angel, and now that I'd actually seen him and touched him, it was easier to accept who and what *I* was. And what my mother had been.

My mother. This creature had bedded my mother, made her pregnant, then left her without protection so that she could be murdered by a man from the Vyantara. How dare Barachiel let that happen? How dare he even call me his daughter?

My hand still against his chest, I pushed. Hard. He hadn't expected it, and though he was twice my size and probably a hundred times stronger, he stumbled backward. One bare foot remained on the mirror as he caught himself.

He scowled briefly before looking amused. "You call me to you, then try to get rid of me so soon?"

I fisted my hands at my sides. "How could you do that to my mother?"

"Chalice!" Gavin shouted.

Barachiel turned his head, his lion's mane of sleek black hair lifting in a surreal breeze, then falling in perfect waves across his shoulders. He glowered at Gavin. "Who are you?"

Gavin stepped forward, straightening the lapels on his jacket before tugging at the neckline of his shirt. "Gavin Heinrich, chief of operations for the North American Vyantara. I have a business proposition for you."

Barachiel refocused on me. "You called me here for *him?*"

Holding my head high, I wasn't sure how to respond. I'd called him for Gavin because he'd ordered me to, but I also wanted to see him for myself. I needed proof that I still had one parent left, be it human or otherwise. Instead of answering Barachiel's question, I asked one of my own. "Why did you hurt my mother?"

"Chalice, that's enough," Gavin scolded, sounding both annoyed and angry. "We didn't bring him here for you to argue with him about your mother—"

"Silence!" Barachiel's voice shook the walls like the boom from a cannon. "Your business proposition can wait. *My* business is with my daughter."

"You say that as if you care," I said, my rapidly beating heart making my voice shake. "You feel as much for me as you did for my mother, which is absolutely nothing."

"Felicia was very dear to me." He laid both his enormous hands on my shoulders and bent forward to gaze into my eyes. "I was once her Guardian, her protector. That was my role until she asked me to father a new knight for the order."

My eyes filled with hot tears of anger and I blinked them back. "That's not what I am."

He appeared confused. "You are my progeny, a knight in the Order of the Hatchet."

I slapped his hands away. "Have you been living under a rock for the past twenty-five years?"

"I don't understand. Did your mother teach you nothing?" He still looked puzzled, though his voice was edged with restrained rage.

My laugh sounded as bitter as I felt. "My mother is *dead!*"

The room went abruptly silent.

After a few seconds, Gavin cleared his throat. "We'll give you anything you want, Barachiel. All I ask is that the gift of invisibility be granted to a few of our clients. You'll be paid with the blood of virgin fey, have all the human women you want, live a luxurious life on the mortal plane if that's more your style. Name your price and it's yours."

Understanding seemed to dawn on Barachiel at the same speed as Gavin's sales pitch. His eyes turned from black to red, and tears the color of blood streamed down his cheeks. One foot still on the mirror, he faced Gavin and the others. Zee looked petrified, her eyes round with amazement, her lips parted in a small O of surprise. My breath caught when I saw that Aydin was no longer there.

His jaw tight with fury, Barachiel pointed at Gavin. "*You* killed Felicia."

Gavin licked his lips. "It was necessary. She had something I wanted, something I needed. But she still got away from me and it took me thirteen years to find where she'd left it so that I could claim it for myself."

My stomach turned as I realized the *it* he referred to was me.

I'd known Gavin had been responsible for my mother's death, but it still hurt to hear. The memory of my abduction came racing back and I relived the sight of Father Thomas collapsing dead in front of me. I heard the thunder of machine-gun fire that followed. Barachiel gently clasped his hands to both sides of my head, his fingers hot instead of the cold marble he'd been a moment ago. His expression changed as he experienced my memories with me. Then his hand slid to the back of my neck, halting on my tattoo. My mark of shame.

Both his hands dropped away, but his eyes never lost their scarlet hue. He stared at Gavin again. "I can name my price?"

Looking eager, Gavin nodded like a bobblehead doll. "Anything."

"I want my daughter. I want Chalice."

Gavin sputtered. "Of course. She's yours, with my blessing."

Just like that? I wasn't some poker chip that could be tossed on the bargaining table. I was a human being. I had rights! Or at least I did until I was cursed. Even so, I wasn't Gavin's to give.

Not one to be ignored in a deal that could potentially involve him, Shui hissed and flared his wings. He wasn't ready to give me up. The two of us still had unfinished business, his being to make a meal out of me someday.

Gavin smiled. "Pay no attention to Shui." He glared down at the gargoyle while sliding his hand inside his jacket. Shui's eyes narrowed as he watched where his master's hand settled. Then he went quietly still.

"Chalice wouldn't stay my daughter for long though, is that right, Gavin Heinrich?" Barachiel glowered at the man who had literally ruled my life for the past twelve years.

"How many hours does she have left before she shifts into a winged devil like that one?" He flicked a finger at Shui, a dismissive gesture as casual as swatting a fly.

He knew. How could he know of the gargoyle's curse? Even Gavin looked surprised.

"I'm not an idiot," Barachiel told him. "These creatures have existed as long as I have, and so has their nefarious curse. But like a promise, the curse can be broken. Once the gargoyle is dead, the curse is broken."

"I already know that," I said softly, hope leaking from me like air from a deflating balloon. For a minute there, I'd actually believed he had the power to set me free. I'd never in my life felt so defeated. "But gargoyles are immortal."

Carefully enunciating each word to ensure he made himself clear, Barachiel said, "Only until one kills the other."

I could have sworn the dark angel actually smirked.

Barachiel shoved his hand out toward Gavin, palm open and fingers splayed. The air shifted like a wave in a pool. And as it did, all motion outside the circle abruptly stopped. Gavin was frozen midleap, Zee looked ready to join him and Shui had risen a foot off the floor while beating his wings to take flight. He hung suspended, going nowhere. Time outside the circle stood completely still.

Barachiel turned to me and said, "You can free yourself of the gargoyle's curse."

I nodded, giddy with this knowledge, but apprehensive about how to do what needed to be done. "There's only one other gargoyle here that I know of."

"It will do."

"But what if Shui kills *him?*"

"The other one must win if you're to be free." He grabbed hold of my hand and held it gently between both of his. "I swear to you, Chalice, that I didn't know what happened to your mother after she conceived."

"You left us."

"Only because I had to." He heaved a sigh, his eyes finally going back to normal. Well, normal for him. It was like looking into orbs of black glass. "I was familiar with humans and their ways, and I refused to become one of them. The only other choice was this."

"Which means you're playing on the wrong side!"

He shook his head. "I'm still an angel."

But he was a fallen angel, a dark angel, who served the enemy. I wasn't okay with that. It was just…wrong.

"If you do fail at breaking the curse," he told me, "there's a way to reverse the change."

"You mean a gargoyle can change back into a human?"

He nodded. "I doubt your Vyantara sorcerer knows this, but once you've changed you must eat the heart of the gargoyle you were bonded with in order to change back."

Eat its heart? "But a gargoyle turns to stone. How can a stone heart be eaten?"

"It can," he said. "I've seen it done many times."

I gazed at the frozen figures beyond the circle and lost my enthusiasm. "I'm their prisoner, Barachiel. I have no power over them. They control *me.* There's no escape."

"There is." He tightened his hold on my hands and it didn't hurt. His touch didn't hurt my skin. Was it because he was my father? Or because he was an angel? "Leave the circle and run from this house. Run as fast and as far as you can until you reach someplace safe."

"There's no safe place for me to go." Then I thought of Elmo's. "Or maybe there is. But they'll follow me!"

"They won't." He tossed a quick glance at Gavin. "I won't let them."

"What about you?"

He gazed at me with such tenderness that I could still see the angel he used to be. Then his expression melted into one of fierce determination. "I have a place to go."

"The black veil?"

"No. Chalice, don't believe everything you hear about us. The Fallen are not demons."

"But if not the black veil, then where?"

"There's no time to explain. Just know that I'll come to you again." He leaned down and kissed the top of my head. Now that his anger had cooled, his touch was like ice on my scalp. "No matter where you go, I will find you. I promise. Now go."

"Now?"

"Now!"

He said it with such vehemence that the very volume of his voice propelled me across the pentagram and through the circle. I sped out the door, but glanced over my shoulder to see the air shimmer around Barachiel. His hold on time continued. His face looked strained, desperate. It was taking all his strength to maintain his grip on the suspended room. He jerked a nod and I ran.

I took the steps two at a time, racing up to the main level, then stopping in front of a tall grandfather clock on the main floor. It had stopped at 1:00 a.m., the second hand motionless. I looked around me to see dust motes hover unmoving in the beam of light cast by a Tiffany lamp on a table. A moth hung suspended in midflight. A ceiling fan had stopped rotating, the blades frozen within a blur of halted motion. Barachiel's freezing of time continued to hold.

Gavin's stone knife! I had to have it, and now would be my only chance to take it without him stopping me.

I turned and raced back down the stairs to the basement, then flew into the summoning room. Without looking at Barachiel, I thrust my hand inside Gavin's jacket, feeling around the pocket until my fingers touched the solid surface of the knife. I tugged it free, clutched it in my fist, and sped out the door and back up the stairs. I don't think I'd taken a breath by the time I reached the building's main entrance. Just as I clasped the door's handle, I felt time let loose. It was over. Barachiel's spell broke and time rushed on.

I yanked the door toward me, but as I dove to cross the threshold, something grabbed hold of my ankle. Still hanging on to the door, I glanced down at the black claw digging into my flesh. I blinked and saw the rest of the demon's body as it clung to me. This was the Maågan demon.

Its red eyes glared at me from a black face as creased as old tree bark. Adrenaline coursed through me with the force of a racing river and I hardly felt the skin on my ankle tear as the demon's nails dug deeper. Gavin's knife still clutched in my hand, I screamed and swung so it cut through the black hide of my assailant's arm. It was like slicing a brick of warm butter. Instantly free, I lunged out the door with the demon's severed limb still attached.

Limping quickly down the sidewalk, I turned to glance back at the house. It looked the same. I slipped an earplug from my ear and caught a chaotic flurry of voices, excited shouts, pounding footsteps, slamming doors. What the hell was going on in there? The noise infused my panic and my limp became a run. In spite of the bond I had with Shui, I had to get away from this place. Once at Elmo's, I'd at least have some semblance of freedom, even if it was only temporary.

I'd run about two blocks when I felt a rumble beneath my feet. I looked behind me for just a second and saw the explosion that blew a good-size chunk from the roof of the Fatherhouse.

fifteen

SMOKE AND FLAME FOLLOWED THE BLAST.
Then came the sirens. Had Gavin and the others made it
out in time? Shui most certainly survived. Immortal gargoyles tended to do that.

Oh, my God. Aydin? There was no way he could have
been inside when the building blew up. He'd left the summoning room before hell broke loose, and I hadn't seen him
in the house when I left. Surely he'd escaped. I couldn't bear
to think he hadn't.

The flames rising from the building illuminated the
streets, and crowds of residents wearing bathrobes and heavy
jackets ventured out into the cold to watch the fire. All of
them were so focused on the catastrophe that no one noticed
a small, dark-haired woman with a limp running by.

As soon as I had the chance, I pried the Maågan's

bloodless and disembodied claw from my ankle and tossed the severed arm in the gutter. When it touched the ground it dissolved into a black stain on the snow.

It was hard to ignore my wound as I ran. It burned as if tainted with poison. My body felt hot all over and my mind flamed with fever. Where was Elmo's Coffee Shop? Down this street? Or was it that one? They all looked the same. Every turn-of-the-century home I passed was covered by leafless climbers and thorny rose vines, the yards filled with holly bushes, blue spruces and skeletal cottonwood trees that hovered over snow-coated lawns.

I felt like a hound that had lost its scent. I crouched beneath a tree and removed my nose filters, seeking the aroma of coffee.

Within seconds, the strong scent of coffee and cinnamon took hold of me like a leash attached to my nose. I stumbled down one alley after another until I ended up in Elmo's front yard. After hobbling down the basement steps, I limped through the tunnel, my naked eyes scouring the walls for an entrance. There was a thin line of light leaking out between the floor and the bottom of a door. The sign hanging outside said Closed.

Shit. I thought Elmo kept his shop open through the wee hours. I pounded on the door. "Elmo? You in there?"

I heard two voices on the other side of the door. One belonged to Elmo, and the other was... "Aydin? Oh, thank God you're here. Let me in!"

The door opened and I fell inside.

"What happened?" Aydin asked as he dragged me up by

the arms. "You're bleeding. And your eyes—" His forehead creased with worry. "You have a fever."

I held on to him as he steered me to one of Elmo's spool tables. I sat and struggled to catch my breath while replacing both contact lenses over my stinging eyes. "Explosion. Fatherhouse."

"We heard about it on the radio." Elmo handed me a glass of water and I gulped it down. "They're still putting out the flames."

I gasped in a breath, my lungs feeling too small to fill with the oxygen I needed to talk. I pointed at my ankle. "Maågan."

Aydin grimaced. "Nasty creatures. Coffee grounds work really well at drawing out the poison. How did you get out of the house?"

Once I was able to breath normal again, I told Elmo and Aydin what had happened with Barachiel. When they asked what had caused the explosion, I shrugged. "I'm not sure. I was already outside when it happened." Though I wondered if the buildup of magic from the Vyantara's collection had attributed to the cause.

"You're lucky to be alive." Elmo made a poultice of coffee grounds for my demon wound and wrapped a dish towel around my ankle to hold it in place. I started to feel better almost immediately. "It's a good thing Aydin left when he did."

"Where did you go?" I asked him.

"Come and I'll show you." He helped me up and I

grabbed him around the waist to keep from falling over as he guided me to the small room behind Elmo's kitchen.

There, lying faceup on the cot, was Quin's body.

"What the hell?" This was the last thing I needed to see. "I thought he was to be cremated."

"That was Gavin's original plan, yes," Aydin said. "I found out Quin was dead just before going to see Geraldine. When I told her what had happened to him, she said I should save his body. That his death was only temporary."

"Are you saying he's a zombie?" I envisioned a mindless, flesh-eating corpse. I'd encountered one in Haiti a couple of years ago and preferred not to repeat the experience. "If he is, we'll have to chop off his head. That's the only way to stop those things."

"No one's chopping off anyone's head." Aydin went on to explain how Geraldine had been immune to her executioner's efforts at ending her life. "She kept coming back until they finally had to cut her into pieces and set fire to her entrails. They'd thought that was the end of her, but they were obviously wrong." He swallowed and jerked a nod at the corpse on the cot. "Once the Arelim believe it safe for him to come back, Quin's soul will return to his body."

I sat in one of the two director-style chairs across from Quin's corpse. My ankle still throbbed and I elevated it on a wooden box Elmo used as a nightstand. "When will that be?"

"Now that the danger is past, he should come back anytime now."

We both gazed down at the angel whisperer's body. His face was white as parchment, his lips pale violet with black scabs where they had split. Several contusions mottled his skin where Gavin had beaten him literally to death. If he lived, he'd be sore as hell for a few days unless miraculous healing was part of the bargain for playing on the good angels' team.

"How did you get him here?" I asked. "I didn't see the Hummer outside. Did you hide it around the block?"

Aydin shook his head. "Remember the harness I told you about? The one I use with Shojin?"

"You didn't!"

"It was the only way to get Quin here without Gavin finding out." He reached down and touched two fingers to the side of Quin's neck, then shook his head. No change. "I intercepted the Hummer at the crematorium and then I, uh, convinced Gavin's men to take a nap."

And experience told me just how he'd done it, too. "So when you came to me at the summoning room, you'd already taken care of Quin."

He nodded. "I managed to get him here, but there was more I had to do. That's why I didn't stay while you performed the ritual. I had to help Elmo get Quin's body inside the shop. Shojin is a loyal friend, but he has his limitations. He's not very agile on his feet."

I shuddered. It still bothered me that Aydin had befriended his gargoyle. Even Barachiel had labeled gargoyles as "winged devils," which I considered pretty damn demonic. Speaking of Shojin, it was time for me to break the big news.

"What is it?" Aydin asked me, one corner of his mouth lifting in a wary grin. "You look happy all of a sudden."

I patted the chair next to me. "You should sit down for this."

Frowning, he took a seat.

"I learned how to kill a gargoyle."

He stared at me, unblinking.

"Use another gargoyle to kill it."

Now he blinked.

I had expected a more exuberant reaction. I leaned forward to clarify my point. "Don't you get it? That's why gargoyles are always kept apart. If they fight, one will die, and the dead one's bonded human will be freed. So we have to get our gargoyles to fight each other...." My shoulders slumped as I made a realization. "But only one dies, meaning only one of us would go free."

Aydin licked his lips and looked away. "I don't want to lose Shojin."

This wasn't going as planned. "Shojin can take Shui, you know he can. He's twice his size."

"And he's centuries older, too, and not half as vicious." Aydin stood and shoved both hands in his pocket. "He's not as strong as he used to be."

I couldn't believe he was balking at this. My freedom was at stake, and so was his. He knew how much it meant to me, how desperately I wanted, no, *needed* to be free. Had he been a slave so long that he couldn't tell the difference anymore? The Vyantara trusted him, allowed him to do whatever he liked, to go wherever he pleased, and his bond to his gargoyle had become more friendship than burden. Freedom didn't mean as much to him as it did to me. "Aydin, I'm begging for your help. Where else can I find a gargoyle to fight Shui?"

He paced from one end of the little room to the other, a disturbing resemblance to Gavin. Thank heavens they were nothing alike. Aydin massaged his chin while looking pensive. "Hundreds of gargoyles exist throughout the world, but the majority are kept on Mahdi Island. It's a deserted rock just off the coast of Yemen."

Yemen? In the Middle East? That was way too far away, but I still had to ask. "Can you find one for me there?"

"Possibly." He looked at me then, his gaze intense. "Only there isn't time."

I didn't understand.

"Your cycle completes in two days. I doubt Shui will be too cooperative after you managed to burn down his house and kill all his friends."

Shui couldn't hold me responsible for what had happened to the Fatherhouse, though I'd happily take credit. The destruction of the house and the evil it contained was a boon for all things good in this world. "That wasn't my fault."

"But it was your father's. Shui won't see the difference."

Knowing Shui, Aydin was right. "You can talk Shojin into fighting, can't you? He's a big, strong gargoyle, not a stocky monkey with wings like Shui. There's no contest.

And I bet Shojin would love to take a bite out of that ugly beast. Can you at least try?"

He gave me a sad smile and jerked a nod.

"Great!" My heart swelled with hope. "Where *is* Shojin?"

"The minute we heard about the Fatherhouse blowing up, I sent him to Quin's house to lay low."

"There's a gargoyle in my house?" Quin's voice sounded weak and froggy, but his British accent was crisp as ever.

As much as I would have liked to get up and give him a hug, my agonized ankle wouldn't let me. I was incredibly happy to see him alive and amazed that his resurrection was even possible. I felt very thankful he hadn't turned into a zombie. "Quin, I can't tell you how glad I am that you're back."

He turned his head to see me better. "No thanks to you."

Nothing like a grudge to kill the buzz of a welcome-back party. But I didn't blame him. I was surprised he'd even speak to me at all. "I'm really sorry about everything. If I'd known how far Gavin would go, I'd have lied to him much sooner."

Quin propped himself up on his elbows. "You summoned a fallen angel? And he's your dad? The Arelim told me all about it, but I still think it's nutters."

Though thrilled to have him back, I didn't like his tone. "You can't fault me for who my parents are. It's not like I was given a choice."

He winced while trying to sit up. Aydin rushed to help him, and Elmo gathered up more pillows to support his back. "I know what you mean," Quin said. "I wouldn't be what I am today without the help of my family's legacy. My gift isn't always well received and it can be troublesome." He frowned while glancing around the room, his lip drawn back from his teeth in distaste. "I never know where it will take me."

"So you're not mad?"

He tilted his head back and angled it side to side, the heel of his hand pushing his chin until his neck cracked. "Ah, better. Oh, I'm upset all right, but it's that awful Gavin character I'm mad at. You're right that I shouldn't blame you."

My shoulders slumped in relief, though I still felt guilty. If my lie to Gavin had come earlier, I could have saved him from enduring as much torture as he had. "Was it painful?"

He shook his head. "The Arelim put me in a trance. I felt nothing." But he did now. His tongue ran over his bottom lip and he grimaced. "I take it the ritual went well, then?"

I nodded. "Barachiel came through, and he was terrific. Protective. And fierce. He even blew up the Fatherhouse."

"Did he now?" Quin appeared mildly impressed, though he should have been astounded by my father's power. On second thought, I had my own reservations about the mysterious dark angel. Barachiel would have to do a lot more than stop time and destroy my enemy to earn my trust. Where was he now? He had some explaining to do.

Quin's face suddenly fell like a bad soufflé. "The hand."

Oh, no. Saint Geraldine's other hand, the one we'd found in Quin's workshop. I'd forgotten all about it.

"It's sitting on my workbench." He began to fidget,

then started rummaging through the sheets and blankets. "Where are my clothes? I've got to hurry home. If the Vyantara get hold of it—"

"Relax," Aydin said. "It's right here." He went to a wooden trunk in the corner and lifted the lid. Inside was the glass case containing the mummified hand.

Quin hissed out a relieved breath and sat back against the pillows again. "Thank you."

I turned an adoring gaze on Aydin and my heartbeat picked up speed. The man was a wonder. Embarrassed by my own thoughts, I blinked away all signs of admiration and said to Quin, "We hid it inside the basement wall right after we found it." Looking at Aydin, I asked, "You went back to get it?"

Aydin nodded. "I've been losing ground with the Vyantara for years. It was just a matter of time before someone figured out they had a traitor in their midst." He threw back a canvas tarp that I had assumed was Elmo's unique style of home decor. Beneath the heavy fabric were stacks of crates, boxes and trunks. They were the same ones that had been in the storage room inside Aydin's house. Settled on top was the small wooden cube that held—

"Ruby!"

The top of the box flipped up and the thimble-size frog hopped out. She leapt into my open hands and chirped.

"Blimey." Quin blinked. "Is it real?"

"She's not a toy." Aydin petted the bejeweled creature with his finger. "And she's taken quite a shine to Chalice."

The feeling was mutual.

"You take your personal possessions very seriously," I said to Aydin. "Does it all have as much sentimental value as our little friend?"

"You could say that." He replaced the tarp.

I glanced at Quin and did a double take. The bruises had lightened to a yellowish green and his split lips were already healed over. The scars looked good on him. It gave his handsome face more character.

"What else do you have stashed away, Quin?" I asked, having wondered that since the day we found Geraldine's hand. "Any more body parts?"

"No." He swung his legs over the side of the cot and leaned forward, forearms on his knees. "I'd like to find them, though. The legend of Saint Geraldine claims that once her head is reunited with her other parts, she'll become whole and live again."

"Do you believe that?" Aydin gazed at him intently.

Quin shifted his eyes with uncertainty. "As there's some truth to every lie, I believe there's validity behind every legend."

When Aydin didn't comment, Quin turned an expectant gaze on me.

"I think you're right." I thought about Geraldine's disembodied head, her loneliness and isolation inside an airlocked tomb in a church basement. I wanted the legend of reuniting her parts to be true. It was a travesty for her to remain a bodyless knight from the Crusades who talked to angels. She should live again as a whole person. No question about it. "If I told you we know where her head is——"

"Stop." Aydin stepped forward. "Don't tell him any more."

Quin's eyes brightened. "I already know. The Cathedral Basilica, right? It's here in Denver. The Arelim told me."

Aydin sat back down in the chair beside me. "How do we know we can trust you?"

"There's no reason you shouldn't." He sounded indignant. "You already know I talk to angels. The Arelim told me about Chalice, about the Order of the Hatchet. And I know Saint Geraldine was one of the first knights."

Aydin studied him, his gaze wary. He was very protective of Geraldine, and I assumed that to be true of all the knights in my order. *My order.* It felt wonderful to think that, even if I only said it to myself. My sister knights. My people.

"We should tell him everything." I looked hopefully at Aydin. "Think about it. We could use his help contacting the Arelim to locate the other Hatchet knights. After what he's just been through to protect the Arelim *and* the order, he deserves our trust."

Aydin closed his eyes, his expression stern but thoughtful.

I reached for his hand and curled my fingers around his. It didn't hurt that much. I'd grown used to his touch. "We have to do whatever we can for the order. And for Geraldine."

He sighed and nodded at Quin. "The Vyantara have had Geraldine's head since the day she was executed."

"My heart goes out to her." Quin's eyes filled with tears. "After all the years my ancestors have searched, their goal to bring her back to the world of the living, and she's been with the enemy all along?"

"Not *with* the enemy," I corrected. "*Owned* by them. She's not on their side, Quin. She'll speak to no one but her fellow knights."

"She's spoken to you?"

"Yes."

Aydin's eyes looked mournful when he said, "And to me."

Quin tilted his head to the side, squinting as if confused. "What do you mean by 'speak?' You're talking telepathically, right?"

"No, I'm saying she talks." I cleared my throat. "She may not have a body, but her head is just fine, and so is her tongue."

He gazed at me like I'd just sprouted a third eye. "Where, exactly, is her head being kept?"

"It's safely stored inside a hermetically sealed vault in the church's basement," Aydin said.

The Arelim had told Quin a lot, but he didn't know everything. It took us an hour to update him about Geraldine and her plan for the Hatchet knights, as well as my role in it. That is, if my humanity survived the gargoyle's curse. Staying human, especially now that Shui would no longer cooperate to keep me that way, would be a challenge. What we did in the next day or two would determine my future, or lack of it.

During our discussion, Quin looked appropriately amazed in all the right places and waved us on when we brought up anything he already knew, like how the Hatchet knights had come to be. He was better versed on the subject than I was, but the Fallen were as much a mystery to him as they were to Aydin and I. He assumed they stayed behind the black veil.

"I thought that, too," I told him. "And maybe some do. But Barachiel said he's from somewhere else."

"Where?" Quin asked.

I shrugged. "He didn't say. But he did tell me I'd see him again. That he would find me."

Aydin glanced at the clock on the wall above Quin's head. "It will be daylight soon and I want to get over to Quin's house and make sure Shojin's okay. He's homeless now."

I rolled my eyes.

Catching the look, Aydin quirked an eyebrow. "I'm concerned because I haven't sensed him since he left here. Quin, is there iron in your workshop?"

"Lots. I work with all metals."

"No wonder I can't sense him," Aydin said. "The iron is blocking me."

I remembered the jewelry we'd seen in Quin's workshop the night he was taken. "I saw your Celestine crystal pendants. You do beautiful work."

He offered me a half smile. "Thanks. I sell them on commission to New Age shops, and online through eBay. It's a hobby, but the crystals do help people stay in tune with their guardian angels."

Now I had to ask him something that had been bothering

me since the day Gavin told me about having his guardian angel murdered. "Quin, can you tell me if I have a guardian angel?"

He hesitated before saying, "I believe so, yes."

So weren't these angels supposed to *protect* people? I found that hard to believe after what happened to me when I was just a kid. I felt the hackles on my neck rise. Controlling the growl in my voice, I asked, "Then where the hell is he?"

Quin blinked, looking uncomfortable. "Chalice, I don't have all the answers. I'd tell you if I knew, but I don't."

"And as long as you're bonded to Shui, no angel will come near you, at least none of the Arelim," Aydin added. "We've been through this. What's important now is that we focus on breaking your bond with Shui. We still have a couple of days, so let's use that time to come up with a plan." He yawned loudly. "I don't know about you two, but I can't concentrate if I don't get some sleep."

I glanced around the little room that wasn't much bigger than a walk-in closet. "There's hardly enough space here for one of us to take a nap let alone three."

Elmo waddled in from the coffee shop's kitchen. "There's an entire house above us with plenty of room."

"Great idea, Elmo, thanks." Aydin clapped the little man on the shoulder. "Lead the way."

It wasn't a large house, but there were three tiny bedrooms and a big old-fashioned sofa in the living room. Aydin opted for the sofa so that he could keep one eye open for any Vyantara who had survived the explosion. There had been so much magic in that place, and a number of portals leading to who knew where, that I guessed more than a few had escaped. How easily they could return from where they'd vanished was anyone's guess, but we didn't dare let our guard down. Especially when it came to Shui, who would be gunning for me the moment he found out where I was.

I tried not to let that scare me. I'd had run-ins with Shui before, and if not for Gavin's intervention, I'd be dead. Things were different now. I was different, stronger, more confident. Best of all, I had Gavin's stone knife, which seemed to have a powerful effect on the gargoyle. But my biggest advantage was knowing how to kill Shui.

There were iron bars on all the windows of Elmo's house. The iron would help keep out any unwanted fey or demon influences, and according to Aydin, the metal blocked telepathy, as well. So any mind readers out there were out of luck.

After Quin and Elmo disappeared behind the doors of two of the three bedrooms, Aydin and I sat together on the sofa to talk about Geraldine. "Do you trust Quin?" I asked him.

Looking unsure, he said, "Yes, and no. I don't think he'd do anything to intentionally harm her, but I can't ignore the chance he might hurt her by accident."

"I understand." Perhaps I'd underestimated how important she was to him. "You still love her, don't you?"

He looked surprised, then chuckled. "You mean romantically? Of course not."

"But you told me you'd fallen in love with her."

"That was nine hundred years ago, Chalice." He leaned back on the sofa and lifted his legs to rest his heels on an early twentieth-century coffee table. The entire house looked as if stuck in a time warp from that era, but it felt comfortable, too. Normal, like a real home.

"For one thing," Aydin said, "Geraldine never loved me back. I'd mistaken admiration and awe for love when it had only been infatuation. I was young and foolish, and the object of a fallen angel's bad joke. I've since learned to deal with my curse, and I've matured enough to know the difference between real love and a crush."

"Have you ever been in love?" I wanted to grab those words as they left my mouth, but it was too late. I'd said it, and I couldn't take it back.

Aydin smiled while giving me an appraising look. His Asian eyes crinkled with amusement. "As a matter of fact, I have."

My mouth went dry and my heart tripped over itself as I hoped it was me he loved. I loved him, or at least I thought I did. Unfortunately, this damn curse kept getting in my way of believing it.

I studied his face, seeing his gentle eyes trained on me as if reading pages in a book. He knew how I felt. He knew everything about me and instead of being annoyed at having my privacy invaded, it turned me on. I had no need for inhibitions around Aydin. It was okay for me to be myself, but I wasn't used to that kind of freedom. What if it backfired?

An awkward silence fell between us so I stood up to leave. "I'll let you get some sleep."

Eyes still focused on my face, he moved both his legs from the coffee table to the couch, then settled his head back against a stack of lacy throw pillows. He winked at me. "Sweet dreams, Chalice."

sixteen

WE SLEPT HALF THE DAY AND WAITED UNTIL
dark before going to Quin's house. We piled into Elmo's
ancient Studebaker that was in surprisingly good condition,
though it took a few tries getting it started. Aydin said Elmo
never drove it because his feet couldn't reach the pedals, but
Aydin would take it out for a spin every few weeks to keep
the battery charged. Maybe Elmo had only bought the car
because it made him feel like an American. Like a human.

There were no lights on in Quin's house when we arrived, which wasn't surprising. While still parked in the
driveway, I removed my nose filters and my earplugs to
scope things out. I didn't smell any intruders, and I especially couldn't smell any gargoyles. That was a bad sign.

"He's not here," I told Aydin. "I know what Shojin smells
like and there's no scent even similar to his."

He looked concerned when he asked, "What *do* you smell?"

"The exact same odors as last week." I inhaled the brisk autumn air and shook my head. "All that's missing is the smell of blood." Which I considered a *good* thing. "I might find more odors once we're inside."

Quin unlocked the front door and the three of us entered the house. It didn't take sensitive eyes to notice the house had been ransacked. Furniture was broken, the stuffing torn from cushions, books were scattered across the floor with the pages ripped out, drawers were upended and their contents strewn from one end of the living room to the other. It was the same in other parts of the house, as well.

Aydin looked at me expectantly and I shook my head.

He and Quin rushed to the staircase leading down to the basement workshop. I could smell Shojin now, but very faintly. It was the residual scent of wet fur and feathers.

The workshop was in just as bad a shape. Tools littered the concrete floor, and chunks of drywall were ripped away as if someone had searched for something in the walls. All the drawers in Quin's workbench were missing.

"What did you have in them?" I asked.

"Crystals, a few angel charms, incense, a bunch of dried herbs. Nothing of any real value. The Aztec scrying mirror was the only artifact I'd kept in there." He pointed at a hole in the wall. "Is that where you hid Saint Geraldine's hand?"

Aydin nodded. "Gavin must have sensed its presence, probably by using a dowsing spell." Seeing loose feathers on the floor beside the workbench, he knelt to pick one up. "Shojin *was* here."

I found an envelope on the worktable with Aydin's name scribbled on the front. I recognized the handwriting. Shit! Gavin had survived after all. My heart racing and my mouth desert dry, I handed Aydin the letter. "Gavin left you something."

Scowling, he took the envelope from me and ripped it open. I watched his expression change from interest to anger in a matter of seconds. His chest heaved with each breath and his hands began to shake. He tossed the note aside and ran his fingers through his hair while throwing back his head to stare at the ceiling. "Not now. This can't be happening *now!*"

An airline ticket stuck out of the envelope and I slipped it free. A one-way flight to Quebec scheduled to leave tonight. I peered at Aydin, whose eyes were unfocused as if in a trance. "What does it mean?" I asked.

"It means Gavin took Shojin." He turned away from me and kicked a box filled with odd pieces of iron cookware. It slid across the floor to crash against the wall, the clang of metal echoing against the basement walls before trailing into silence.

"I still don't get what the ticket has to do with—"

He grabbed the ticket from my hands and shook it at me. "It means I have to leave. Now. Tonight."

Of course. Without Shojin, he would succumb to the curse and transform. I wondered if Shui was there with Gavin, but I didn't think so. I may not be able to communicate with him telepathically, but I sensed his nearness. Shui was still here in Denver.

I picked up the letter Gavin had left and began to read.

Aydin, my old friend—

I may as well forego any pleasantries and cut to the chase. I realize now that your loyalties lay elsewhere, therefore I'm giving you the opportunity to make a choice. Chalice's dark angel destroyed what was home to a dozen Vyantara members, including you and your gargoyle, so those of us who survived the conflagration are moving to the Fatherhouse in Canada. It took forceful persuasion to encourage Shojin to join us, and it is now up to you to make sure your bond with him remains intact.

I believe your latest cycle concludes early tomorrow morning. Therefore, this plane ticket will guarantee your reunion with Shojin in plenty of time.

I know Chalice is with you. She has proven to be a disappointment, but I will miss her company, as well as her impressive skills. Be assured that her future life as a gargoyle is imminent, and I have already arranged her bonding with a necromancing witch who's in need of some extra motivation. I have no doubt the new Chalice, whom we will rename Sha'ling, is just what our recruit needs.

I look forward to seeing you soon.

Sincerely, Gavin Heinrich

P.S. Chalice, if you're reading this, be aware that the

knife you stole from me won't stop the inevitable. Your fate is sealed.

Sha'ling, huh? Gavin was renaming me before I even had a chance to sprout wings and claws. His confidence was premature. My fate sealed? Like hell it was.

I fumed over his letter as we drove to the airport. We had Quin take the Studebaker back to Elmo's after rethinking our original idea that it was safe for him to return home. Then we took his Acura. There was no time for Aydin to pack a bag, though he didn't intend to stay in Canada long enough to need one. Once he got what he needed from Shojin, he and his gargoyle would vanish to somewhere not even Gavin could find. But I didn't want him going too far. I needed Aydin to come back to me.

"I wish I could, Chalice," he said, after parking the car in the airport parking garage. "But the first place Gavin looked would be wherever you are."

I closed my eyes to calm myself. A variety of scenarios went flying through my head as I considered what I was up against. Shui was out for blood and in the end, it would be either him or me. I touched the stone knife inside my jacket's inner pocket and believed I could use it to control Shui. I'd not allow my body to change into a hideous monster just for the Vyantara to use however they liked. If it came to a choice, I'd die before letting things get that far.

"You're sure about this knife?" Aydin asked, not sounding sure himself.

"Since I don't have another gargoyle to do the deed, it's a chance I have to take."

"Gavin is set on you going through the change. That means he'll do what he can to keep Shui away from you."

And Gavin knew Shui would kill me if given the chance. If Gavin had his way, he'd capture me, then torture me into making the change. Shui, on the other hand, was ready for a fight. And so was I.

"Gavin can't control him anymore, so Shui can do whatever the hell he wants. I'm counting on it."

"If Shui can't find you, he can't touch you." Aydin's chest heaved with an exaggerated sigh. I understood he worried, and I appreciated that he cared, but he had to realize how determined I was to put an end to this curse. I'd do anything to be free. Anything.

"There's only one way to let Shui know where you are," he said. "Have you tried contacting him with your mind?"

I shuddered. "Not yet."

"Then you better start practicing." He slid out of the driver's seat and held the door open for me to take his place behind the wheel.

I stood beside Aydin in front of the open car door, my heart aching as I thought about how much I'd miss him. He had been my mentor, my savior, my friend. And to be honest, I wished he'd been even more.

He lifted his hand to smooth back a tangle of shaggy hair from my face. My spiky haircut was at that bottle-brush stage, the ends dry, the roots greasy. If only I had inherited my father's perfect hair.

Self-conscious, I yanked my head back from his touch. It wasn't a rebuff, but the wounded look in his eyes said he took it that way. I grabbed his hand and held it firmly in my own. Smiling, I told him, "Don't stay away from me too long, okay?"

He gave my fingers a squeeze, but the smile he returned was melancholy. "You're breaking my heart, you know that?"

"Mine is already broken." I brought his hand to my cheek. "Believe in me?"

He frowned. "Of course I believe in you."

"Then stop worrying." I pressed a light kiss to his palm. "Just knowing we'll be together again gives me incentive to survive, and to survive as a human."

"You're making it very hard for me to go."

I gently dropped his hand and took a step back. "You have to. It's the only way for you to stay human." And I wanted nothing more than for both of us to remain human *together.*

His smile broadened as he reached for me. I let him take me by the waist and pull me into him, his rock-hard chest pressing against my breasts.

He held my gaze, his pupils expanding like tiny balloons. I recalled how I'd felt when his ghostly body merged with me, his mind sharing my thoughts as his essence filtered through my blood and bones. I wanted that again, but now was neither the time nor the place for intimacy. We'd have to wait. And it gave me something to look forward to.

One hand at the back of my head, he held me while slowly touching his lips to mine.

I inhaled a shaky breath just before our mouths touched. It stung at first, but then our lips seemed to melt together, warm and soft and natural. It was a sweet kiss with just a hint of passion underneath. A promise for the future.

I leaned back to study his face. "Do you think Geraldine will be okay about us?"

He held my chin and ran his thumb lightly over my bottom lip. "She'll be fine. She wants what's good for me, and I want the same for her."

My voice breathy from the adrenaline surge Aydin's kiss had caused, I said, "Speaking of what's good for Geraldine, I plan to steal her head from the cathedral vault. We have one of her hands and I know where to get the other one. Once we find her feet, we can bring her back."

Still holding me, Aydin nodded and his eyes brightened with hope.

I hugged him, resting the side of my head against his shoulder. He held me closer, sighing into my ear, his moist breath like a kiss of warm air. It would be harder than ever to see him go now. Within a few short minutes we had moved from close friends with a sexual attraction to something deeper, just as I'd hoped we would. It was too good to be true.

He eased away from me and headed for the double glass doors leading to the elevators inside the airport. Once halfway across the parking lot, he turned to face me and walked backward while waving goodbye. I waved back, my heart growing tight, the first stage of yearning taking hold. The sensation was bittersweet; I felt happy that he cared, yet sad he had to leave.

"Goodbye, Aydin," I whispered, knowing he couldn't hear me. "I…" But I couldn't say the rest. It hurt too much.

I turned off the I-70 and was heading for downtown Denver when I decided to drive past the ruins of the Father-house. According to news reports, very little of the building had survived the blast and the fire. The fire marshal reported it an accident, saying a source of natural gas had ignited and literally blew the top off the house. The building used an energy efficient wood-and-coal burning furnace, so there was no gas line. The source of the gas remained a mystery.

How Barachiel had managed to drum up a gas explosion without gas had me curious, but I strongly believed the buildup of power created by the Vyantara's collection was the cause. Looking at it that way, it was apparent they'd blown up their own Fatherhouse. How ironic.

As I drove past, I saw the remnants of display cases and storage cabinets, and I knew some of the collection must have survived. Too bad. I made a mental note to return later and retrieve what I could.

I didn't stop the car, but inched along the curb. A couple of the stone gargoyles had fallen from the roof and shattered on the ground. A head here, a wing there…but what caught my eye was the color of the stone. I stopped the car and picked up some of the broken chunks. They were marbled purple and red with thin veins of black running through them, just like the stone knife I'd taken from Gavin.

Now it made sense. Gavin's knife had been created out of the body of a dead gargoyle after it had turned to stone. That's why Shui was afraid of it. Using the knife to kill a gargoyle would be the same as one gargoyle killing another.

I imagined there were precious few of these blades in existence because such weapons would make it too easy to eliminate the winged beasts. If the Hatchet knights were armed with knives made of gargoyle stone, a fatal attack by a gargoyle assassin might not be so fatal. The women would at least have a fighting chance. I just prayed Gavin and his Vyantara pals would never find the knights to begin with.

My gaze wandered back to the ruins, to within the shadows of broken brick walls and shattered concrete. The ghosts hadn't left the premises. In fact, at least one new one had been added. I quickly recognized the hippo outline of my not-so-dear friend, Zee. That meant she hadn't made it out in time, and I wasn't heartbroken about it, either. Her shade peered at me through ebony holes that used to be her eyes, her vaporous visage morphing into pure fury. Oh, dear. She was seriously pissed.

Walking into the ruins, I navigated through a sea of bricks, boards and broken furniture, just to get to the stone gargoyles.

Vaporous shapes tried to impede my progress. One in particular leapt in front of me, even on top of me, in an effort to make me stop. It was Zee, of course, and I ignored her. She was a newly made ghost and therefore too weak to do any harm.

I gathered chunks of stone from the broken gargoyles, the edges so sharp that one of them sliced through my winter gloves and cut my palm. Blood flowed, though not very much, and within seconds the piece of rock crumbled to dust. That was strange. I hadn't squeezed the rock hard enough to break it, and it had been firm as a chunk of iron. If that's what blood did to these rocks, I'd have to be careful not to cut myself again or I could lose my entire collection.

I loaded my cache of gargoyle stones in the car's trunk, then slid behind the wheel. Zee's specter flew toward the car like a demon possessed, as she likely was, and I stomped on the gas pedal. Gazing in the rearview mirror, I caught sight of her hulking form as it levitated to the middle of the street, her attention focused on me. I cringed as the car behind me drove straight through her. The mist of her ghost-body dispersed, then simply gathered back into its original shape.

I doubted she'd follow me since ghosts are pretty much attached to either their murderers, or to the locations of their deaths. Even so, I drove up and down random side streets, continually checking the rear and side mirrors to be sure her reflection wasn't staring back. After a half hour, I blew out a relieved breath and headed to Elmo's.

Excited over my revelation about Gavin's knife, I couldn't wait to tell Quin and Elmo. When I did, it surprised me that neither of them was as enthusiastic as I was.

"You're sure this will work?" Quin asked. Elmo hung behind him with a sick look on his face.

"Sure I'm sure."

"So when will this battle to the death take place?"

I checked the clock hanging on Elmo's shop-kitchen wall. "In two or three hours. It's best that it happen before sunrise. I imagine the noise will attract the cops, so it has to be done quickly while the neighborhood is still asleep."

Quin raised his eyebrows. "Exactly *where* are you planning to do away with the unwary beast?"

"I'm so glad you asked." I peeked into the room full of fey, who cheerfully swigged and sipped their fancy coffee drinks. The usual rock music rumbled through speakers set high on the wall, and none of Elmo's customers appeared the least bit interested in our conversation. I still kept my voice low to avoid questioning stares. "The Cathedral Basilica."

"Isn't that where Geraldine's tomb is?" Quin asked.

I nodded. "Which brings me to our other order of business. We need to get her out of there."

Both Quin and Elmo looked uncomfortable. "Do you realize her head has been in that vault since the late 1800s?" Elmo asked.

"So?"

"So moving it could be tricky." Looking thoughtful, he laid a finger alongside his nose and frowned. "The security is really tight. I remember Aydin telling me about someone trying to steal Geraldine thirty years ago. That's when Gavin changed the vault door from the old Diebold crane hinge that banks used in the early twentieth century. The lock is digital now."

Aydin never told me about that. "Who was the thief?"

"One of the Hatchet knights." Elmo cleared his throat and shifted from one foot to the other. "It was your mother."

My stomach dropped so far I thought I'd have to pick it up off the floor. "My mother tried to steal Geraldine's head?"

Elmo nodded. "She would have gotten away with it, too, if she'd had help. But she was alone, and though she had no problem unlocking the vault door, she wasn't strong enough to pull it open. It weighed close to two tons. The alarm sounded and she had to run off to avoid getting caught."

My breathing picked up speed. Taking over where my mother had left off would be a thrill, not to mention a tribute to her memory. Cracking this vault should be a piece of cake. Not only would I have help because Quin would be with me, I also had experience with the type of digital lock Gavin had installed. I'd heard the series of beeps when he keyed in the combination and I could duplicate it just like I'd done dozens of times with similar locks. It was getting away with Geraldine's head safely intact that had me worried.

"I'm in," Quin said, his eyes overly bright. "If you can open the vault door, we can get Geraldine to safety."

"How?" I asked.

"Through the veil."

"The silver veil? But humans can't pass through any of

the veils." Goose bumps trotted up and down my arms because I knew I *could* pass through once I was curse-free.

"Geraldine is special. The Arelim would allow her passage."

And me, too. But not as a gargoyle. And not while I was still bonded to one.

"Quin, can you put together a container to hold Geraldine so that she isn't damaged when we take her from the vault?"

He looked at Elmo, who said, "I have all sizes of boxes and packing material in my storage room. Take anything you want."

"Just point me in the right direction."

Elmo gestured toward a doorway carved in the earthen wall.

Once Quin left us, Elmo motioned me to a table and asked if he could get me anything.

"I'll have one of those caramel macchiatos that Aydin likes so much."

The old elf nodded, then cocked his head to the side and studied me. "You miss him already, don't you?"

I closed my eyes and jerked a nod.

"Me, too."

Elmo left for his kitchen, returning a few minutes later with my coffee, as well as one for himself. He slid into the seat beside me, his feet barely touching the floor despite the short stool he sat on. "Is Aydin coming back?" His small, close-set eyes gazed at me in earnest.

"He will as soon as he can." I took a sip of my coffee.

Delicious. I suddenly realized this would be my last cup of coffee as a bonded slave. Or as a human. I preferred believing the former.

Elmo tilted the small cup to his lips and blew air across the steaming surface, though he didn't act interested in drinking it. He must be sick of the stuff after serving it every day for who knew how many years. I wondered just how long it had been. So I asked.

"Fifteen years now." He set his cup down and laced his short sausage fingers together while squinting in thought.

"I'm amazed Aydin has been able to keep you and your shop a secret all these years."

"He's been a good friend." Elmo's eyes had a wistful look as he stared into the distance. "We've helped each other a lot. We make a good team."

"I bet you do." Elmo's Coffee Shop had been Aydin's port in the storm, and now it was mine. And Quin's. "I'd like to know more about the fey. And about white magic. Would you teach me?"

His grin split his face from ear to ear, his cheeks bulging like two ripe plums when he smiled. He was an attractive old elf. More on the ancient side, but still handsome.

"I can start by helping you learn how to use Aydin's collection of charms," he said.

"Charms?" I had no idea what he meant. "What charms?"

"You've already met one of them. You're okay with Ruby, right?"

I liked the little frog, but she wasn't a charmed object. "Yeah. So?"

"What do you think are stored in all those boxes you saw in my back room?" He pulled a pendant out from under the collar of his shirt. It was a rose crystal tied with a leather thong and several tiny sparrow feathers. It looked Native American. "Aydin gave it to me. It deflects prying spells like the kind witches and sorcerers cast to spy on people. I just have to be careful not to get too close to iron or the charm's energy will weaken."

Now I knew the contents of those boxes from Aydin's storage room. He must have pilfered a number of charms over the course of his thieving career and the Vyantara didn't have a clue. He probably planned to distribute them among the Hatchet knights, which is why he'd seemed so uncomfortable about me staying in that room. He knew how I felt about magic. Yet he'd still taken the time to explain how charms could help protect my sister knights. I wanted to learn anything Elmo could teach me.

A breathless Quin emerged through the kitchen. "I'm ready." He held up a bowling bag.

"I forgot that was back there," Elmo said.

"Do you mind?" Quin asked.

"Not at all."

Quin held a red bowling bag emblazoned with a logo that looked like a flaming angel and said Heaven's Warriors.

"You bowl?" I asked Elmo.

"It's not mine. It belonged to Aydin when he played on a team. He was quite the bowler in the fifties."

That man was full of surprises. "It looks flimsy to me."

Quin opened the bag for me to see inside. "I put a couple layers of padding along the sides. It makes a nice cushion in case the bag gets banged around."

"Good job. I think we have everything we need." My pulse quickened and the coffee I'd just swallowed churned in the pit of my stomach. "Is there room to fit the hand in there, too? Might as well keep her parts together."

"There's room," Quin said.

Elmo tucked his pendant back in his shirt. "I bet a charm or two in Aydin's collection could protect you during your battle with the gargoyle."

"Thanks anyway, Elmo, but even if there were, I'm immune. It wouldn't help me."

I didn't make a big deal out of saying goodbye to Elmo. Though there was a chance I'd never see him again, I considered it a slight one. I wanted to believe the odds were mostly in my favor.

seventeen

ARMED WITH NOTHING BUT A KNIFE MADE
from the stone body of a dead gargoyle, Quin and I took
the bowling bag with Geraldine's severed hand and drove
his car the few blocks to the cathedral. We had at least two
hours until daybreak, and the streets were as quiet as a ghost
town. I'd removed my contacts and my nose filters so that
my raw senses could warn me of possible danger. So far, I
saw nothing more unusual than a handful of ghosts lurking
in the shadows around houses in the neighborhood. I made
a point of looking for Zee, but there was no sign of her.

Quin and I didn't talk along the way. I was too focused
on sending a mental message to Shui. Though it turned my
stomach, I had to let him know where I was so that he'd
come to me. I couldn't tell if my attempts were successful
or not, and if they were, he didn't respond.

I sensed he was close, but no one else was. Not even the homeless were out and about on these dark, abandoned streets, not that I expected to see any. It was freezing out, too cold even to snow. I gazed up at a black velvet sky studded with stars, the lack of cloud cover bringing temperatures below the teens.

We parked the car on the street near the church. I picked the cathedral's lock as I had the first time I'd broken in. The janitor must have used an extra-strong cleaning solution on the floors because the smell of ammonia wiped out every other scent inside the church. That and the wood polish used to clean the pews. We kept the lights off until we reached the basement, and then I let Quin flip on the low-watt hallway light so that he could see.

When we arrived at the tapestry that covered the vault door, I removed one earplug and pressed that side of my head to the electronic keypad. I closed my eyes, trying to remember the sequence of beeps I'd heard while listening to Gavin key in the combination.

Panic edged Quin's voice when he said, "It's not opening."

"Hush." I refocused, feeling the vibrations in my fingertips when I touched the keypad, each tone syncing with the next. After just one try, the air lock released and the door's seal popped free.

"Quin, before we go in, I need to warn you about a couple things." I described the condition of Geraldine, letting him know it might be more illusion than reality. I guessed it was her method for self-preservation; as long as she appeared dead, the Vyantara left her alone. "I don't know if she'll talk to you."

"Why not?"

"She won't talk to just anyone."

"I'm not just anyone. I talk to angels just like she does. And besides, she spoke to Aydin."

Did I hear a note of jealousy in his voice? "Only because they've known each other for more than nine centuries. That breeds a certain kind of familiarity, don't you think?"

"I suppose." He straightened his spine, pulling at the collar of his sweater and smoothing the sleeves of his suede jacket. "Do I look all right?"

I peered at the scars on his face, which had faded to almost nothing. I gave him a sniff. He smelled like coffee. "You're fine."

"It isn't every day you get to meet a live saint from medieval times."

"Technically, she's not a saint." And the *live* part was debatable.

He frowned and pushed his glasses higher up the bridge of his nose. "I suppose you're right." He looked wistful when he said, "She's like me, Chalice. She talks to angels the same as I do. I've never known anyone else who could do that."

"Don't tell me you've never met other psychics."

"Sure I have, but none of the ones I know can channel angels." The corners of his mouth turned down when he said, "It's a special gift that can get you into trouble if you're not careful."

He was living proof of that. Or I should say re-living proof. And so was Geraldine.

He held the door open for me and I preceded him into the tomb. Her silver aura appeared unchanged, but her mummified skin remained dry and sunken like a nine-hundred-year-old corpse.

I glanced at Quin, whose upper lip curled in disgust.

"Stop it. You'll hurt her feelings."

Scowling, he looked from me to Geraldine and back again. "There's no way this thing is alive."

"She's not a thing!" I watched her for a minute longer, but there was no change. I wondered why. Didn't she trust Quin? Was she okay? Well, she obviously wasn't okay, but had something happened to make her worse? I waited for a warning about my impending fight with Shui. Nothing. Why wouldn't she speak to me?

"We can't wait any longer." I listened for an alarm, but there was none. No one but Elmo knew we were here. Gavin was in Canada, so was Aydin, and Zee was dead. Perhaps some members of the Vyantara had stayed behind, but that was doubtful.

I sniffed the air for signs of Shui, but I didn't detect his unique gorge-rising stench. There were no smells at all in-side the tomb. And no sounds. I felt a twinge of wrongness grab the base of my spine.

"Get her into the bag. Hurry!"

Quin slid on a pair of latex gloves and gently lifted the mummified head from the table. He slipped it in the bag and zipped it closed.

"Stay here," I told him, and crept to the open door. That's when I smelled him.

"I knew I'd find you here." Gavin's voice had never sounded so cold.

I practically choked the second I saw him, but struggled to keep my cool. Reaching inside for my anger, I let it coat me from head to toe in an effort to hide the truth from Gavin. He didn't know Quin was inside the tomb and I was desperate to keep it that way.

My knees wobbly as a newborn colt, I sauntered out of the vault and pushed the door shut behind me. I watched Gavin's face for a change in expression. There was none. He looked as bland as ever.

"What are you doing here?" I asked.

That made him smile. "As if you didn't know."

Okay, so we were just filling space with meaningless words. I stalled for time as my mind buzzed like crazy, my mental wheels spinning on a plan. Any plan. Something. But I came up empty.

"Where's Shui?"

He shrugged. "I haven't a clue. He flew off after the explosion and I haven't seen him since."

There weren't many places a gargoyle could hide, unless he camouflaged himself among the statues on any number of historical buildings downtown. Denver's older architecture was known for its ornamental statuary. Shui would blend right in.

"I thought you were in Canada."

"I had a few things to wrap up here first." His crooked

smile was snide as ever and I wanted to smack it off his face. "One of which is to collect Geraldine and take her to the Fatherhouse in Quebec. There's a lovely old cathedral in town that I think she'll be fond of."

I stepped aside to give him access to the vault. "Be my guest."

His smile faltered. He suspected something was up, but not what. I didn't dare hope he'd be stupid enough to walk past me without expecting a knife in his back.

He suddenly crouched and looked up at the ceiling, bowing his head and throwing up his arms as if to ward something off. I reacted as well, though I hadn't seen anything. My first thought was that Shui must have responded to my telepathic call and was swooping in for the kill.

When I shifted my attention away from Gavin, he rushed in and grabbed me from behind, pinning my arms so tight that an ounce more stress on my bones would surely break them. He was damn strong for an old man. A hell of a lot stronger than me. I kicked backward and he squeezed me tighter, forcing my shoulders back so far that I thought the bones would pop from their sockets.

He pressed his face against my cheek, his lips touching my ear. I felt drops of spittle fleck my skin when he breathed. "Hold still or I'll break both your arms."

"Not if I break yours first."

He chuckled. "Such a dreamer. As always, your reach exceeds your grasp." He grabbed both my wrists in one powerful hand while using the other to search inside my coat. I knew what he was looking for, and a sick, lost feeling filled me from the toes up. If he took the knife away, my chance at freedom was lost.

His hand slid up my rib cage and over my breasts, making me gasp. He'd done some horrible things to me in the past, but never had he molested me sexually. I'd let him do it now if it would distract him from what he was really after. His hand changed direction to feel the lining of my coat, searching for an inside pocket. When he found the knife, he yanked it free and pushed me away.

I fell to the floor, both my arms aching, but I could still move my fingers so I knew they weren't broken. I jumped to my feet and Gavin brandished the knife, waving it within an inch of my face. I automatically reached behind my head to grab my Balisong, but the sheath was empty. Zee had liberated me of my blade several days ago. I was helpless.

"It's such a fine piece of craftsmanship," he said, tilting the knife and swiping it slowly through the air as if wielding a sword ten times its size. "I can understand why you wanted it so badly. I think you know why I had to take it back."

"That's why Shui left you." My heart beat so hard and fast I heard it echo inside my head. But adrenaline kept me alert, and it also sparked a few extra brain cells as new understanding clicked into place. "He left because you lost the means to control him."

Gavin poked the blade at me and jutted his chin toward the stairs. "But I'm in control now. Let's go on upstairs, shall we? There's more room up there to…move around."

I had to stall him, distract him. I'd lost the knife, but if

I made it to the back door, I could run to Quin's car and grab the gargoyle stones from the trunk. One shard would be enough to create a knife of my own.

"Wait," I said, walking backward down the hall and away from the stairs. "I need to ask you something."

He looked down his nose at me. "There's no time. We have a dinner reservation and we can't be late."

I licked my dry lips, knowing exactly whom that reservation was with. I also knew what was on the menu. Me. "Before I die, the least you can do is tell me about my mother."

Following me down the hall, he stopped waving the knife and pierced me with a grave stare. "Felicia is dead and gone. She no longer matters."

My cheeks burned with anger, but I was determined to keep it together. "Tell me why you killed her."

"You know very well why. She had what I wanted. She had *you* in her belly."

A chill ran through me as I considered my next question. "But why was she here in Denver?" I was almost to the end of the hall now, my back facing the door. "I know she tried to steal Saint Geraldine from the vault."

He stopped dead, his pallid skin going one shade lighter. "Who told you?"

"Does it matter?" I swallowed, fearful of the answer to my next question, but the mystery of my mother had to end. No more secrets. "You brought her here to see Geraldine. You wanted my mother to help you find the

Hatchet knights. What I don't understand is how you found her to begin with."

Gavin grinned, his thin lips stretching over teeth gritted shut. "I didn't find her." He grabbed me by the throat and shoved me hard against the door that rattled on its hinges from the impact. "She found me. And her attempt to kill me failed."

I struggled to breathe as his hand tightened around my windpipe. His skin was rough, the multitude of scars on his palms and fingers digging into my flesh. The healed sigils that branded his will with the dark side burned me like fire.

I aimed a kick at his groin and missed. The knife was only inches from my heart, but I'd rather he stab me than slowly strangle me to death. Gavin got off on torture, the slower the better. I wouldn't give him the satisfaction of prolonging my death for his own entertainment.

He yanked me away from the door and flung me down the hall toward the stairs. I tripped and fell, landing hard on my knees.

"Get up. And get moving."

I did get up, but I didn't *give* up. I gagged for breath as I staggered down the hall, my mind racing. I had to get my hands on those stones.

He planted his booted foot in the small of my back and pushed. I lurched forward, then spun around to make a run for the back door again. But Gavin knew me too well.

He stood in my path, fingers splayed, a green ball of energy gathering between them. He balanced it in the palm of his hand. "Remember your friend the monk, and how he died?"

How could I forget? He held in his hand that same energy that had sucked the air from Brother Thomas's lungs, stunning him so that Gavin could shoot a bullet through his head. I wasn't fated to meet the same end. I still had too much left to do. So I turned around and obediently trudged toward the stairs.

"That's a good girl." His footsteps tapped loudly on the linoleum floor behind me. "Your mother tried to steal from me, Chalice. It was only fair that I steal something from her. Too bad she got away from me, but I still won. You were quite a prize."

Owning me was his revenge against my mother? "How did you know she was a knight?"

"Like I told you many times. You have your mother's eyes."

I led the way upstairs and tried to figure out how I could gain myself a few extra minutes, but a few minutes wouldn't be good enough. I wanted it all. For a chance to win *my* prize, my freedom, I'd have to play Gavin's game.

Shui hadn't come to me when I called because I'd had Gavin's knife, and he knew I would use it on him without hesitation. He was a ferocious creature, but also a coward. He might not even bother to show up, forcing me to turn into a winged devil just like him. Except that now Gavin had the knife, and Shui would surely heed the word of his master. My fate was in Gavin's hands.

I walked down the red-carpeted aisle between the pews and stopped at the altar.

"That's far enough." Gavin lifted his wrist to let light from the full moon illuminate his watch. "He should be here any minute."

"And then what?"

He grinned. "And then I'll let him have you."

My heart leapt into my throat. "What about your plans for the new me? I believe my new name is to be Sha'ling."

"You belong to Shui now." Gavin gave me a pitying look. "He's been a good and loyal servant for years, and he deserves his reward." He turned the beautiful knife in his hands and its surface reflected red-and-purple light from the full moon's glow through the church windows. "His mouth has been watering for a taste of you for a long time. It's only fitting that I let him dine on his bonded human."

I inhaled deeply, rooting for Shui's scent. The overpowering odors of polish and disinfectant were all I could smell.

"In anticipation of your screams, I cast a soundproofing spell on the church. You could light a stick of dynamite in here and no one would hear the explosion." His eyes danced with menace. The man really was insane. "This will be a private dinner party, yes? We don't want the police interrupting Shui while he's feeding. It could get ugly."

I glanced at the windows set high into the cathedral's vaulted ceiling. Something far larger than a bat flew this way. I jerked my gaze back to Gavin, who continued admiring the knife. "It wasn't made in the mortal realm, you know. Nothing so perfect could come from such a benign plane as this one."

"Where did you get it?" I cast another furtive look at the sky. The winged creature circled, waiting, thinking.

"From hell." He swiped the blade through the air again. "I don't know how old it is, but it's the only one of its kind. And it belongs to me."

I needed more time. "I saw Zee's ghost. Too bad she didn't survive the blast."

The skin around Gavin's eyes tightened. "And you're wondering how I did, is that it?"

I said nothing.

"The paintings in the first room you were assigned weren't the only portals in the house." He winked at me, as if sharing a secret. His voice lowered to a conspiratorial whisper. "Poor Zee was too big to fit through."

I threw another quick glance up at the window.

Gavin huffed. "How typical. You're about to lose your life and you have the audacity to roll your eyes at me? Why am I not surprised?"

The words had barely left his lips when a huge crash sounded from above, the stained-glass window exploding to rain shards of color over our heads. I ducked beneath the altar and Gavin scrambled for shelter beside a huge statue of the Virgin Mary. Shui flew around the ceiling, his extended bat wings almost too large to flap effectively inside the church. So he glided in graceful circles, around and around, like he had all the time in the world.

Gavin slithered out of hiding to stand out in the open.

"I've missed you, Shui," he called to his winged monkey. Sweeping an arm out at me, he added, "Look what I brought you."

Like he was the one responsible for bringing me here? Shui wasn't that stupid. And just to prove how stupid he wasn't, he swooped down, heading straight for Gavin.

Gavin didn't have time to hide again. He held up the knife in a threatening manner, and I assumed the blade is what got Shui to target him in the first place. From the look of hatred on the gargoyle's face, he was finished taking orders. He was done slaving for Gavin. He'd become a rogue gargoyle on a murderous mission.

Shui's talons gripped Gavin's wrist before he could wield the knife. Wings flapping to stay aloft, Shui clung to Gavin so tight that the man screamed in agony. After a few more seconds the hand holding the knife separated from Gavin's bleeding arm and fell with a bouncing thud to the floor.

Staring in disgust at the severed arm, I rushed out from beneath the altar to retrieve the weapon. But again Shui swooped, using his front claws to grab both hand and knife from the floor. He charged Gavin again, only this time he plunged the knife into the old man's chest. Just as it had done so easily with the Maågan demon, the blade slid into Gavin's body.

Gavin gawked at the gargoyle, his eyes bulging with shock as blood spurt from his mouth. The bloody stump where his hand used to be reached for the creature as if pleading. But the deed was done. And if a baboon could smile, Shui did a great imitation of one. His lips drew back from dripping fangs, and he let out a long roar of triumph that shook what little was left of the glass in the windows above.

As ghastly a scene as it was, I rejoiced in the monster's victory. He'd done us both a favor. We both watched as Gavin collapsed to the floor and went still.

I looked from Shui to the knife still protruding from Gavin's chest. Shui tensed and so did I. But before I had a chance to make a move, the knife crumbled to dust right in front of us.

"What the—?" I started to take a step toward Gavin's body, but Shui issued a warning growl. "How did that happen?" I imagined the answer was the usual one when it came to most magical objects. Once the weapon had done its job, it was spent. Game over. "Shit!"

Shui peered at me from where he stood beside his dead master's corpse. His lips spread in a parody of a smile. Oh, he was loving this. Having me at his mercy was a dream come true.

He lunged at me, knocking me onto my back, then sitting on my chest to hold me down. I could hardly stand the stink of him. His gray scaly skin was stained red by whatever poor creature he'd devoured last, and I knew for a fact he hadn't showered in months. As for his breath? It was all I could do to stay conscious.

I was scared out of my mind, but I did my best to hide it. Even so, Shui had an uncanny knack for sensing emotion. He might have been a coward, but he was a shrewd coward, extremely self-centered and always hungry. He smelled my fear and from the gleam in his eyes, he found it delicious.

"I'll make a deal with you," I told him. "Stick with me, give me what I need to stay human, and you can wreak havoc wherever and whenever you want." Yeah, like I'd ever let that happen.

He gave a derisive snort. He knew I was bluffing. His mouth opened, then widened to show a double row of pointed teeth sharp as razors. Leaning in close, he gave me full view of his impressive dental equipment. I breathed hard and fast, calling on that part of my intellect that wasn't consumed by fear.

Then I thought of Aydin. Courageous, protective Aydin who was the best and only friend I'd ever had. He'd stolen my heart, and now it was breaking for him. I blinked back the tears that gathered, savoring the few memories I had left of a life too short to be fully lived. I mourned my sister knights spread all over the country, the only family I had left that I'd never get to meet. I even grieved for the fallen-angel father who had tried to save my life. Would I get to see him in the afterlife? Would I see my mother?

Warm saliva dripped from Shui's open mouth onto my forehead and dribbled into my eyes. It stung like salt water and made my vision blur.

Just as he lowered his open maw toward my face, the sound of beating wings ripped his attention from me. He leapt back as the taloned feet of another gargoyle swept across his shoulder, slicing through flesh and drawing blood. He roared in surprise and pain, grabbing his arm and glaring up at the ceiling with hatred in his eyes.

I retreated back to my hidey hole beneath the altar and gazed up at the winged beast that sailed up to the ceiling. I expected to see Shojin, Aydin's gargoyle, but it wasn't him.

Had Aydin already found another winged monster to fight Shui? I squinted and spotted a monster as striking as Shojin, but more feline than hawklike, and not nearly as big. Larger than Shui, though. Its flying was wobbly as a baby bird on its maiden flight. The leathery appendages looked shiny and new, like something freshly hatched. Then I saw its eyes. Its ice-jade eyes bright as two stars shining from an animal face covered with brown fur.

I couldn't believe it.

eighteen

"AYDIN?" I CRIED. *PLEASE, GOD, DON'T LET IT be him.* When I had dropped him off at the airport, he still had a few hours to get to Shojin and he'd had plenty of time to make it to Quebec.

But he must have purposely missed his flight. He'd thought I would fail at fighting off Shui, and he had been right. Aydin sacrificed his humanity for my life, and for my freedom.

I didn't know if Shui recognized whom he was fighting, but the shock of a sneak attack had worn off and he was now in full battle mode. What little fur he had stood up in spikes along his scaly back and he hissed at the new gargoyle flying above him. Hesitating barely a second more, his powerful wings lifted him up and off in the direction of his enemy.

I had to do something. Shui was small but vicious, and he'd have no trouble ripping out Aydin's throat. I thought of the broken gargoyle bodies from the Fatherhouse ruins stored in the trunk of Quin's car. The chunks of stone were sharp enough to do the job I needed done.

I rushed down the aisle, aiming for the back door of the church. Once outside I raced to the car parked at the curb.

Remembering how sharp the stones were, I removed my jacket and used it to wrap the pieces so that I could carry them back to the church. These stones were the answer to my prayers. Now I could kill Shui so that Aydin would live, and then…

My heart turned over when I considered what he'd become, but I knew how to reverse the change. Barachiel had said, *Once you've changed, you must eat the heart of the gargoyle you were bonded to.*

I didn't try to stop my tears this time. They froze on my face as quickly as I shed them, and I wiped my cheeks with my shoulder, the yarn from my sweater sticking to my frosty skin. Careful not to trip and fall on my lethal bundle, I forced my stiff legs to run to the church.

The two gargoyles were locked in a fierce embrace, their wings beating wildly in an effort to stay airborne. I saw Shui's teeth clamped on Aydin's arm, but Aydin's talons had sunk deep into Shui's side. Blood rained down on the pews below them. I ran beneath the wrestling pair, who appeared to be weakening. They were losing altitude. Suddenly, they both plummeted in a tangled heap to the ground.

My first instinct was to run to Aydin, but Shui stood in

my way. He growled, teeth bared. I peered at the downed gargoyle that lay on his side, unmoving.

One wing unfolded, then Aydin grew still again. He hadn't turned to stone. He was still alive.

I had to stay strong. I couldn't help Aydin if I were dead. And I couldn't turn into a gargoyle now even if I wanted to. Shui would see to that. All I wanted was to be with Aydin. If I lived, he had to live, too.

I opened my bundle and dropped my load of rocks, watching the larger pieces break into long shards that glistened in the moonlight. Good. The more sharp bits the better.

I glared at Shui. "Come and get me, you wrinkled, ugly, smelly son of a bitch."

Shui howled and charged. He wasn't too steady on his feet to begin with, so when his talons hit the lake of blood on the floor, he went sliding. Just as he began beating his wings for lift off, I jumped at him, both my feet extended, and kicked him in the ribs where Aydin had already done some damage. Shui doubled over, landing on his back atop the broken bodies of his dead comrades.

Stone shards pierced the gargoyle's body, the angular tips forced upward to protrude from his chest and belly. He screamed, his eyes stunned wide, his mouth agape and showing yet another rocky point that had pierced through the back of his head. He gasped one final time before his body stiffened. A sound like shattered crystal filled the church as his scaly skin solidified, his wings becoming webbed granite, his eyes glazing over like glass marbles. In an instant, his entire body turned to stone.

The back of my neck began to sting, then burn, and I panicked. Freedom should feel calm and beautiful, not agonizing. But tentacles of fire bored through my body and snaked down my spine. They curled around my arms and legs, choking my neck. Just when I thought I would pass out, the pain subsided. A bone-deep chill replaced the burning. My body spasmed, my teeth chattered, and I toppled backward to the floor, my head banging against the blood-soaked carpet as I went into convulsions.

Seconds later, it was over. A sublime peace fell over me and I knew I'd survived the worst of it. I was finally free. I touched the back of my neck and the flesh there was tender to the touch. When I brought my hand away, it was damp with blood.

As good as this news was, I didn't feel like celebrating. I still had Aydin to worry about.

I rolled over to my hands and knees, my joints complaining at every move, and crawled toward the injured gargoyle. Aydin's chest lifted and fell with slow breaths. His shoulder showed puncture wounds, but he wasn't bleeding as much as before, not like Shui had been. Regardless, he was still hurt. And he needed me.

"Aydin?" I smoothed my hand over the ruffled brown fur covering his face. He still retained some semblance of his former self. It was his crescent-shaped eyes the color of sage leaves that made him recognizable. I'd know him no matter what kind of creature he became. "Aydin?" I said again, coming closer and petting the injured shoulder that was already starting to heal.

He blinked and widened his feral eyes. Seeing me, he scrambled to his feet and hobbled backward, moving as far away from me as he could without tripping over a pew.

Choking back a sob, I said, "It's me, Aydin. It's Chalice. Don't you recognize me?"

He blinked again, then bowed his head, shoulders slumping as his wings drooped from his back. He wouldn't look at me.

I stepped toward him and a warning growl rumbled in his chest. I wasn't sure how much someone's personality changed with the transformation into a bloodthirsty killer, but I no longer believed all gargoyles were murdering fiends. Take Shojin, who seemed as gentle as a house pet. Aydin wouldn't hurt me.

"I know how you can change back," I told him.

He looked at me then, cat eyes narrowed and ears flattened to his wedge-shaped head.

"Barachiel told me. It's easy. All you have to do is kill the gargoyle you were bonded to, then eat its heart."

He snarled, a series of grunts and growls pouring from his mouth as he tried to talk. Shaking his head, he hissed and made a fist with his paw.

"Please, Aydin. You have to do this!" I didn't like the pleading tone in my voice, but I was desperate. "It's the only way for us to be together. No one can pull our strings anymore. You can become as free as me."

He shook his head again and backed away even farther.

"We have a duty to my sister knights. You can't let Geraldine down."

At the mention of the saint's name, he looked around the church, his gaze settling on the staircase that led to the basement. He pointed.

"She's safe," I assured him. "Quin is with her."

He closed his eyes and his face relaxed while he exhaled a slow breath.

I took a chance and stepped toward him again. He heard me come closer and his eyes snapped open, his lips peeling back from his teeth to show an impressive set of fangs. I recognized a faker when I saw one.

"You don't scare me. I'm on to you, you know." I slid my hand over the incredibly soft fur on his feline face. He nuzzled into my touch and I came closer, sliding both arms around his thick neck to hold him close. He hesitated, then wrapped a paw around my waist to hug me back.

We stood like that for a full minute before he stiffened and drew away. His wings spread out behind him and he threw back his head to let out a mournful wail that tore right through my heart.

"Aydin, find Shojin. You have to find him and kill him. Please, do it for us and do it for yourself. Do it for the Hatchet knights!"

He roared again, his eyes shining with standing tears. One powerful flap of his wings sent him straight up toward the ceiling, where he circled once before heading out the broken window and into the predawn sky.

"Aydin!" I couldn't let him leave me. Where would he go? How would I find him again?

I stared up at the gray sky and watched him disappear into the distance. I felt so empty, so alone. It reminded me of what I'd experienced right after Aydin's ghost left my body in the summoning room. Now I knew why I'd felt that way. He had become a part of me, and losing him was almost like losing a piece of my soul. I had to get him back. And if he wouldn't kill Shojin to consume the gargoyle's heart, I would do it for him.

I stood in front of the tapestry that covered the tomb's door. How was I going to explain what had happened to Aydin? Would Geraldine blame me? Hell, *I* blamed me. If only I'd worked harder at convincing Aydin I could handle Shui, he never would have let the change take him. He'd have gone to Shojin as planned and would still be human right now. And I would be dead.

Instead, Gavin was dead, as was Shui. And Aydin was... Still alive and had a chance to become human again.

It was fully dawn now, though clouds had rolled in to cover the late-autumn sun, making the day appear even more dismal. I heaved a shaky breath and keyed in the vault's combination. The door swung toward me, and I held it open to let light in for Quin.

But there was no need. The room was lit up as if inside the sun itself, though it had no windows for sunlight to shine through. What the room did have was a gleaming-white angel, and he glowed brighter than a dozen roman candles.

I blinked, certain my eyes would burn right through my brain, but it didn't hurt. The light cast by the angel had no adverse effect on me, though the glare obscured my view of Quin.

"Quin?" I shielded my eyes and saw the outline of a man standing beside the angel. "What's going on?"

He stepped forward with Geraldine's head cradled in his arms like a baby. He jerked a nod at the angel. "We have a guest."

"I see that." I squinted at the being whose white hair and white wings pulsed with unearthly brightness. "Can he tone it down a little?"

Quin shook his head. "It's what angels do."

Geraldine looked more alive than I'd ever seen her. She blinked at me and smiled.

"I take it you and Quin are getting to know each other."

"Oh, yes," she said. "And I'm so sorry about earlier, but I sensed Gavin waiting outside and couldn't take the chance of him hearing me."

"He's dead now." I tossed a look over my shoulder, half expecting to see the old man standing there. It would take time for me to get used to his absence and I was looking forward to it. "His death was pretty awful."

"We know," Quin said. "We watched through the silver veil as it happened."

I blinked in disbelief. "You did what?"

"Quin's getting ahead of himself." Geraldine sounded

annoyed. "First off, I'd like you to meet your guardian angel, Rafael."

To say I was shocked would be an understatement. Was he really *my* angel, like Barachiel had been my mother's? Knowing how it had turned out between the two of them, I stared up at Rafael and felt a little woozy. He had to be at least seven feet tall and was silent as a tree. I assumed he'd had to keep himself a secret until now, seeing as how my curse was newly broken.

"Can't you talk?" I asked him.

His forehead wrinkled, making his expression stern. "What would you have me say?"

"Nothing. Never mind." This was too surreal. I shook my head and redirected my attention to Geraldine. "How were you able to watch everything through the veil?"

"I opened it in here," Quin said, sounding matter-of-fact. He held up his right hand and I saw the pink scar of a sigil that was nearly healed. "I also opened the one inside the church upstairs. The result was a lot like watching a movie."

"But you couldn't go through it to get out of the tomb?"

He shook his head. "I'm human. I can't pass through the veil, remember?"

I still had so much to learn about this new life of mine. "I thought your ability to communicate with angels made you an exception."

"It doesn't work that way," Rafael said.

I squinted up at him, then at Geraldine, realizing she knew what had happened to Aydin. I would have hugged her in sympathy if she'd had a body to hug. "I feel horrible about Aydin. It's my fault." I swallowed back my grief, trying to stay strong. He would want me to hang tough.

"It's not your fault, dear. This was Aydin's destiny. You couldn't have prevented it."

I refused to accept that. "He should have let Shui kill me."

"He couldn't," she said. "You're too important to the other knights. Your mission is to unite your sisters, to teach them how to defend themselves with curses and charms, to share with them what you know of the Vyantara and their allies. Aydin was sworn to protect them, and therefore to protect you."

How could she be so casual about this? Aydin had turned into a monster. His life would never be the same, at least not until I did something to fix it. "I promised to help make him human again."

Her pretty pink forehead creased with a frown. "I'm not sure you can."

I held a hand to my chest to keep my heart from bursting with anguish. "Yes, I can. Barachiel told me how."

"Are you so certain the dark angel told you the truth?" she asked.

"Why would he lie?"

"He's one of the Fallen, Chalice. It's what they do."

"I don't think so." I thought back to the ritual that had brought Barachiel to me. "He saved my life, Geraldine. And what he told me about how to kill a gargoyle was true. He wouldn't lie to me about this."

She sucked in her bottom lip, looking thoughtful. "I suppose all you can do is try."

And I would succeed. Geraldine knew next to nothing about the Fallen except that her mate had turned into one. He may have been a bad seed, but Barachiel wasn't. I owed him my life.

Since the gargoyle stones I'd used to kill Shui had ripped up my coat, I knew I would freeze the moment I walked out the cathedral doors. But I had to return to Elmo's and let the elf know what had happened to his friend. I'd get Quin's help in fashioning knives from the gargoyle stones still in the trunk of his car. Then I would head for Quebec, track down Shojin and take his heart. My mind spun with all the tasks I'd set for myself, not the least of which was to connect with my sister knights. It's what my mother had asked of me before I'd even been born.

I looked at the angel, wondering why he was still here. I said to Quin, "We have to go back to Elmo's. It's not safe for us here. There's no telling how many more Vyantara maniacs are still in town, and I don't like to think what they'd do if they found us."

"They won't find us," Quin said. "Because you're not going back to Elmo's. You of all people need to lay low for now. As for me, everyone thinks I'm dead."

"He's right," Geraldine said. "We want the Vyantara to believe Shui managed to kill you before he died. If they think Aydin is the one responsible for Shui's death, they'll respect him more. If they catch him, they may even treat him better than they treated Shui."

"If I don't go back to Elmo's, where will I go?"

"You'll come with me," Rafael said.

"I don't even know you." The idea of hanging out with an angel made me uncomfortable. "And where would you take me?"

"Beyond the silver veil." He waved a hand at the wall and it shimmered with silver light. "You'll bring Geraldine with you."

My mother's rune divination had predicted I would cross over, and now that the curse was broken, I was free to do just that. Though I wasn't a hundred percent sure I wanted to. "My sister knights? They'll be there?"

"Some will be, yes," the angel said. "We bring them through if their lives are threatened, then relocate them to a safer place."

Goose bumps rose the hairs on my arms. "What's on the other side?"

"You'll find out in a minute," Quin said. "I'm sorry, Geraldine, but I need to put you back in the bag."

"No problem. I'm ready."

And so was I, or at least as ready as I'd ever be. But I would never forget my promise to Aydin. I wondered if the doorway through the veil might be the means to finding Shojin, and then Aydin, wherever he was hiding. If so, I planned to take full advantage.

Quin handed me the bowling bag with Geraldine's head and hand zipped up inside. Rafael held his hand out to me and I took it. His skin felt warm, not icy like Barachiel's had been, though the texture was equally soft. The first thing

I noticed was that he had no calluses. Aydin used to have thick calluses on his fingers and palms. Now he had paws.

I sucked in a breath, feeling the tears gather behind my eyes again. I had to be brave for Aydin, and for myself. I looked over at Quin. "Tell Elmo I'll be back."

I slid my gaze to Rafael's piercing blue eyes. I'd have to depend on this angel, the same as I had Aydin, to instruct me in my new life. Doing so would feel like a betrayal. Someday soon I'd have Aydin back the way he used to be and we'd pick up where we left off. I wasn't giving up on him. Not ever.

I nodded at Rafael and he guided me to the silvery curtain that separated the mortal realm from the divine. I knew it was a way station of sorts, but I hadn't a clue what I'd find there. Holding my guardian angel's hand, I glanced over my shoulder at Quin, who grinned and flapped a farewell wave. My gaze swept the windowless tomb one last time before I passed through the shimmering veil and into an uncertain future.

★ ★ ★ ★ ★

 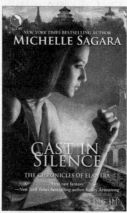

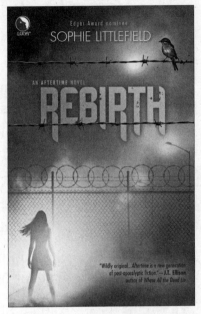

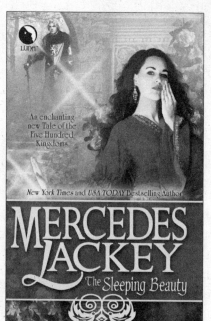

Domino Riley hates zombies.

Bodies are hitting the pavement in L.A. as they always do, but this time they're getting right back up, death be damned. They may be strong, but even Domino's mobbed-up outfit of magicians isn't immune to the living dead.

If she doesn't team up with Adan Rashan, the boss's son, the pair could end up craving hearts and brains, as well as each other….

SKELETON CREW

Pick up your copy today!